GENESIS MORTALIS

GENESIS MORTALIS

BOOK ONE OF THE TAKE IT TRILOGY

A.E. HEARN

NEW DEGREE PRESS

COPYRIGHT © 2021 A.E. HEARN

GENESIS MORTALIS

Book One of the Take It Trilogy

ISBN   978-1-63676-725-3   *Paperback*

             978-1-63730-042-8   *Kindle Ebook*

             978-1-63730-144-9   *Ebook*

"The guilt of morality will always catch up to us as we deviate from what is right. Unless you're a sociopath. Lucky you, then. The sociopath will never succumb to the turmoil of human emotion. For the rest of us, for me, it will eventually consume our body, mind, and soul."

—JUN JAE-HO

CONTENTS

AUTHOR'S NOTE

———

Thank you for choosing to read *Genesis Mortalis*, Book One of the *Take It* Trilogy! This has been an incredibly long and thrilling journey for me. I first started working on this action book series in 2011. Back then, I was only beginning to draft short ideas for exciting spy missions to take Madisyn and Marcelle Montevega on.

In high school, I was only just starting to develop my writing style, so while I had drafted the plots of what I wanted this book series to look like, I didn't exactly know how to write it. By the time I got to college, I had the first quarter of *Take It* drafted when I decided I wanted to tell this story as a screenplay instead.

Cinema played a huge role in developing these ideas. At an early age, I fell in love with the suaveness of *James Bond*, the action of *Mission: Impossible*, the gore and badassery of *Kill Bill: Volume 1*, and the relatable female characters of *Totally Spies!* All these pieces of media influenced the type of story I knew I wanted to write.

Music also played a crucial role while writing *Genesis Mortalis*. Each climactic moment of this book has a song behind it—sometimes they're slow songs, sometimes they're fast-paced. Either way, music is integrated into this story. Whenever I came across a song that moved me, I wrote down the name of the song or piece. Pieces from "Carmina Burana" to Russian lullabies to Logic's "Fade Away" shaped Madisyn and Marcie's story. Anyone who knows me understands just how important music is for me. I always say my background in violin and piano allowed me to fully appreciate a wide range of genres.

So, with the naive hope of someone just starting out in film, I started adding all the songs I wanted in my movies into the most intense action scenes. I thoroughly notated how many seconds into a song the action of that scene should be (so when people read it, they could listen to the song and clearly picture the exact moments of musical *genius* I had seen in my own mind). I took screenwriting classes in school to help me fine-tune my screenplays and delved more into film directing, all while taking all the creative writing classes I could. During these years in college, I actually finished the screenplays to both the first and second books of this series.

As I learned more about filmmaking throughout college, I started to realize just how difficult it is to get screenplays picked up and how intense directing your own films can be. So, I changed my mind yet again! I made the decision to convert both of these scripts back into novels, as I assumed getting a novel picked up by a publisher would be easier than having screenplays picked up by Hollywood. (I was right.) Plus, I figured I would leave the making of my movies up to the professionals. I had discovered I had no real passion for movie directing and simply wanted to have total control over this series being turned into a movie.

The other big factor for converting my scripts to books was that I had learned in film classes that screenwriters should *never* add their own music to a script. This bothered me a lot as I truly consider myself a music connoisseur and an artist. No one could know the right songs for certain scenes of my book better than me. Regardless, and having put my ego aside, I finished the first two drafts of these novels in January 2020, and I was able to preserve some of the songs I wanted to be included by writing them into the text where they fit well.

Another significant change for this book and the series as a whole was deciding on my audience—something that, according to my mentor (bestselling author of *Party Girl*, Anna David), I should have thought of before ever starting to write! The problem with starting a book in high school and not finishing it until after college is how muddied your focus can get. I had originally written my characters to be middle-school age, but as I got older, the characters seemed to grow with me. After going back and forth on the age, I settled for teenage characters with content that was still much more mature for teenage readers themselves. Thankfully, my editor, Kristin Gustafson, was able to reign in my focus so that my book would be YA (Young Adult), a fiction genre that can span from ages twelve to eighteen. While this meant cutting a lot of content I wanted to explore further, like teenage sexuality, I also realized how this would help me tremendously to reach a wider audience and increase my chances for the books to be picked up as a movie series.

Regardless of all the changes my book and the entire series have undergone, I am extremely grateful for all of it. Even while there were certain aspects of the book that had to be cut (that I thought were some of my best work), it has been extremely enlightening to see my book's full potential and to finally have a direction to take this series in for YA readers.

As someone once said, there's a time and place for everything, and this especially applies to writing books. I am excited to get this first series out there for the world to see and to explore other genres with novels I already have outlined and drafted: romance, drama, and a thrilling (fictional) military story that is inspired by my time in the United States Army.

Thank you so much for purchasing this book and supporting me as a new author. I can't wait for you all to read the next book in the trilogy. The Montevega twins have lived in my imagination for so long now, I am relieved to have their story down on paper and out of my head. If you enjoy *Take It: Genesis Mortalis*, please consider leaving a review or recommending it to a friend.

To follow my journey, you can find me on social media! I am on Instagram, Facebook, and LinkedIn. I also have a website coming soon—stay tuned.

Thank you again for your support!

CHAPTER 1

——

A mass of clouds, luminous like argentine, leisurely parts ways in the sky. The sun stretches its arms through, shining over the Amazon basin. Reaching across the earth, determined to illuminate every obscure corner, it seems to halt its pursuit upon approaching a forest hidden amongst a grassy mire. The thick, unwilling canopy of the wide span of trees resists the sun's rays, sending the beams dancing playfully off the tops of its dense leaves. Slyly, a beam of light just manages to penetrate the branches, finding its way to the forest floor, beaconing the earthy green abyss.

Deep inside the heart of the newly lit forest, and dangling upside down from a tree, is an unconscious British teenager—sixteen-year-old Madisyn Montevega. Her ankle is caught fast by a rope, and she hangs from the branch cataleptically. Her eyes are closed and her hair, wrapped tightly in a ponytail, hangs toward the ground between her limp arms. Dressed plainly in black, her face is encrusted with mud, and her pants are ripped near her thigh from her fall through the trees. Through the tear, a small wound can be seen—not quite seeping but coated with thick dirt and dried blood.

A capuchin monkey sitting high in a neighboring tree swings over to sit on the branch on which her foot is caught, rustling a few of the loose leaves and causing them to fall gently to the forest floor. Madisyn stirs from her unconscious state, opening one eye, then the other. She blinks a few times and surveys her surroundings, completely overtaken by the colors of the forest and the noises all around her. For a girl stuck in a tree, she is rather calm. Tilting her head slightly upward, she notices the knot wrapped tightly around her left boot.

I could untie it, she thinks. *But then somehow, I'd have to climb down a tree and run through the forest with one shoe...*

Madisyn sighs and lets her body go limp. She takes in the forest from her upside-down view, pondering a way to get out of her predicament. Drawing in a deep breath, she reaches up to her foot and pulls a small hunting knife from its sheath inside her shoe. She grips it tightly in her hand and lets herself hang loosely again, releasing a loud exasperating groan. The startled capuchin screeches and leaps up to a higher branch.

Taking another long deep breath in preparation, she grits her teeth and uses all the strength she can muster to pull her entire body up to her ankle with another groan. She uses the knife to saw viciously at the rope, her teeth clenched as she feels her ankle swelling painfully inside her boot and her ponytail swaying violently at her back with every motion.

"Come on," she grunts, a bead of sweat dripping down the side of her muddied face. She is anxious, if anything. Her mind races with scenarios leading to certain death, and it pushes her to speed up. If only she had stopped to think of all the much worse situations she had been in before, maybe she wouldn't have been so concerned. But she had never been stuck in a tree before—especially not a tree in the middle of a jungle.

And *where* were her friends? Where was her sister? Why had they even been there in the first place?

She can't seem to remember any of it. She can only focus on the knot. And the branch. And the squawks and squeals coming from all the rainforest's noisy inhabitants. The only thing that terrifies her more than staying caught in the tree is the moment she would finally cut the knot-free and plummet twenty feet to the ground. Or what if the branch broke first? Then she would *still* descend twenty feet to the ground, only she'd have a thick branch waiting to crush her body.

"Ah," she groans, trying to shake the racing thoughts. She needed to stay focused if she was to accomplish anything.

Her palms become slick with sweat, and her body shakes from holding herself up for so long, a task that even her daily Pilates had not prepared her core for. She pulls the knife from the unwilling rope and lets herself hang down to catch her breath. With a couple of breaths, all her worries ease, and she becomes calm again. She listens to the animal noises that surround her, including the squeals of the capuchin sitting high in the tree above her. She stares up at it. The monkey is happily distracted with a shiny black object stuck between some branches—the AR-15 she had dropped on the way down through the trees.

She scoffs at the monkey, the way it seems so happy and carefree... and not involuntarily hanging upside down like she was, for that matter. It looks down at her and squawks.

"Are you mocking me?" she demands. The capuchin only looks away.

Madisyn grunts and pulls herself back up, determined to finish the knot once and for all, when her earpiece starts beeping. She had almost forgotten she was wearing one. But moment after moment, saw after saw, the buzzing still in her ear, she gradually remembers where she is and her purpose for being there...

The Amazon rainforest. She pieces the situation together. *Marcie and Robbie shouldn't be too far away, hopefully. Had to land the plane somewhere? No... we took parachutes. Didn't we? Where's mine, then? Did I really jump from a plane with only a gun? That'd be absolutely mental, even for me... Bad guys should be nearby. Must get to the highlands, acquire critical information, destroy target...*

The beeping in her ear continues, breaking her train of thought. Holding on to the branch with one hand, she presses the button in her ear with the other to answer the call and continues sawing away at the rope.

"I'm a tad occupied," she begins with a hint of irritation. "But I could *really* use some serious help here if you don't mind."

"Madisyn Montevega! It has been *hours* since I tried to get hold of you!" comes her mother's familiar voice.

"*Mother? How* did you get this number?" She saws harder against the rope, her mother's yelling causing more frustration.

On the other end of the call—standing on the grand patio of their luxurious villa just outside London, England, with a hand on her hip and the phone pressed to her ear—Reese Montevega paces back and forth. "Just because you were on holiday all the way across the world doesn't mean you get to add an entire week more to your trip. You and your sister were supposed to be home three days ago for that damn debutante party your great-aunt insisted on putting together!

How do you think that makes me look when my own daughters aren't present for their own party?"

"Mother, we told you we weren't going to that ungodly circus act anyway, and we all know you didn't want to host it! So, what's the big deal?" Madisyn stops her sawing, hearing the voices of an approaching group of men. She holds onto the branch to look off into the trees. "Shit!" she whispers to herself and saws harder than ever at the stubborn rope.

"The nerve you girls have these days!" Reese shouts into the phone.

Ignoring her mother's distress, Madisyn hears the group of men getting closer, shouting a slew of curses in Portuguese and carelessly firing their weapons in the air like madmen. One of the bullets hits her tree and causes the leaves above her to rustle and fall. "Mother!" she shrieks. "I am in the middle of a very important... *game*, and I am about to die, so I'm hanging up before you get me killed!"

Before Reese can protest about her lack of interest in what she assumes to be meaningless child's play, Madisyn ends the call. She's close to cutting the rope free as the men run wildly in her direction, still blindly firing their weapons until one of the shots hits the branch where her AR-15 lies. The capuchin squeals in fright, swinging away to safety as the branches above Madisyn come falling down.

The knife falls from her grip as she attempts to shield her face while holding on to the branch. The gun falls straight into her free arm but jabs her in the nose, jerking her head back and giving her a proper nosebleed—Madisyn groans in pain.

"*Lá está ela!*" one of the men hollers, pointing at her from a little under ten meters away. "*Agarrá-la!*"

They holler and run through the trees, charging at their newly spotted target. Madisyn, still caught by the rope around her ankle, skillfully lets herself hang upside down and fires the semiautomatic at the group of men, their bodies falling to the ground like dominoes.

She sighs with relief, her heart pounding in her chest. Glancing up at her body, she smiles—*unscathed yet again.*

"That could have been messy." She looks up at the capuchin sitting nearby. "Coward," she chides, to which the monkey squawks and bounces on the branch.

"Madisyn!" An approaching voice echoes through the trees.

She whips her head around and spots her twin sister Marcie, who wears a similar black outfit with her hair swept over her shoulder in a long messy braid, running toward her. Madisyn lets the gun, out of bullets and useless to her, fall to the ground nearby as Marcie comes to stand under her, gesturing at the dead bodies.

"God, what've *you* been doing?" Marcie asks, somewhat accusingly.

"Dangling from this bloody tree the entire time, what else?"

Marcie puts her hands on her hips, staring up at her twin. "I told you taking those chutes through trees was a bad idea. You never listen." Marcie squints, her gaze moving further up into the trees to look past her twin. She spots the camouflage-pattern parachute blanketing the treetops roughly forty meters away. "How did you even manage to cut yourself out of your pack but get stuck again? So much for smooth sailing, Madi," she chides, clicking her tongue.

"Do *not* call me that," Madisyn retorts, seething from her sister's use of the nickname she absolutely abhorred. Marcie smirks at her twin's reaction and folds her arms. "I had some extra rope and thought I could use it to climb down. I must have slipped and hit my head or something."

The tattered knot around Madisyn's ankle, barely holding by a thread, snaps and releases her foot, sending her plummeting to the ground with a mouthful of curses. Marcie opens her arms in an attempt to catch her, but on impact, they both fall over, groaning.

Marcie shoves her twin off of her. "Remind me never to try and catch you again."

Getting to their feet, Madisyn wipes the blood from her nose. "As if next time I'd ever let you," she mutters.

"A simple 'thank you' would suffice."

Ignoring her, Madisyn looks off into the trees, her memory flooding back in. "We need to get a move on. We're close to the highlands. And we have to be in and out by nightfall." Stepping over her AR-15 rifle, Madisyn picks up the knife she dropped earlier instead and shoved it back inside her boot. She knew they would need to travel light from then on and quietly. Standing up straight, Madisyn fixes her high ponytail.

A Portuguese guard moans from where he lies in the dirt, severely injured from his bullet wounds but not quite dead, to Madisyn's dismay. Going for the quick and easy option, she picks up the gun of one of his dead friends nearby and walks over to the man, aiming it right at his face as he attempts to sit up, holding on to his bloody abdomen.

"Madisyn, we're not supposed to kill anyone. We're supposed to be ghosts on this mission—not murderers!"

"Aren't we, though?" Madisyn keeps the gun pointed at his head and squints her eyes. Marcie walks over and shoves her arm away, the weapon accidentally going off and shooting the man in the knee instead. He screams in agony and curses at them in Portuguese. Madisyn frowns at her twin. She drops the gun and unhooks a pair of brass knuckles from her utility belt, sliding them onto her hand. Dropping to one knee, Madisyn drives her brass-covered fist into the man's face, making him fall over unconscious.

The capuchin sitting high up in the tree squeals down at them. Standing back up, Madisyn glares in its direction one last time before looking at her sister. "Come on. We'll have to split up again when we get closer."

"At least this time, it'll be on purpose," Marcie retorts, to which Madisyn rolls her eyes. They take off running through the rainforest, leaping over tree trunks dark from moss and dodging dangling wet branches in their way.

Deep within the Mantiqueira Mountains in the Brazilian Highlands, a modern building lies atop one of its highest cliffs. Inside this lair, in a room that was much too vast to be an office, a Brazilian businessman named Matheus Azevedo takes in the breathtaking jagged curves of his homeland. He stands in front of the glass wall, a figure of South American political defiance for the two suited men behind him.

"*Meus amigos,* we are a force to be reckoned with. We will assert our dominance over our American allies, but only when the time is right. I trust you'll hold your alliance until then, *falou?*"

Azevedo turns to face his partners, Braulio Rocha and Estevan Barros. The latter nods in agreement, though Rocha purses his lips uncomfortably. "We'll see how today goes," he says.

The door to the office opens, and American businessman Christopher Ryan, a burly man in a suit with a distinctly bushy mustache, comes in, followed by his partner, Richard

Wickham, who is slim with facial hair pristinely sculpted to his chiseled jaw. Behind them is Ryan's adviser, Alexander Smith, a gentleman quite older than the rest in the room, with graying flecks in the full tuft of hair on his head, his clean-shaven face showing the wrinkles in his aged skin. Azevedo moves through the Brazilian men to greet their guests.

"At last, Mr. Ryan." He shakes the man's hand and gestures to a massive conference table long enough to seat thirty men. "Let's get right down to business."

The six men take seats in the middle of the table, Ryan cracking open his briefcase and spinning it around to reveal large stacks of freshly printed cash. "I've never cared for small talk anyway," Ryan says. Barros and Rocha exchange careful poker faces, unimpressed by the showy American.

Azevedo laughs and sits back in his seat. "We're not interested in your money, Mr. Ryan. It's your trust we want. VedoPetrol is growing *muito rápido*: one of the largest petroleum companies in Brazil, a multinational corporation with influences all over South America, the United States, parts of Europe, Asia… You came to me five years ago with certain promises of growing my American investors exponentially."

Ryan sighs and closes the briefcase. "Yes, and we have. But laundering money can be a tricky business. Word keeps getting out of a VedoPetrol 'scandal,' and it's starting to worry some of the buyers. No one wants to be associated with this kind of widespread global corruption. Your own people are protesting in the street, calling out Brazil's head politicians for their involvement. It's just not good for business."

"*Cabeça dura, essa,*" Rocha mutters to Azevedo. "*Ele nunca vai mudar.*" Azevedo clicks his tongue to settle his partner's obvious dislike for Ryan.

"We'll handle the media," Barros chimes in. "And there are ways to get a new president. One the people trust before things get too out of control." He looks to Azevedo for confirmation, who simply nods, giving his partner the go-ahead. Barros pulls out his phone and types a message to an anonymous source. A sly smile pulls across his lips as he tucks his phone back into his pocket. "*Feito.* It's handled."

Turning back to Ryan, Azevedo raises an eyebrow as if to say "your move" to his American counterpart. Ryan scoffs. "What do you want us to do, set up some scheme to assassinate *our* president? You know, things just don't work that way in America. And come on, did you really fly us all the way out here just to ask for our trust? I've been on your side from the beginning. Now, I have a hearing tomorrow morning I'm due back for. I don't have time for games."

"Well, see, *that* is exactly why we are all here *cara*," Rocha adds. "We heard about the hearing, and it worries us."

Ryan scoffs and looks over to Wickham for support, who clears his throat and straightens up in his seat. "What exactly are you implying? We've tied up our loose ends. Micky Rosetto is going to go to prison of his own accord. He has no connection to us."

Azevedo leans forward, holding up his finger to silence them. "Then *why* is Christopher Ryan so interested in his hearing tomorrow?"

Wickham and Ryan exchange glances, lacking a good response to set the Brazilians at ease. Barros chimes in, "How are we supposed to do business with you when your *caras* keep getting locked up? None of our *caras* are going to prison."

"All we're saying is that perhaps, it might be useful to have law enforcement on our side, *tá bom*?" Rocha adds, making Smith laugh.

"You want us to pay off the cops? That's much too risky, even for us." Smith looks to Ryan and Wickham and shakes his head at this idea.

Azevedo sits back in his seat with a smile. "We already have our guys aligned with *our* intentions." He grabs a remote sitting nearby on the table and swivels around to aim it near the vast wall across the room behind his desk. A hologram screen flickers on to show the news, revealing a chaotic scene of the Brazilian president being shot and arrested by local law enforcement for allegedly murdering his own wife and kids only minutes ago. The Americans look to one another slyly but try not to reveal too much of their own distaste for the way their Brazilian partners did business. Barros grins before Azevedo flicks off the screen again, his point having been made. He turns back to the Americans. "It's time you measure up. I don't care *who* you pay off to do it."

"He's right," Wickham wearily sighs as if he had always known it would eventually come down to this. "We must ensure the security of our business. Any mistakes on the US end and we could potentially lose… well, everything."

The men are quiet, the Brazilians holding stern gazes on their American counterparts. Azevedo searches Ryan's wary face for enough doubt to send the Americans packing.

In another part of Azevedo's lair, a vent cover in the wall of an empty hallway pops out of place and is set gently on the ground. From the opening, a black briefcase is pushed out onto the floor before Madisyn scoots out behind it. She fixes the cover back in place and struts straight down the hallway, briefcase in hand.

A security guard turns a corner into the hallway, and Madisyn swiftly chucks the briefcase at him like a Frisbee. It hits him square in the face, making him clutch his nose with a groan. Madisyn slinks coolly toward him, pulling out a small gadget from her belt and popping it open. She throws it at the man with the curl of her wrist, which sends the collar-shaped taser zipping through the air. The gadget snaps around the man's neck, electrocuting him, and he falls unconscious to the floor.

Picking up the briefcase first, Madisyn takes the man's gun from his holster and continues down the hallway. She presses on her earpiece. "Robbie, I'm in."

Parked somewhere within the mountains in a white Jeep Wrangler, sixteen-year-old Robbie Ancens, Madisyn and Marcie's best friend since childhood, sits in the backseat typing furiously on his laptop. He pulls up an interactive map of that facility which shows the girls inside. "Get to level three—west wing," Robbie advises through his earpiece. He uses the map's data to pull up a clear route for her. "There's another vent channel there."

Madisyn heads that way, creeping up a flight of stairs and down another hallway until she comes across another large vent. She sets down the briefcase and pops open one of its secret panels, from which she pulls out an electric screwdriver. She uses the tool to remove the screws in the vent just as another security guard comes around the corner.

"Hey, you!" the man shouts in Portuguese. He starts to pull his gun, but Madisyn is quicker and grabs the one she stole, shooting the man twice in the chest.

"What the hell, Madisyn!" comes Robbie's voice in her ear. "We said not to kill anyone!"

Madisyn picks up the tool again and finishes removing the vent. "*No, we agreed we would try not to kill anyone unless absolutely necessary. That guy just had to go!*" And who was Robbie to judge from the safety of his vehicle? She was the one in any real danger.

Robbie takes a deep breath and just shakes his head. "Whatever. Back in the vents you go, missy."

Tossing the briefcase inside the vent, Madisyn climbs in after it and fixes the vent cover back in its place behind her. Crawling through the air ducts and pushing the briefcase along in front of her, Robbie chimes in her ear again. "One minute until fans turn on. I can't switch them off without disrupting the system—so hurry."

Madisyn grumbles as she continues to crawl until she reaches a large fan that blocks her way. She wedges herself between its blades, contorting her limbs to fit the awkward angle. Sweat drips down her face as she hears the whir of the system booting up.

"Five seconds, Madisyn!" Robbie adds, annoying her more than being helpful.

She just barely gets her foot out before the fan's sharp metal arms swoosh in a circular motion fast enough to cut someone in half. Slouching on the side of the vent, Madisyn lets out an exasperated breath, the air from the fan blowing obnoxiously in her face. She continues in the opposite direction, crawling until she gets to her final destination.

On his laptop, Robbie keys in a complicated code to shut off the sensors to the vault room. "I can only keep these off for seven minutes," he tells her. "Anything longer, and they'll notice it missing on the grid. Jump right in."

Madisyn drops the briefcase inside first and then jumps down from the vent, landing flawlessly in a crouched position on the floor. She stands slowly, her attention consumed by the titanium metal vault door in front of her. She can't help but think of all the shiny things that surely lie behind it. This was the very moment that kept her doing mission after mission, no risk or danger too mighty to steer her away.

"Marcelle," she breathes through her earpiece, eyes locked on the door. "Please tell me you have those codes ready."

In a dark office somewhere on the first floor, Marcie sits behind a desk, hacking files from the computer onto her hard drive. She finds the password for the vault. "Prepare to copy: five, two, alpha, seven, whiskey, six, delta, four."

Madisyn types the code into the vault's keypad, and the vault lock clicks open. Madisyn's mouth eagerly twitches as she twists the lever to pull the heavy door back. She stands in the opening, taking it all in. "God, I fucking love rich people."

Robbie sits back in his seat, also taken aback by the camera on his screen. He hollers in excitement. "That's a lot of cocaine!" He grabs his hair with his hands, psyched at their discovery.

Back in the office and too occupied to join in on the celebration, Macie's face twists into worry as she types frantically on the computer. "Something's wrong, guys."

Refusing to let her sister pull her back to reality, Madisyn continues stacking the briefcase with cash and coke, only becoming distracted suddenly by the glass case that sits in the middle of the floor holding a very large diamond. She had never been a girl to care much for jewels, but she could only imagine its worth. Moving over to the case, she opens it and picks up the gem, her eyes sparkling in its mesmerizing reflection.

"Marcelle, what is it?" Robbie asks, becoming serious again.

At the desk, the computer flashes bold red letters that read, "SECURITY BREACH." Marcie jabs on the keyboard, trying to override the system. "I think some of the files are corrupt! They must have hidden them as a protection. We need to leave right now!"

A security guard walks into the conference room and approaches Azevedo. He leans down to whisper in Portuguese as Barros and Rocha listen in. "Sir, there seems to be some kind of infraction in the system."

"*Que infração?*"

"We can't pin its location yet, but—"

Azevedo immediately stands. "Sound the alarms. We can't risk anything!" The guard rushes from the room. Barros and Rocha draw their guns and rush toward the door. Businessmen or not, they were still going to protect what was theirs.

The American businessmen squint their eyes at the frantic Brazilians, standing from their seats as well. "Is there a problem, gentlemen?" Ryan asks.

"Madisyn, you have to get out of the vault!" Robbie screams into his earpiece. "You don't have time to grab all of it!"

Inside the vault, Madisyn looks up at the flashing alarms. She pops open a small compartment in the top frame of the briefcase and pulls out a tiny metal cube the size of her palm. She stares at it, eyes twinkling. Etched across the top of the cube is the acronym "UCOCA."

"I don't intend to take it all. This is just collateral," Madisyn replies to Robbie, her gaze still glued to the cube in her hand as she raises it higher, examining it. "The rest of it... I'll destroy."

"I just finished transferring the files," Marcie declares through the earpiece. "We have enough evidence to put these guys away for a long time. Let's get the hell out of here!"

Robbie panics from inside the Jeep, pounding on his keyboard. "They overrode my system breach! Madisyn, get out *now*!"

Madisyn carefully sets down the metal cube in the diamond's previous place inside the glass case. She presses in the letter "O" on the acronym before leaving with the briefcase, sealing the vault door behind her. Shooting a titanium line with a grappling hook from a small pen, it soars upward inside the vent opening above her, and when it catches to the roof, it pulls her up with ease, briefcase, and all.

"Marcie!" Robbie exclaims. "They're coming right at you! Why haven't you left yet?"

Marcie ejects her hard drive at the desk and jumps up from her seat as a group of security guards burst through the door.

"Window! Window!" Robbie screams into her earpiece.

As the security guards draw their guns to shoot, Marcie flips over the massive desk with a groan, blocking the bullets coming at her. She grabs the pistol from the holster on her hip and shoots at the glass wall behind her before throwing herself through its broken pieces.

Marcie lands on the small area of grass outside the window overlooking a cliff and gets up to dash around the front of the building, the guards following in hot pursuit. Without hesitation, Marcie runs right off the edge of the mountain. The guards halt in their tracks, looking down.

Twenty feet from the ground, Marcie throws down a gadget that lands beneath her, producing a magnetic force field that halts her from plummeting into the jagged surface – her body hovering above it momentarily before she hits the dirt.

Robbie punches the seat of his car excitedly and hollers. "*Fuck*, Marcie! Antigravity Forcefield? I can't believe you actually pulled that off!"

Inside the vents, Madisyn pauses when she hears the comment. "Damn you to *hell*, Marcelle! You know I wanted to be first to try that!"

Brushing dirt off her shirt and pants at the bottom of the mountain, Marcie rolls her eyes at her sister, though she can't help grinning, satisfied that she beat her more competitive twin to the punch. She always felt like she was hiding in her sister's shadow, so why shouldn't she have her moment for once? "Quit your griping, Madisyn, and get down here!"

As the American businessmen scramble to their car, Azevedo heads down to the vault with his security. He curses at them in Portuguese to unlock the door to the room faster and runs over to type in the vault password.

When he opens the vault, Azevedo notices his diamond has been replaced with a metal cube. Enraged but not quite understanding its significance, he moves closer to read the word etched across the top. "What the fuck is UCOCA?" he yells, turning to his guards, who shrug dumbfoundedly. "*Merda*! *Idiotas*."

The metal cube starts to crack apart like an egg. The businessman and his security take a step closer to watch as a little spiderlike robot crawls out first. Suddenly, the bot splits itself in two, those two splitting apart as well, as the bots continue to double until an endless stream of the pea-sized metal creatures swarm the glass case. Azevedo's mouth hangs open. Some of his men run from the room as the tiny bots double and triple until Azevedo can no longer see the floor, all making an earsplitting high-pitched squealing noise.

The bots destroy everything in the vault, and some swarm over Azevedo, who shrieks as they eat away at his flesh. The rest of the bots swarm out of the vault, attacking what is left of his security.

Outside in their limo, Ryan has his phone pressed to his ear, Wickham and Smith sitting across from him, leaned in close to hear a frantic voice on the other end. "We were ambushed! Everyone's dead. Everything in the vault was destroyed. It was some group called UCOCA? They hacked the network—stole everything! All the files are *gone*."

Wickham shakes his head, burying his face in his hands. Smith only sighs heavily and leans back into his seat. Ryan throws his phone and screams, infuriated at the sudden turn of events. He grabs his hair, a tortured expression turning his face purple. "*Goddamn it!*"

Somewhere at the bottom of the mountains, Madisyn meets up with her sister. Together, they race to some bushes nearby where they uncover their hidden motorcycles, stashed earlier by Robbie for their easy escape. Madisyn stores the briefcase on the back of her bike and straps it in.

"On our way, Robbie," Marcie says. The twins rev their bike engines.

"What did I tell you, sis?" Madisyn beams. "If we want something, it's ours for the taking." Marcie winks at her, and they put on their helmets.

On the other side of the mountain in the Jeep, Robbie closes his laptop and hops into the driver's seat. "Hell yeah, let's bring it home!" He stomps on the gas pedal, jolting the Jeep forward.

The twins take off, kicking up a cloud of dust as they make their way down the winding dirt road.

CHAPTER 2

FIVE YEARS EARLIER

Eleven-year-old Madisyn Montevega sits at the piano playing a devastatingly beautiful yet somber version of "Lacrymosa" from Mozart's "Requiem" during her mother's cocktail party. Guests nearby watch her with impressed smiles on their powdered faces while sipping on flutes of champagne. Others stand around the room engrossed in snobbishly polite conversation. Everyone in attendance wears their finest evening wear, the Montevega twins included. Marcie stands amongst the adults, dressed up like a doll with dainty curls in her hair, a mirror of her sister.

Before taking on the fascinating lives of vigilantes or their own warped interpretation of bringing justice to the world, this was the Montevega twins' boring reality, entertaining at luxuriously overdone dinner parties every weekend to celebrate nothing more than their parents' continuous rise to success.

Their father, William Montevega (an accomplished businessman and notable English billionaire), mingles with a group of other dashing men in suits, accessorized with glasses of scotch. He glances across the room at his breath-taking wife, Reese Montevega, who stands talking with another woman. Both dressed impeccably in fine jewels and slender gowns, wearing forced smiles that desperately hope to convince the other of their feigned interest.

Marcie, observing the room and catching her father's entranced gaze, looks up to her mother beside her. After all those years, he was still madly in love with her. But who wouldn't be madly in love with a woman as defiant and inter-esting as Reese Montevega? A much newer billionaire, Reese spent most of her time running Rossi—an English luxury sports car manufacturer and global automobile brand with over one hundred dealerships on six continents. The busi-ness was an inheritance that had been part of her deceased first husband's family since the early 1900s. This, of course, caused many to speculate that her first husband's death was part of a bigger plot for Reese to become the richest black woman in England. Madisyn and Marcie liked to believe so as well, as it added mystery and drama to their typically boring lives. Scandal or not, Marcie had always seen more of her mother's bold, rule-breaking personality in her twin, though she couldn't help but wish that she too would some-day blossom into even half the woman her mother was.

A few people away, the twins' best friend and neighbor, Robbie Ancens, sits in a chair next to his parents, Jonathan and Chey Ancens, notable Korean billionaires. His father is half Korean and half Polish, and his mother, Korean. The Ancens were constantly traveling back and forth to Asia with-out Robbie for "business"—at least that's what his mother told him, though he had come to find out after listening in on one of his parent's private conversations that his mother's family was involved in some kind of Korean mafia business, a part of her life she felt obligated to but wanted her son to take no part of. When they were home, though, they always made an effort to attend the Montevega's parties, more so to show their gratitude for watching Robbie. He didn't mind their absence, though. With his parents always gone, he spent more time with the Montevega family than his own and had come to much prefer their company. Bored out of his mind during the party, Robbie locks eyes with Marcie. He gestures across the room to the twins' older sister, Mackenzie, and mocks her prissy attitude with a silly face, pursing his lips and swishing his shoulders. Marcie covers her mouth to conceal a giggle.

Fifteen-year-old Mackenzie Montevega sits on a couch surrounded by three teenage girls, all toting glasses of champagne, as no one would surely question their consumption of alcohol at such an exclusive event and gossiping about the latest drama at school. Mackenzie very rarely came home from her private boarding school, but she always seemed to make time for appearances at her parents' fabulous dinner parties. She never had much of a relationship with her younger sisters, whom she found to be irritating more than anything—though maybe it was more out of jealousy from her parents' "special treatment" of the twins, deeming them too good for "regular" school. While Mackenzie didn't care much for being homeschooled anyway, the incredible amount of freedom the twins had to travel the world is what really annoyed her most (or rather, it was *her* lack of freedom to use the family's private jet), even though she knew their freedom came with a price.

At the piano, Madisyn's eyes wander up as her fingers move across the keys. She examines the guests around her with fierce, narrowed eyes, all of them gawking at her like an animal at the zoo. Ever since they were three years old, the twins were subjected to "entertaining" at their parents' parties, taking turns playing a newly learned piece of music from that week's lessons. As the more obedient twin, Marcie found it hard to complain of her parents' power move showing off their perfect children as a way to demonstrate their incredible wealth. They were raised with truly ideal lives, having the best of everything. The least they could do was cooperate and play the parts they were meant to perform.

When the twins turned six, Reese and Bill decided they could broaden their minds through homeschooling. They had watched their eldest daughter become consumed in more superficial interests going to school with other children, but they were determined to have Madisyn and Marcie explore their full potential studying from home. Robbie joined them, of course, as this allowed his parents to work more in Asia. After careful screening, the Montevega's hired Valentina Dementieva, an eighteen-year-old yet highly decorated and quite strict Russian tutor whose expertise showed well beyond her age.

In their home library, Valentina would make Robbie and the twins sit at the table with perfect posture and read for hours, watching them with stern, unblinking eyes until they finished. They learned every subject taught in school, plus more, at a much faster pace than average students. With an interest in technology, they each acquired skills to challenge even the most highly classified computer hackers on the National Crime Agency's most-wanted list by the age of eight. And per their parents' request, they spoke nine languages by the time they were nine. Valentina insisted they learn Russian first, but then the children went on to learn

Korean, French, Japanese, Italian, Spanish, Portuguese, and Mandarin Chinese.

For extracurriculars, Valentina convinced Reese and Bill that instead of the children wasting their talents on meaningless activities like sports, they learn physical activities that could benefit them and possibly protect them, as children of billionaires could often be targets to criminals. Not a day went by where they weren't training under a martial arts expert as Valentina stood off to the side watching, cold and emotionless, almost militant, with her hands linked behind her back. The twins and Robbie soon earned their black belts in Jiujitsu and Krav Maga and specialized in weaponry, including sword and chain mace fighting, Tantojutsu, and Eskrima, all by age ten. Reese and Bill never seemed to question the necessity for their children having top-notch skills of trained assassins, and in fact, figured "why not?" when their children should surely have the best of everything.

But what Madisyn, Marcie, and Robbie all loved the most from their homeschooled education was taking the family jet any and everywhere in the world, having convinced their parents that their trips were purely educational—though most of the time they were simply to satisfy their curiosities. And to make friends, of course. Whoever said homeschooled children were unsocial obviously didn't own a private jet.

With all the resources money could buy, the Montevega twins and Robbie were perfect at practically everything—thanks to Valentina. And as a notion of gratitude to the young, devoted tutor, Reese and Bill invited her to live with them and become a full-time nanny, which again was especially convenient for Robbie's parents as well. The Montevegas built her a home attached to theirs by a long glass hallway that arched over the driveway.

Valentina, now twenty-three years old, stands in the door-way of the party, just close enough to keep an eye on the children but far away enough to not be expected to socialize, something she found very trivial. Her hands rest behind her back in her usual stance. To Valentina's dismay, a woman comes up to her, laughing ridiculously at her own joke—clearly the product of one too many flutes of champagne. The stern-faced nanny nods: the only forcibly polite gesture she can muster to keep from appearing disrespectful to her bosses' guests. Losing interest, Valentina looks over to an obedient Marcie, still standing quietly by her mother.

The corner of Valentina's mouth almost seems to pinch into a smirk of admiration. She was often praised for her work of raising geniuses. Some people called the twins prodigies. Reese and Bill called them "flawless creations of strong genes," which perhaps had something to do with the twins' genetic modification—something their parents had often slipped into the conversation to further flaunt their wealth. But what most people *didn't* see was what lurked beneath the surface. Something inside Madisyn was brewing—something, not even Marcie and Robbie could see coming.

With a desire to end her piece early on the piano, Madisyn abruptly slams her fingers on the keys in an ear-shattering chord, her eyes fluttering up again to take in her audience's reaction, a faint rather pleased smile sneaking across her lips.

Everyone in the room gawks at her, gasping at the small outburst from their usual order. Reese's nostrils flare, trying to hide her anger for the sake of her polite company. Marcie's eyes grow at her twin's defiant gesture.

An unapologetic Madisyn stands from the piano, taking pleasure in glaring back at the curious eyes on her presence. She had never gotten this kind of satisfaction from a performance before. She decided there must be more of this glorified disobedience in her near future. Without a word, Madisyn struts from the silent room: the only movement amongst a crowd of seemingly paralyzed partygoers.

As people start to murmur about the spectacle, Reese and Bill apologize for the disruption, attempting to liven the party again. While her mother is occupied, Marcie sneaks away from her side to run after her twin, and Robbie dutifully follows. Both run past Valentina, whose emotionless gaze follows the children from the room.

A brooding Madisyn sits in a thronelike chair in a dark corner of the twins' bedroom, the dim light of a single lamp nearby casting a shadow across her face. "Omnia Sol Temperat," a more dismal and measured section from Carl Orff's "Carmina Burana," the complete opposite from the lively infamous "O Fortuna," plays softly in the background. Her face rests in the "L" of her right hand, as the melancholic lull of the minor key allows her to entertain her vices. Her blank and unblinking eyes stare off into the distance. Inside of her burned a deep desire for something more—more than performing at dinner parties and being a puppet dangling from her parents' fingertips.

The bedroom door opens, and Marcie cautiously enters, seeing her more dramatic twin in a trance. Robbie lingers back in the doorway. Marcie walks up to her sister and slowly reaches out to poke Madisyn's cheek, but her twin does not move or even blink, for that matter. Marcie settles to her knees in front of the chair. With rising concern, she places her hands on top of Madisyn's in her lap. She stares up at her, longing for even the faintest sign of life, but as the music drones on, Madisyn stays lost in her daze of deep contemplation.

Hours later, Marcie awakens in her bed, disturbed by noises across the room. She sees Madisyn sitting on the floor, surrounded by a mess of papers that list names and long numbers. Madisyn scribbles out another list and sorts through the pile with a feverish need.

Marcie slips out of bed and moves over to her twin. On a single sheet of paper, Madisyn writes the word "UCOCA" in bold red letters. She sets down the marker, realizing this is the acronym she was looking for. She holds the sheet out in front of her. With wild eyes, Madisyn looks over her shoulder at Marcie, who stands behind her, her eyes as big as saucers at her twin's erratic behavior. Madisyn does not smile nor speak, but her eyes communicate a seriousness about the word—one that would change the meaning of their lives forever.

CHAPTER 3

——

PRESENT DAY

Madisyn struts through the front doors of the Rossi car dealership in London—sporting a black, over-sized, designer blazer as a dress, with knee-high stockings and white, patent leather Prada sneakers—her hair in its usual high ponytail, and her eyes masked by wide black, Gucci frames. She had once seen her mother wear the exact same outfit in a photo, except she had been wearing black sling-back pumps as she held on to the small hand of baby Mackenzie. Even back then, she had been the image of a powerful woman who was just starting a family but was never too afraid of her own sex appeal. This was the exact persona Madisyn had decided she would take on to run her own empire, when she wasn't scaling mountains and infiltrating secret lairs of the world's richest men, that is.

Unmoved by the breathtaking, two-story, glass building sparkling with luxury vehicles, she passes sixty-year-old Chadwick, the front desk man and long-time friend of her mother's. "Top of the morning, Miss Madisyn," he chimes.

"Chadwick," she greets him coldly, without so much as a glance from underneath her tinted shades, focusing all her energy on the day ahead.

She heads to her mother's office down the long glass hallway. Closing the door behind her, Madisyn looks back to make sure no one is around before ripping the shutters down over the doors and windows.

Removing her shades, she sits at her mother's desk and runs her hand under it until she feels a small indention. She pulls on this secret latch. One so obscure in its placement, not even Reese herself had ever discovered it. Madisyn swivels around in the chair as a secret elevator opens in the wall. She gets up and hops inside, and its door closes behind her.

At the bottom floor, a hundred feet underground, the elevator opens to reveal the entrance to the UCOCA London Headquarters, a place built five years ago when Madisyn cooked up the idea for her, her twin, and Robbie to go rogue. Meeting many others like themselves, teenagers bored of their families benefitting from the woes of capitalism, during their traveling, they built five other locations under Rossi car dealerships. These locations were run by their most entrusted friends in discreet areas that would allow them the most advantageous global reach: Seattle, NYC, Japan, Brazil, and Ukraine. The twins borrowed large amounts of money from their father to start "investing," which boosted his entrepreneurial spirit so much that he even set them up with their own bank account with a starting loan of £50 million. Just what they needed to get their empire up and running.

Five years later, their organization was fully operational. They were officially the Unorthodox Capitalists Organized Crime Association, though instead of preying on the innocent through trafficking and drug trade etc., their goal was to target the richest bad guys in the world and steal everything from them.

It was about power. It was even somewhat about greed. But most of all, it was Madisyn's way of sending a great big *fuck you* to a rule-abiding society and anyone who thought they could control her. They were playing by her rules now.

Madisyn struts down the long, clinically white hallway until it opens up into a massive room. Teenage agents work at computers with headsets, huge monitors splayed behind them on the wall showing digital maps, targets, and visuals on the other UCOCA locations. As founders, Madisyn, Marcie, and Robbie always had first dibs on missions from their other locations if UCOCA London wasn't working on anything themselves, but this rarely occurred. Madisyn made sure their headquarters always had promising targets lined up around the world, utilizing teams from the UCOCA location closest to the targets as a backup along with taking her own trusted team from London to get in on the action. But as they still ran an operation meant to bring in extreme capital, and simply because Madisyn knew she couldn't be in two places at once, they still expected each of their locations to take on at least one target each month on their own. For Madisyn, it wasn't even about getting a cut of the profits. She just wanted to ensure her teams were kept sharp for when it came time for UCOCA London to use them for more dangerous missions.

The rules of their operation were simple:

1. **Rule #1.** Utilize cash whenever possible for purchases (if they needed something that required a credit card, they would use funds from the investment account their father

had set them up with, being careful to stay under £10 million when withdrawing).

2. **Rule #2.** Never use stolen drugs (Madisyn enforced a very clean operation that allowed her agents to be as focused as she was).

3. **Rule #3.** Get rid of any drugs, gold, and jewels by trading on the black market for cash (allowing them to uphold Rule #1).

4. **Rule #4.** Carry out "drop-offs" each month—an idea Marcie had held over Madisyn's head until she had reluctantly consented, arguing for them to anonymously donate leftover portions of their spoils to worldwide organizations that fight poverty, hunger, and trafficking. This had piqued Marcie's interest when they began studying world history with Valentina, which had been around the same time they started building upon Madisyn's idea for UCOCA. Back then, for whatever reason, Valentina had felt the need to make sure her billionaire princesses (and prince) were fully aware of the brutal hardships different people around the world faced, like modern-day slavery, starvation, and human trafficking, through intensely graphic educational videos. Marcie had threatened to withhold her participation from UCOCA completely and even risk jeopardizing her twin's insane plan unless they would use their stolen goods to help the less fortunate. Eventually, Madisyn negotiated her down to donating whatever was left after all their agents had been paid their fair share.

5. **Rule #5.** Never abandon a fellow agent, no matter how risky the mission (this was one Madisyn, Marcie, and Robbie equally agreed was necessary, knowing that the

moment the three of them ceased to have each other's back, which would be the demise of their entire operation).

UCOCA would be both business and leisure for them, as long as the three of them stuck together as founders. They all had different reasons for running the organization, though. For Marcie, UCOCA was meant to play a part in the world's social issues. For Robbie, it was just good fun. Humanitarians or not, Madisyn knew that money was the key to her overall happiness. Whoever had said "money isn't everything" clearly didn't know how to use it. To her, money was *freedom*. It allowed them to build a worldwide operation with wicked-cool secret lairs. It allowed them to fly on private jets and sail the high seas on expensive yachts. Madisyn had even built a hidden weapons room in their own room at home without their parents ever knowing. And her favorite part was the state-of-the-art weapons lab she had installed in their London headquarters, where her most high tech and proficient agents designed, built, and tested gadgets and guns, unlike anything the world had ever seen before. Stealing was much more than just a really good sport now for Madisyn. It was a way of life that created extreme wealth and opportunity without having to become boring businesspeople who lived mundane lives like their parents.

Spotting her twin and Robbie across the vast operations room in the main office, in the center on a raised platform surrounded by cylindrical glass walls stretching up to the ceiling, Madisyn makes her way over to them. Inside, Marcie sits behind a desk, her chair facing Robbie, who leans against the wall looking her up and down. Marcie can't help but giggle nervously. She crosses her legs, leaning back in the chair. "Robbie Ancens, why on earth are you staring at me like that?"

Robbie shakes his head with his usual dazzling smile. Ever since they were little, Marcie had always been taken with his charm. And now, he had grown into an even more handsome boy with a strong chiseled jaw and a flirty, cool attitude to match. Marcie couldn't quite pinpoint the moment he became such a hunk, but she could sense a shift in his mannerisms after his family's trip to Korea a year ago. She couldn't help but wonder what mischief he might have gotten into there…

"Nothing. You just look…" he trails off, not meeting her eyes. "It's just impossible for anyone to take you seriously." He laughs at his tease, and Marcie purses her lips. She adjusts her navy, gold-buttoned blazer, draped across her shoulders to match her sleeveless black bodysuit and leather pants. They might have been criminals, but that didn't mean their double life couldn't hold a certain allure. After all, they were practically adults now. And they had only ever watched their mother slink around the house in showy getups that could still make their father drool after all those years of marriage. Her presence was mystifying to men, and her daughters all longed to be just like her.

As Madisyn enters the office, Marcie and Robbie awkwardly look away from one another. Marcie clears her throat and sits up straighter, running her hand down her long braid that hangs over her shoulder. She forces a smile toward her sister. Marcie's intention was never for her twin to know how much she liked Robbie. He was their childhood friend, after all, and Madisyn technically had dibs on him just as much as she did. She figured the right thing to do was to accept an unspoken truce for neither of them to pair off with Robbie. So as much as Robbie tried, she always dodged his advances.

"Call a meeting," Madisyn says. "I've come across quite the subject for our next mission. A fun one, if I must say so myself."

"*Fun?*" Robbie asks, amused. "And *you* found this one?" He laughs, and Marcie tries to stifle her own. Over the years, Madisyn had become rather uptight since they began running their UCOCA operation. Madisyn was convinced she was simply doing what it took to be a fearless leader since neither Marcie nor Robbie were willing to step up to the plate. Somebody had to be the bad guy, which was a role she had no problem taking on.

"Shut up," Madisyn retorts, rolling her eyes and not finding Robbie's joke even a little bit funny. "We'll need to connect Heidi with UCOCA Seattle. They'll help us with this one." She turns and leaves promptly, never being one to linger in meaningless chitchat. Through the glass, Robbie and Marcie watch her strut through the main room.

"Why is it that whenever *I* find a mission, it gets dismissed? But when Madisyn finds one, everyone has to be involved or gets their head chewed off?" Marcie pouts. Robbie just laughs and pushes off the wall.

"You know how sensitive she is about UCOCA. It's her 'baby.' Me and you? We're just along for the ride, sweetheart." He pushes through the door, leaving Marcie behind. She hated that she always got the short end of the stick, but there wasn't really room for both her and Madisyn in the spotlight—she would just have to settle for being "along for the ride."

Inside the dark conference room, the twins and Robbie sit at a large doughnut-shaped table resting on an elevated platform, each spot at the table holding embedded touch screens for each agent to view digital files on.

Other UCOCA agents fill in the table, including two of their top agents, sixteen-year-olds James McEvoy and Drake Calley, best friends and work partners. The two of them were so close, one could hardly ever find one of them without the other. They were known as "the other set of twins" because of this, though they looked nothing alike. James was chisel-faced with a buzz cut and mocha skin, just a shade darker than the twins. Drake was fair-skinned with a full head of dark wavy hair. Both were tall and noted by most of the girls who ogled them constantly—both were extremely attractive.

Madisyn uses the built-in control panel to call up UCOCA Seattle. A hologram cube appears over the center hole in the table, showing a sixteen-year-old blonde named Heidi Pennington, leader of their favorite UCOCA site in the US and one of their closest American friends.

"Hello, UCOCA London," Heidi chimes.

"Heidi Pennington, everyone," Madisyn introduces her, as was a formality. "From our headquarters in Seattle."

"Heidi!" Marcie exclaims girlishly. "It's been so long. How *are* things? How are tiny Jackson and the evil soon-to-be step-mummy?"

Heidi beams lovingly at her friend. "Aw, they're so great! How's—"

Madisyn clears her throat loudly. "Ahem."

Marcie scoffs, giving her twin an appalled glance, but Madisyn simply ignores this and moves the cubed hologram with a flick of her finger to a monitor on the wall. The hologram disappears as Heidi's face reappears on the monitor now. A sour-faced Marcie looks to Robbie for support, but he only lifts his eyebrows at her, unfazed by her twin's behavior.

Madisyn types on the control pad and pulls up a hologram of two men in the center.

"Here we go," she begins. "Two American senators—the one on the right is Jacquard 'Jay' Saunders, and this one…" She notions to the left. "This is Patrick McLean. They're leaders of a secret society of wealthy men who… like to participate in some particularly fucked up activities. Real *bad* boys." She smirks, getting a few laughs at her sarcasm. "I've been keeping a close eye on them, though I find McLean to be a most *interesting* character."

TWO WEEKS PRIOR—TEXAS, USA
In the Texas State Capitol, Senator Patrick McLean stands in front of the mirror, checking himself out. He fixes his tie, adjusts his suit jacket, and then winks at himself flashing his winning smile. With a thick Texan accent, he blurts out his awful, self-indulging campaign slogan: "the name is Patrick McLean, and we'll do the thang!" He laughs with an air of confidence the way only a white man in politics can, as his assistant, twenty-something-year-old Catherine Schwalb, opens his office door.

"Senator, your meeting starts soon."

He spins around to face her, still smirking. "Oh no, no! I'm not going to that boring meeting. That meeting is for men who like to talk! And *I* am a man of action, Ms. Schwalb, isn't that right?" He winks at her, and Catherine forces an unsure smile.

"But sir, it's just that—"

"Walk with me, Catherine." He gestures her out the door and follows. They walk down the hallway together. "We have to be very careful this month, and I mean *very* careful, on this new set of bills. Hey, how are ya doing, Bobby?" He greets a man passing by, paying less attention to Catherine, who only nods and walks closely behind, practically scurrying to keep up with his cocky strides.

"Yes, sir. And there's also been a lot of talk about the budget."

He waves his hand at the subject. "The budget's fine. The people of Texas need to learn how to cooperate. I say we already get plenty of money that takes care of everybody."

Catherine purses her lips at this. "Well, sir, it's just that people are expressing their concerns for education and schools."

Senator McLean swings around to click his tongue at her, shaking his head as they stop in front of a doorway. "Catherine, you know what's wrong with Texas? It's not the schools; it's not the quality of education or our funding. Its people are *greedy*. Plain and simple." He tilts his head down at her with a look to nudge his mousy assistant into agreeing. Catherine sighs and nods, forcing a smile that satisfies him. "What do I always say, Catherine? 'The name's Patrick McLean, and we'll do the thang!' Don't you worry, darlin', the people *love* Pat McLean."

The senator laughs, ignoring the waning faux grin on her face as she turns around to leave. Senator McLean enters the doorway of the meeting room filled with men around a table, talking before the start of the meeting. He makes his way to a group of men standing and pats one of the guys on the back. "Jay, good to see ya!"

Senator Jay Saunders spins around to shake his pal's hand. McLean pulls him slightly aside and lowers his voice, keeping his usual smile plastered on his face to appease any onlookers. "We're moving the date earlier this month. Say, next week?"

Jay chuckles lightly, keeping his own smile wide and innocent. "Sure, I'll let everyone know."

Both men laugh, and Patrick slaps him again on the shoulder, leaning just a tad closer to his comrade to talk into his ear. "I'm blowing off this meeting for a little rendezvous of my own. We'll talk business at the party." He squeezes Jay's shoulder and heads for the door.

That evening, Senator Saunders's wife Darla hosts a lavish backyard garden party at their home in downtown Austin. Well-dressed guests mingle about in the yard, some sipping tea, others martinis and mimosas, while a string quartet plays lively classical music in the far corner of the patio. Next to a vast spread of hors d'oeuvres near the center by the pool, Senator McLean and his wife Annie stand talking with Jay and Darla.

"Oh, Annie!" Darla coos. "Jay and I are always so glad you two make time for our little shindigs."

"Yes, it means the world to her that you come," Jay adds, forcing a less enthused smirk. Patrick raises his eyebrows at him in an attempt to hurry the conversation along.

"Honestly, though," Darla continues. "I barely had time to put this one together. Jay wouldn't dare let me host it next weekend! You know, with their little boys' trip to LA to watch the men's national soccer team final." Annie almost spits out her drink to stare at her husband, but Darla doesn't notice. "Daniel's going too, right Patrick? Where is he tonight anyway?"

Patrick downs half of his drink to avoid his wife's glare. "Danny's actually at the office still, finishing up a little business for me."

"Aw, you work that son of yours so hard!" Darla says. "But it's really great he gets to intern with you guys right after high school. Like father, like son!" Darla toasts with a nod before taking a sip.

Annie tugs at her husband's sleeve to pull him closer, lowering her voice. "Were you planning on mentioning this to me at all?"

Patrick laughs uneasily, looking from her to Jay. "You know how these things are, hun."

Jay turns to Annie in an attempt to defend his friend. "Forgive me, Annie, it was really my fault for bringing it up so last minute. A lot of important people are going to be at this game, and Patrick just has to be one of them!" Annie purses her lips and looks away from Jay and a still-smiling Darla to glare at her absent-minded husband, who never seemed to include her in anything anymore. "In fact," Jay continues, nodding toward the house. "A couple of them are here tonight. Pat, why don't we leave the ladies to their gabbing, and I'll introduce you."

Jay starts to lead Patrick away, and Patrick forces a laugh to lighten the mood. He kisses Annie on the cheek and presses his lips to her ear. "We'll talk about this later. Just smile and keep it together." He kisses her on the forehead while she slightly shrinks away, avoiding his eyes.

Darla gushes, refusing to let her friend's sour mood kill her garden party. "Gosh, you know how boys are. They wait until the last minute to plan. It's a miracle they get anything done!" She shouts after the men, "No business tonight, boys! I mean it, Jay!"

Both men laugh and raise their glasses to Darla. Patrick swipes a crab puff from the table before following Jay.

Passing guests on the vast porch leading into the house, Jay and Patrick both nod and tip their glasses. Inside, they turn down an empty hall, heading toward Jay's home office by the front door. Jay lets Patrick inside first, closing the door behind them. Patrick moves to a chair in front of the desk as Jay sits behind it, setting his drink down.

"We've got some new investors this month," Jay starts. "*Big* ones, too." Patrick chuckles with excitement as Jay hands him a file from the stack of papers on his desk. He opens the manila folder, sifting through its content. "Two of the biggest crime lords on the West Coast."

Patrick's smile wanes. "West Coast crime lords, huh?" He holds up a page with a profile on one of the men. "Ian Day?"

"He runs The Motterdal crime syndicate. Their focus is mostly drug trafficking. Worth around two hundred million dollars. And I hear his influence stretches all the way down to Mexico." Jay's eyes flare with delight. Patrick looks from his friend back to the paper and flips to the next, pursing his lips. "Alfie Morgan's the other guy; arms dealer; supplies some of the biggest gangsters around. Now, Pat, these guys aren't going to fully put in until they're satisfied with the stability of our group. But you have to trust me on this one. I think we could get more than a few million for the pot."

Patrick sighs and sets down the file. "I don't know, Jay. Mafia boys? Isn't that a little risky? Even for us?"

"What's life without a little risk?" Jay shrugs, though Patrick appears unconvinced. "Pat, these guys are *very* interested. And it can't pose much risk to us. It's actually beneficial for them, developing a relationship with senators. They wouldn't jeopardize that."

Patrick nods his head, slowly at first but open to being persuaded. "Well, I am familiar with Mr. Morgan's work."

Jay grins, sensing his pal coming around. He opens his desk drawer and pulls out a vintage pistol and holds it up. "Me too," he laughs. He carelessly tosses the gun on his desk, not realizing it's still loaded when the gun fires loudly on its own. The shot hits Jay's scotch glass, which bursts into pieces and causes both men to throw themselves to the floor.

"Holy *shit*, Jay!" Patrick says through a strained whisper. "What the fuck was that?"

Jay, still cowering behind his desk, looks up. "Did they hear that?" he asks, his voice shaking. He gestures to the door as Patrick mouths a silent "what?"

"Quick, go check the door! Go see if anybody heard!"

Patrick hesitantly gets up and slinks over to the door. He peaks his head out, not seeing any guests down the long hallway. He closes the door and sighs heavily, wiping the sweat from his forehead. "Jesus, Jay," he breathes. "It's fine, it's fine!"

Jay laughs uneasily at his own stupidity. He stands, fixing his jacket. "Shit. I'm so sorry, I had no idea it'd do that!" Both of them chuckle uneasily. Jay walks over and picks up the gun, removing the bullets from it before putting it back in his desk. "I guess we should leave the guns to Alfie, huh?"

Patrick shakes his head with a smirk. "Yeah, let's do that."

Jay sighs and sits down at his desk again, leaning back. "I'm telling you, Pat, I'm feeling lucky about this one. I mean, *really* lucky."

"Well, Jay…" Patrick grabs his unbroken glass off the desk and takes a sip. "I'm not really worried about who wins, who loses. I like the pastime. We're already wealthy, established men. This is all just good business… and real good entertainment. Say, what the hell—Let's get Ian and Alfie in on this!" The men laugh again, much more at ease now. Jay picks up what's left of his glass and clanks it with Patrick's, the latter gulping down his drink.

PRESENT DAY: UCOCA LONDON

Having tuned out most of her sister's blabbing about her findings, Marcie scrolls through the file on her touch screen with information about the senators. "So, this is a game of Russian roulette?" she asks.

Madisyn nods. "Held every three months. And the location is always different. I had Drake and James do some digging." Marcie and Robbie exchange glances. Normally they were *her* right hands when it came to mission research.

"Our intel reports this one will be held somewhere in Los Angeles," Drake announces to the room. "It's been hard to pinpoint where exactly, though."

"The locations of these events are very hush-hush," James picks up his partner's point. "No one involved is allowed to say or digitally send the exact coordinates of the secure site for fear of being caught. Obviously, the senators would face pretty hefty repercussions, as well as any of the other big names involved..."

Marcie scoffs. "So how on earth do they know where to meet? What, do they use those god-awful carrier pigeons from the *Harry Potter* movies or something?"

"Those were owls..." Madisyn retorts, to which Marcie rolls her eyes.

"We suspect they write the coordinates on paper and memorize it," James answers.

"But there might be a way for us to intercept this," Drake says.

Robbie shakes his head. "What? We pretend to be someone who wants in on the game?"

"That'll never work," Madisyn says, having already pondered this option. "They only invite very high-profile people, and it's already a week away. We'd have no time to create a fake persona they would be interested in."

"Jay Saunders is a huge football fan, though," Drake adds. "He invited head coach Giovanni Sacchi of the US men's national soccer team to take part in their… 'game.' He makes a little over two million going into the last year of his contract. And the US national team—"

"Plays in LA next week!" Heidi adds from the monitor. "They're playing Mexico. It's one of their huge qualifying games before the World Cup."

James nods. "Right, Heidi. The senators are going to be there before meeting Sacchi and the others for their game that same night."

Robbie sits back in his seat in awe. "That's brilliant. They'll definitely be in premium seating. Can we still get passes this last minute?"

Madisyn looks up from scrolling on her touch screen. "Robbie, sometimes I think you're buried so far deep into our double life that you forget who your own bloody parents are," she chides. As if children of billionaires would ever lack anything they wanted or needed, especially something as simple as tickets to a football game.

Robbie leans forward in his chair, his hands sprawled out on the table and wide-eyed at the hypocritical retort. "*You're* one to talk!" he retorts. She rolls her eyes.

Heidi cuts in, hoping to quiet their bickering, "I actually already have tickets! I'm taking my soon-to-be stepbrother, Jackson. We can grab more passes, premium seating, of course."

Still facing Madisyn with narrowed eyes, Robbie says, "So, you're saying, all we have to do is go to the game and do *what* exactly?"

"We could kidnap one of the senators and force them to tell us where the next game is?" Marcie suggests. Robbie sighs deeply and rubs his temples at the absurd idea.

Madisyn rolls her head over to squint at her sister. "We have to be *way* more discreet than that."

"So how do you suppose, then?" Marcie asks, raising an eyebrow and tapping her fingers on the table impatiently.

Lacking a direct comeback, Madisyn bites the inside of her cheek. "I'm not sure yet. American public officials usually hire sizable security teams at public events, especially ones of this magnitude. But there is someone who might be a little more reachable…" She pulls up a hologram of an attractive blond-haired boy. "Patrick McLean's son, Daniel."

"He's very close with his father," Drake says, informing the group. "Just turned nineteen and put off going to college to start interning with his dad. This was actually the senator's idea. He expressed that a college education was a waste of time for someone with his bloodlines. He's taken Daniel under his wing substantially. So, I suspect he'll not only be at the football game—"

"He'll probably be with his dad later that night, too!" Marcie finishes excitedly as if she just solved a puzzle.

Madisyn sits back in her chair, her gaze lingering for a moment on the hologram's dangerously cute face. "I'll be the one to get close to him," she volunteers. "He's definitely our way in." Her head snaps over for James to continue.

"So the estimate for the winner of this game is about ten million," he says, not missing a beat. "It's the biggest bet in the last five years." A few agents whistle in awe. Madisyn uses her keypad to make the hologram disappear as he finishes. "As far as how the game actually works: The Gamblers force people desperate for money to be players. Only one player is alive by the end of the game. He and the man that bets on him win the pot, in this case, ten million dollars."

"Probably not split very evenly," Marcie says what everyone is thinking. James shakes his head, confirming her suspicion.

"All ten million is kept on location during the game," Drake continues. "Senator McLean's bright idea."

"Who can blame him?" Robbie says. "I'm sure the smell of cold-hard cash really plays nicely with the stench of fresh corpses." A couple of agents laugh.

Madisyn clears her throat, establishing order. "We steal the money and intercept the game before anyone's head gets blown off. Sounds fairly simple, yes?" The agents murmur with anticipation.

"It sounds like the US Senate is corrupt," Robbie adds, getting more snickers around the room, including from Marcie.

Madisyn narrows her eyes at him for a second, slightly annoyed at his attention-whorish behavior. "What else is new?" she says, waving away the comment. "This a great opportunity to have some wicked fun and make a pretty penny at the same time."

"Well still," Robbie rebuts. "None of it means anything without even knowing this mystery location..." Madisyn breathes heavily, forcing herself to remain calm. It seemed she and Robbie were always butting heads lately, though, in this instance, he made a very valid point. She purses her lips at this realization, unsure of how to respond just yet, but she would be sure to contemplate long and hard on a solution when she had some peace and quiet later on.

"Don't miss the point here," Marcie cuts in. "We'll be heroes." The room grows silent. Only a year into their full-fledged operation, and it seemed like they were all forgetting the noble cause that lay behind UCOCA's existence—the one reason that had originally convinced Marcie to go along with her twin's obvious growing insanity. "Let's pretend we have morals for once. If we actually go through with this, we'll save innocent lives. We're not just thieves! We take things from *bad* people. It's the least our sorry selves can do to contribute to the world. Most of us in this room were born with everything we could ever want. Don't you all feel any kind of responsibility to give back and make the world a better place?"

Some of the agents nod quietly in agreement. Robbie averts his gaze with a small amount of guilt. Like Madisyn, he too often got too wrapped up in what they were capable of and forgot the positive impact they were actually making on the world. In the midst of a silent moment, Madisyn scoffs at her twin's soppy speech.

"God, we're not superheroes! Get over yourself," Madisyn retorts. "I just want to scare those pricks so much they shit their freaking pants. Can you imagine their faces?" A few agents laugh as the mood lightens. Madisyn stands, ignoring the sour look on Marcie's face. "Heidi, start preparing your team. This game is scheduled for next week. Let's get ready to play."

CHAPTER 4

A half kilometer down the road from the Montevega villa, and on the family's vast piece of land, Madisyn stands in one of the stalls of their stable, grooming her favorite black stallion Buckley. She runs the large brush down the horse's mane and gives him a pat on the neck. Since they were six years old, riding had been the only fun-time activity Valentina had allowed the twins to indulge in, and as they grew older, it became a ritual for the sisters to go out on the trails together. Setting down the brush, Madisyn grabs the cherry-oak leather saddle from the wall. She places the saddle on Buckley's back, atop a black saddle pad, just as Marcie comes into the stable wearing a matching riding outfit of white breeches, a black blazer, and tall leather boots, her usual braid swooped over her right shoulder.

"You're late," Madisyn says without so much as a look back.

Marcie purses her lips, looking down at her diamond-encrusted, rose gold Jaeger-LeCoultre watch. "I'm right on time," she retorts, moving over to her own horse, a bay mare named Freesia.

Madisyn dons her black riding helmet before checking her girth and bridling her horse. She hops onto the stallion with ease, swinging her right leg effortlessly over his back. "You should always be five minutes early with enough time for preparation." She touches Buckley with her leg, and he eagerly walks out of the stable.

Rolling her eyes, Marcie quickly tacks Freesia before mounting her, taking off after her twin through the tall grasses of the backcountry fields. She finds Madisyn waiting right at the start of the dirt trail. Together, the sisters ride side by side through the woods at a brisk walk.

"So I was thinking," Madisyn begins. "For the upcoming mission, we'll want to take the jet up to Seattle rather than straight to LA. That way, we can meet up with Heidi and the team at our headquarters. Plus, I don't want any correlation with our jet landing in the same city where our mission will take place. The tabloids have been having a field day with our close presence to the last couple of murders, so I don't want to take any chances." Madisyn smirks. "And I have an idea about using the senator's son. I'll be the one to take charge on that, of course, but don't worry, you'll still have a good time too."

Marcie exhales loudly, something clearly on her mind but refusing to talk. She nudges her horse into a trot. Madisyn peers over, raising an eyebrow at her sister's reluctance to speak. She faces forward again, urging her mount to catch up to Marcie's.

"Don't you have anything to say?" Madisyn asks, becoming impatient. Their weekly rides were some of the only times the twins got to be alone together to share their thoughts without someone overhearing them, something that became crucial for Madisyn with having Robbie around them all the time.

"Honestly, Madisyn," Marcie says. "Does everything really have to be about business with you? Don't you miss hanging out with me at all?" Madisyn furrows her eyebrows and frowns. "I mean, I feel like we never get to catch up on normal things. We only talk about UCOCA."

Madisyn scoffs. "Of course, I miss hanging out with you!" she gushes, almost too over the top. Madisyn purses her lips, seeing that her twin saw right through her. "What exactly *should* we talk about then? It's not like we have anything else in common…"

The sisters ride in silence for a moment, and Marcie sighs. "Remember when we were little? Mum and Dad would take us to the South of France every summer." Marcie peers over at her sister, a slight grin tugging at Madisyn's lips.

"We would all hang out at the beach," Madisyn adds with a nod, the memory resurfacing. "Mum complained about how weird the French are after we accidentally went to that nude beach." The two of them laugh. "Dad was always busy with work. We'd have to practically pry his phone and laptop away from him so he'd get in the water."

Marcie smiles, watching her sister's face light up. "Mackenzie wasn't so bad back then either. She actually used to talk to us, remember?"

Madisyn laughs and shakes her head. "Oh, God! And she had that disgusting crush on that awful French boy! What was his name again?"

"Pierre!" Marcie shouts, cracking up. "He was quite sweet to her, though." Madisyn's grin starts to wane into a pout. "Don't you miss the old us? Before everything got so serious? Before we all grew up into obnoxious teenage girls who hate each other." Marcie teases, trying to lighten her sister's mood.

"We don't hate each other, Marcelle." Madisyn looks over at her. "We all just grew up."

Marcie remains quiet.

"Of course, I miss it sometimes…" Madisyn admits after a moment of silence for her lost innocence. "But things are different now. Mum and Dad are busy—they don't have time to take us on family trips. Plus, we're not little girls anymore. We don't need them to have fun. Mackenzie's got her own friends, and she doesn't want to be bothered. That's why I started UCOCA."

Marcie purses her lips, her gaze wandering off into the trees. Madisyn knew what exactly she was thinking—that running their operation wasn't always exactly "fun" for Marcie. That Madisyn "always had to be in control." Maybe things would be different if they were just able to talk about it…

"I don't think we're always on the same page when it comes to UCOCA," Madisyn says, easing into the subject. "For instance, in Brazil—you took our Antigravity Forcefield from the weapons lab without even talking to me. I hadn't even had a chance to test it out and deem it safe in a controlled environment! I mean, honestly, what if it didn't work and you had been killed?"

"Oh, come on!" Marcie says, calling her bluff. "You're telling me that had nothing to do with you just wanting to be the first to do it like you are with everything!"

Madisyn rolls her eyes. "I know, so maybe we should talk about that! You know how hard it is for me to let go sometimes. I don't know. Maybe you can help me be a little better about that."

"I want to talk about things that actually matter, Madisyn." Marcie continues, oblivious to Madisyn's UCOCA-related statement. "Like... I don't know, what new things are you into now? I've been reading this new book I found the other day by an up-and-coming author in the city, and it's really good actually. It kind of reminded me of how—"

"*God*, Marcelle!" Madisyn exclaims, pulling Buckley to an abrupt halt. "See what happens when I actually try to put myself out there? This is why I stopped opening up to you." She closes her eyes and takes a deep breath.

Marcie pulls Freesia over and turns back to face her sister. "I'm not trying to ignore what you want to talk about, but I just feel like we don't really know each other anymore."

Opening her eyes, Madisyn sucks on the inside of her cheek. "Well then, who's fault is that? Because this is *exactly* who I am." She nudges Buckley into a canter, taking off down the path and leaving her twin behind in the dust.

Later that night in the library of the Montevega villa, twenty-eight-year-old Valentina restocks the bookshelves from a pile of thick, old books on the table. She touches the spine of one and opens it, distracted from her task. Most of her nights were this quiet and peaceful now that the twins were older. The solitude was known to make her anxious. Her mind filled with turmoil from a dangerously lived past that no one around her could quite understand—not yet anyway.

The door cracks open, and Valentina cocks her head, listening as Marcie enters. Valentina closes the book and places it delicately on the shelf before picking up another, not bothering to look behind her.

"Is this what you do all day now that you're not teaching us anymore?" Marcie grins, sitting on the edge of the table next to the pile of books. She picks one up and flips it open.

"Don't you have studying to do?" Valentina asks, referring to their sixth form studies, which would help them pass A-Levels and get accepted into an esteemed university. The twins had no plans of actually studying for a traditional college education, though they often kept up the impression to avoid their parents asking what they were actually doing to keep busy. Valentina was no fool, though she played along with information the twins *thought* she knew.

Avoiding the question, Marcie sighs and sets down the book on the pile. "V, I need to tell you something," she says, addressing the woman with the nickname she, Madisyn, and Robbie had come up with years ago. The name "V" had been Madisyn's idea, of course, as Valentina had always been a rather mysterious and intimidating figure and deserved to go by a name that reflected her personality. "You've always been our mentor. And…" Marcie pauses, almost unsure of what she was about to say next. "I feel like we can trust you."

Valentina finally turns away from the bookshelf to face her for the first time. "You shouldn't trust *anyone*, Marcelle. Haven't I taught you that?"

Marcie swallows hard and looks down at her fidgeting hands, knowing her long-time tutor would disapprove of her weak demeanor. "We've done terrible things though… well, I guess not exactly all bad. I don't regret any of it, but… I'm afraid… of what it's doing to Madisyn. I don't know who else to go to."

Valentina opens another book from the stack and runs her fingers down the yellowed pages. She picks it up, bringing it to her face and closing her eyes to take in the smell of the old book. Marcie looks up, squinting at her, wondering if Valentina was listening at all. Valentina closes the book. "You and your twin have always been so different," she says.

"Madisyn is direct. Headfirst. Very Russian. *You* are heart-first. But you are both perfect: the way I taught you to be. And whatever it is you're hiding—do you think I don't already know?" Valentina cocks her head at Marcie, who swallows hard. Her unwavering gaze causes Marcie to shyly turn away before sliding off the table's edge.

"Well, like you said, it's late, and I should go study for sixth form. Or how else am I going to get into Oxford?" Marcie forces a laugh and makes her way across the room. As she gets to the door, a throwing knife comes flying at her and sticks into the wooden door mere inches from her face. She whips around. "*Really?*"

Valentina grabs another from between the tattered pages of an open book on the table, chucking it toward her with the grunt of a practiced karate master. Marcie dodges the second knife as her tutor circles the table with an icy, calculated expression, balancing a much thicker book on top of both palms. Knowing exactly what this meant, Marcie grabs the two knives from the door as Valentina flips open the book and pulls out two more throwing knives with gold handles. They sparkle like they had just been polished. She waits for Marcie to make the first move, as was routine in these sporadic outbreaks of combat that Valentina liked to put on to keep her protégés sharp. Marcie lunges at her. The two collide, wielding and blocking each other's slashes.

Marcie kicks one of the knives from Valentina's hand and uses hers to knock the other from her grip as well. Always a proponent of a fair fight, Marcie tosses her two knives aside and lunges at Valentina, pushing her backward onto the table. Valentina throws Marcie from on top of her onto the floor, causing the pile of books to tumble over. Valentina grabs her by the throat, but Marcie knees her in the stomach and climbs on top of her. Valentina swiftly pulls her by the hair and rolls them over, pulling out a fifth knife and pressing it so close to Marcie's throat that it just barely causes a bead of blood to appear on her skin.

Valentina shakes her head before she hears the click of the cocked handgun Marcie holds to Valentina's side. Impressed, Valentina cocks her head with narrowed eyes. She smirks and removes her knife from Marcie's throat, and stands, extending her hand to help Marcie to her feet. Marcie cautiously puts the gun back into its holster hidden under her black silk pajama set. She could never be too sure when Valentina was truly done giving her a "lesson."

Examining her, Valentina nods her head. "I underestimated you, Marcelle. Sometimes heart comes prepared. You are ready. I wonder about Madisyn and Robbie, hmm?"

Marcie swallows hard. "What are you talking about? And I really hate when you do that."

Valentina kneels to pick up the books that fell off the table, and Marcie bends down to help her put them back on the table. "I will go with you to America. Los Angeles, yes?"

Marcie's head snaps up, her body was frozen. "How do you know about—"

"Don't talk. Listen." Valentina looks her in the eyes, both of them still crouching on the floor, books in hand. "Do you think I wouldn't notice? And your silly parents are so busy, they don't even care. But I've watched you. And I've watched Madisyn when you two created that monster organization. I sat back, observed. I would wait until the time was right."

Marcie swallows hard again, trying to control her thumping heartbeat, which surely confirmed Valentina's suspicions. She had no idea how the woman always seemed to know everything. Maybe there was more to Valentina than they had initially thought. Why *had* she come to them all those years ago?

"We'll see just how good you all really are at this," Valentina adds. An evil smirk creeps across her face, and she shakes her head. "As if any of it would be possible if it weren't for me. If I hadn't made you exactly what I wanted you to be."

"What are you saying?" Marcie breathes, terrified to know the truth.

Valentina's faint smile disappears, back to her usual cold face. "We'll see just how prepared you are, or if everything I taught you three was just a waste of time." She stands, placing the books on the table before leaving. Marcie's gaze follows her from the room.

In the kitchen, Madisyn pours a pot of warm milk into a cup and sits down on a tall stool behind the countertop. She spoons cinnamon from a jar and stirs it into her milk. She would often come down to the kitchen late at night just to be alone. She treasured moments like this: moments of solitude that gave her a chance to let her hair down—moments where she could at least pretend to be a normal teenager.

Robbie walks past the doorway and sees her sitting with her back turned, her long hair flowing down her back. "Isn't it past your bedtime?"

As he comes further into the kitchen, Madisyn lifts her head over her shoulder to look at him, his smile waning. "Oh… sorry, Madisyn," he continues. "Didn't realize it was you with the hair down and all. I thought that wasn't your thing, you know, with it usually always being up or something…" He uses his hand to pat the air above his head, referencing her usual ponytail. He laughs at the awkward gesture, stuffing his hands in his pockets.

Madisyn forces a smile and sips on her milk. Hesitating at first, Robbie goes to sit at the tall counter, leaving a stool between them. She looks over, noticing the void between them that seems to sum up their entire relationship over the last few months. Madisyn could remember just last year when she and Robbie were probably the closest they had ever been, even closer than he was with her sister—something anyone would have found quite hard to believe seeing them now. Robbie had just come back from a family trip to Korea last year, and like Marcie, she too had noticed a significant change in him. She had watched Robbie, around the age of twelve, develop a sudden shyness around Marcie where he stammered and often refused to look her in the eye during a conversation, which Madisyn knew was because he was starting to like Marcie as more than a friend. This peculiar behavior lasted for the next three years and suddenly seemed to disappear around the same time Robbie returned from his family trip. Not as naive as her twin sister, Madisyn knew what exactly happened to Robbie that summer: he had lost his virginity.

At that moment, a year ago, Robbie had gained her full respect. As silly as it sounded, he had beaten her to the punch. She had never been interested in Robbie in that way, but Madisyn was eager to be first at anything that would separate her from others in terms of what she considered to be maturity. She had practically begged Robbie for days to help her, something she would be embarrassed now to admit, but with steady persistence, she had convinced Robbie to take her virginity, with the agreement that they would keep it a secret from Marcie, of course. Surpassing their initial proposal, though, their hooking up continued on a somewhat regular basis up until a few months ago when Robbie had decided he couldn't keep lying to Marcie, which left quite the bruise on Madisyn's ego. The only kind thing Madisyn had ever done for him, though, which Robbie had been extremely grateful for, was to keep their promise to not tell Marcie about it.

"We used to share each other's darkest secrets," Madisyn begins softly, breaking their silence, her gaze still locked on the empty stool. "Why aren't we close anymore, Robbie?"

Not knowing how to answer a preposterous question like that at first, Robbie laughs. He shakes his head, his own eyes on the counter. "I don't know... probably because you're always insisting on being alone to brew up some kind of evil scheme." He had often tried to forget their sordid past and hoped Madisyn had too, though it was obvious things had never been the same between them since. Madisyn smirks at his comment and lets her gaze drift away. "Or... because you're too into yourself."

She snaps her head back over with less of a smile now. "I'm not into myself. I'm into UCOCA."

Robbie nods, still avoiding eye contact with her. "Well, maybe that's because UCOCA *is* you. And for the last five years, it's consumed you entirely."

"It's not like you're a victim in this exactly. You're involved just as much as I am."

Robbie smirks at this. "*No one* could be involved as much as you are..."

Madisyn stares into her milk while stirring it with a tiny silver spoon, watching the swirls of cinnamon chase each other inside the cup. She sighs deeply. "So... I've noticed you tend to stick around late at night to hang out with Marcie." Robbie looks slightly away from her, squeezing his fists and bracing for whatever horrid thing she might say next. "Have you gotten lucky yet?"

Robbie looks over at her finally, though her gaze stays down. "Uh…" He shakes his head, biting his lip. "We just hang out. And talk. And kiss sometimes." He looks away again, color rising to his cheeks.

Madisyn squints into her cup. She had never quite understood her twin. She could remember when she and Robbie had first started hooking up. Marcie had approached her one day in their room with crossed arms. She had figured out Madisyn's secret—that she had started having sex. Madisyn had refused to tell her who it was with, saying it was one of their agents, obviously. There was a moment where Marcie had hesitated and asked her if it was Robbie. Madisyn had immediately denied the assumption, deeming it preposterous.

Seeing how relieved Marcie was, Madisyn had gone on to ask her why *she* wasn't sleeping with Robbie. To this, Marcie had explained she was scared to lose her virginity for what it would do to her. Even though everyone around her always wanted to be more mature, she just wanted to take life slow and enjoy her childhood for as long as possible. Back then, Madisyn had scoffed at her for this and told her to "grow up." But looking back now, Madisyn found her sister's stance to be quite noble. She was doing the thing no one else around them was doing, and if anyone knew how incredibly hard it was to go against the grain, it was Madisyn.

Robbie sucks on the inside of his cheek. "So… have you come up with a plan yet for the football game? You know, with the whole Daniel McLean scheme. How's that going to play out?"

Grateful for the change of subject, a slight smile forms on her lips. "I'm going to seduce him. And then I'll slip a tracker on him." Placing down her spoon, Madisyn picks up her milk and takes a long sip, her lips stopping on the edge of the cup as Robbie sort of laughs.

"Oh yeah?" he asks. "You know how to seduce a guy? That requires you to be soft and loving, you know."

Madisyn looks over as she pulls the cup from her lips, placing it delicately on the table. "I once seduced you, remember? A couple of times, I might add."

Robbie's jaw clenches, averting his gaze uncomfortably. "That's different," he says, after clearing his throat. He spins around in the seat, readying himself to get up and leave. "It's late. I should go."

Sensing his urgency, Madisyn stops him. "Robbie, wait." She pushes back her stool and moves to stand in front of him. Sometimes she hardly knew what crazy idea was coming into her head until it was already too late, her body already in motion to carry out what her mind was too slow to comprehend. All she knew was something in her wanted him back. Tilting her head, she runs her hand through her hair, making her almost favor her twin's movements.

She runs her fingers slowly up his thighs, pushing them gently apart to stand in between them. Robbie swallows, letting his gaze drift down to just above where her thin pale-pink tank top starts. He gently moves her back, nervously chuckling to himself.

"Come on. We talked about this," he says, unable to look her directly in the eye.

Madisyn runs her hand down the side of his face as she brings hers closer to his before locking lips with him, softly at first, until Robbie can't help but kiss her back. As they're making out, Madisyn hoists herself onto his lap with her legs around his waist. She places his hands on her upper thighs, guiding them up to where her pajama shorts end. She moves her own hands away from his to grab his face.

Robbie hesitates, pulling his lips away as he feels himself slipping. "I can't..." he breathes softly, his eyes closed, a touch of pleasure in his voice.

Madisyn pulls his face back up and kisses him anyway, slowly grinding her hips on his groin. It had been too long since she felt him that way. It wasn't even that Robbie was an incredible lover or that she couldn't find someone better. Madisyn liked the challenge of taking what didn't belong to her. Robbie's heart may have belonged to her sister, but Madisyn wanted to remind him that she could have him whenever she wanted.

She pulls her face away slightly, brushing her lips across his cheek. "See? You used to like this, Robbie. I can be much nicer. I promise I'll be gentle this time." She slips off of his lap, carefully undoing the drawstring of his pajama pants, staring him in his weakening eyes. She knew that she had him.

Wrapped up in the moment, Robbie stands, moving her to lean against the countertop and reaching up her shirt. He buries his face in her neck, kissing her, and she pulls his head up by his hair, pressing her lips to his ear. "That's it, Robbie. Just pretend like I'm her." She kisses him, and he moans softly, completely lost in the steamy moment and ready to give himself to her until—" Sweet... *innocent*... Marcie."

At the mention of her sister's name, Robbie jerks away. "This was a mistake," he says quickly, tying his pants back up.

Madisyn glares at him. "Are you serious? Don't be such a baby!" When he doesn't look up at her, Madisyn scoffs in disbelief. She shoves him hard, making Robbie stumble slightly backward. "You always liked her better," she spits, feeling more embarrassed than ever. She hated losing, especially to someone as weak as her twin sister.

Shoving past him, Madisyn storms out of the kitchen. Robbie stands there staring at the floor, feeling more ashamed than anything else. He figured he could blame the entire situation on Madisyn, anyone who knew them would surely take his side, but he just couldn't get his mind wrapped around the fact that he could still make such stupid mistakes. There was no excuse, and there was no way Marcie would ever understand or forgive him for keeping something like this from her and for so long at that. He would have to keep this a secret for now, possibly even go to the grave with it. He knew Madisyn would do the same. There was too much at stake with UCOCA to cause drama between the three of them. It would have to be his and Madisyn's hatchet to bury. The guilt would just have to be something he lived with.

CHAPTER 5

LOS ANGELES, CALIFORNIA

That weekend, spectators seated in the packed Rose Bowl stadium cheer as American and Mexican football players run down the field. Maneuvering through the crowded stands, Madisyn cringes out of the way of a smelly shirtless fan with red, white, and blue paint covering his chest and face. He chugs the beer in his hand and lets out an enthusiastic *whooo*, clearly inebriated from what looked like his fifth drink, a growing pile of empty bottles resting at his feet.

"Filthy Americans," Madisyn mutters under her breath. She dodges another's large billowing flag and quickly makes her way up the endless row of stairs to get in position.

All the way up in the premium seats and right outside the private club lounges, sit Marcie and Robbie, both wearing dark shades and blending in with other high-class premium seat holders, all dressed for a yachting excursion more than a rowdy football game. Marcie lifts the lip of her sun hat to see better, sporting a striped navy blue and white tube top with a matching skirt. Robbie almost matches her in an elbow-length, rolled, white button-down, navy shorts with a brown belt, and tan Sperrys. Marcie glances over to him, admiring their coincidental choice in attire. She squints at him curiously, trying to catch his attention. He had been rather cold to her the past couple of days. She expected him to tease her at least, to joke about how they looked like an annoying couple who wore each other's faces on matching shirts, but he hadn't so much as even looked at her.

Heidi walks over in a beige dress and sun hat, holding the hand of her six-year-old, soon-to-be stepbrother, Jackson. The pair take their seats next to Marcie and Robbie. Facing inconspicuously forward, Heidi says to them, "Madisyn's just got to the bar, but I don't think she's found Daniel McLean yet. Did I miss anything interesting?"

Marcie leans in and discreetly gestures down with her chin to a group of men smoking cigars in seats overlooking the balcony. "That's Jay Saunders, far left." The senator puffs smoke from his cigar before raising his arms in the air, contributing to the tumultuous roar from American spectators.

"Was McLean inside?" Robbie asks, keeping his eyes on the senator below who stands from his seat, beaming. Saunders pats his companion on the shoulder before heading up the stairs.

"I didn't see him," Heidi says.

Their gazes all follow the senator as he passes them to head inside. Turning back around, Robbie looks through binoculars, scanning the field below. "There's Giovanni Sacchi, right by number twenty-four on the sidelines." He passes the binoculars to Marcie, who looks through them.

She spots the head coach below, a tall bald man in a USA-themed polo. Even from the back, they could only assume his face would be quite stern. He stands with crossed arms until his players run past him on the field, Sacchi then pointing and yelling for them to get the ball back. Marcie hands the binoculars back to Robbie, who doesn't so much as look at her as he takes them.

Unable to take any more of his strange behavior, Marcie lets out a frustrated huff. "You haven't said a word to Madisyn since we left the UK. Is something going on?"

Robbie puts down the binoculars and pulls out his phone, looking down at it as he responds. "It's nothing. These trips just seem to make her psycho. You know how hard she is to deal with."

Marcie leans in, hoping to make him look up, her brows furrowed in confusion. "But not any more than usual…" she points out. Something else was definitely on his mind.

Jackson pulls on Heidi's dress from his seat, looking up to her with a mouthful of crab cake. "I need to go to the bathroom." She scoffs at him in disbelief.

"Jackson, we've been inside all that time, and you didn't think to mention it then?"

Robbie clears his throat and stands up, needing an excuse to avoid Marcie's prying. "I'll take him inside. This game's not that good, anyway."

The boys head inside, and once the door closes, Heidi immediately whips around to Marcie. "When did Robbie start hating Madisyn and develop such a fond interest in *you*, missy? Have you two done it? Spill!"

Marcie blushes. "What are you talking about?"

"Oh, please. The three of you used to be inseparable. I just didn't think two of you would ever pair off…" Heidi nudges Marcie's shoulder teasingly.

"No one's pairing off, Heidi. Robbie and I just get each other… most of the time, at least."

Heidi rolls her eyes, biting her bottom lip as if she had just been given the juiciest gossip. "Madisyn can't be taking that well. She's never been fond of losing."

Marcie shakes her head. "It's never been a competition, Heidi!"

"Maybe not to you," Heidi beams. "But when you think about it, it's like, you two are these beautiful billionaires with everything you could ever want, and equally too because you're, like, twins. *Except*, you've got the guy now! That's the only thing Madisyn's missing that you're ahead on. Come on, she's the most competitive person in the world! You'd be a fool to think she hasn't noticed."

Pursing her lips, Marcie looks away as Heidi starts fiddling with her phone. Was she right? Could Madisyn have actually resented her for her friendship with Robbie? No, Heidi had to just be looking for drama. She may have been their childhood friend, but how could she be so sure of anything when she hardly saw them anymore?

Marcie takes a deep breath, bracing herself to defend her case. "Heidi, I just want to say that it's really—"

"You still haven't answered my question," Heidi cuts her off, looking up from her phone.

Marcie squints, shaking her head. "What question?"

Heidi sets down the phone, her full attention on Marcie. "Have you and Robbie done it?"

Rolling her eyes, Marcie looks away. "Why is that the only thing anyone wants to know?"

Heidi gasps, her face twisting into more of a frown. "Oh, my god. You haven't?"

"Robbie and I connect on a much *deeper* level!"

"Obviously not *balls* deep," Heidi mutters, sounding a tad judgmental. "Maybe that's why he's been so bitchy to you today. It only makes sense..."

Marcie whips around to face her, ready to tell her off but then reluctant to speak. She treads cautiously. "Wait, what? Why would you say that?"

Heidi fully turns to face her friend, her eyes as gentle as a mother giving her daughter advice on boys for the first time. "Marcie, Robbie is a sixteen-year-old boy. Sex is all they want at this age. From, like, *now* to when they're old and dying, all they can think about is where to put their boners! All I'm saying is that if you don't want to lose him to some girl who actually lets him, then you may want to reconsider this whole polite good-girl image you've got going on." She puts a hand over Marcie's. "We *kill* people for Christ's sake," she says, lowering her voice. "We're not these normal virgin girls that go to private school and dress up for tea parties! Don't just act the part, Marcelle. *Be* the part." Heidi twists forward again, putting on her sunglasses to watch the game, Marcie's gaze lingering on her.

Inside the club area, Senator Saunders passes by a table of food where Daniel McLean—a dirty blond, frat-boy type, wearing a pale blue button-down with rolled-up jeans and boat shoes—shoves down chips and salsa. Saunders wraps his arm around the boy's shoulder. "Daniel! Why don't you come join me at the bar for a drink?"

The boy wipes his mouth off, swallowing his food. "Jay, I'm nineteen—the press would have a field day! And my dad would kill me, you know that."

Saunders hugs him tighter, slightly turning the boy in the direction of the bar and leaning in closer to him. "You're missing the point, son." Jay raises his eyebrows in the direction of a girl standing at the bar in a yellow sundress, her back to them. Daniel's gaze lingers on her. The girl's ponytail swings as she turns slightly, revealing half her face.

"If I was your age," Jay says. "I'd be talking to *her*. An intern like you should be networking. And she's here with someone important if she's hanging in *our* club area." He pats the boy's shoulder before letting go.

"Hey, wait, Jay!" Daniel stops him from going. He looks over his shoulder first, lowering his voice. "With it being my first game and all tonight... I was just wondering... do you have any advice?"

The senator laughs. He leans in close to the young boy, Daniel keeping his eyes on his surroundings for onlookers. "I'd get in a drink, or *three*, if I were you. Most have a hard time seeing a man die for the first time. But after the third man goes down... it's actually a good time." He laughs again and winks at Daniel before sauntering off.

Daniel looks after the man for a moment. With a gulp, he looks around frantically to check for eavesdroppers. He swallows another mouthful of chips and salsa as he notices the girl again at the bar. Daniel sets down his plate, wiping his mouth first before making his way over to her.

As he comes to stand only feet away from the girl in the yellow dress, Daniel smoothly waves the bartender down. "Ginger ale over ice, please."

"Got it, Mr. McLean," the bartender says, reaching under the counter to grab a can and pouring it into a fresh glass with ice. He slides Daniel his drink on a napkin.

Madisyn raises her head just slightly to smile at him, and he catches her glance. "Hi," he says shyly, quickly clearing his throat after speaking.

Giggling softly at his obvious nervousness, Madisyn turns her attention on her phone, pretending to text on it. She takes a sip from the straw in her glass bottle of Pellegrino.

Daniel tilts his head, almost confused but laughs at her evasive gesture. He slides closer to her with his drink. "What's your name?" he pries.

Setting down her phone on the bar counter, Madisyn turns to fully face him, looking Daniel up and down—his gaze mimicking hers. "What's *your* name?"

Breaking an awkward moment of silence, the two of them laugh, Daniel squinting at her. "You don't know who I am?" Madisyn raises her eyebrows and innocently pouts for him to continue. Daniel laughs again. "I'm Daniel McLean. *Senator* Patrick McLean's son. Ring a bell?"

"Oh! Wow, a senator's son!" she breathes in exaggeration. "Yes, I do believe my father knows yours well, though I must admit I have a horrible memory."

"Hmm, usually people in this club area know my father fairly well, *and* Senator Saunders."

Madisyn tilts her head cutely. "Well, you must forgive my rudeness."

"Maybe…" Daniel slides closer to her, willing to let it go. "But you'll have to tell me your name first."

Blushing, Madisyn holds her gaze on his. "Why? So you can report me?" Daniel bites his lip, looking shyly away and wondering how his advance came off so hostile. Noticing his concern, Madisyn laughs. "Jenna Banks. My father's Robert Banks, the real estate investor."

"Impressive! My father's a senator, your father's in real estate…" He gushes. "How old are you, Jenna?"

"Old enough…" Madisyn puckers her lips around her straw and sips her sparkling water with heavily mascaraed eyes on him. He may have been three years her senior, but she was often reminded that she was *quite* mature for her age.

Daniel bites his lip to keep from smiling too much. "I won't be in town much longer after today, but… maybe before we leave, I can get your number? I can fly out and see you sometime. I'd love to get to know you better."

Madisyn smirks and reaches into her purse, pulling out a business card with her fake identity. She offers him the card, but when he tries to grab it from her, she doesn't let go, holding Daniel's gaze. He laughs at her boldness. She finally lets go of the card.

The crowd outside the lounge explodes with cheers as the game comes to an end with an American victory. Madisyn looks over her shoulder and then back to Daniel. "I'm sorry, Danny, but I have to go. I promise I'll see you again soon." Biting her lip, Madisyn backs away a few steps. She then turns around to head toward the door, Daniel's gaze lingering after her.

"Mr. McLean," the bartender interrupts. "The girl—she left this." Daniel looks over at the phone on the bar counter. He grabs it, holding it in the air just as Madisyn heads out the door.

"Hey, wait! Jenna!" he calls after her. Daniel runs after her with the phone. He pushes through the door into the crowd.

Madisyn shoves through the waves of people, keeping her head down. A few people back, Daniel spots Madisyn's yellow dress and high ponytail, but as more people flood from their seats, he loses her. He spins around in the crowd, standing on his tippy toes to look for her.

Madisyn pulls the band from around her noticeable ponytail and tousles her hair to blend in. She reaches up her dress and pulls down a hiked-up pair of black leggings and presumes to shimmy out of the dress. Some people in the crowd eye her suspiciously, but most are too drunk to care. Stripped down to a thin black tank top and leggings, she rolls up the dress, hugging it closely under her armpit. Madisyn looks back to see if she had lost him, but instead, her eyes land on a very familiar-looking woman sitting very still in a seat—almost too still, making her stand out amongst the bustling crowd heading toward the exits. As people push by, Madisyn loses sight of the woman for a second but then spots her again.

Valentina, wearing large dark shades, turns her head robotically to face Madisyn's direction, a small smile spreading across her face. Madisyn squints in her direction, not recognizing her long-time tutor. As more people shove past her, blocking her view, Madisyn tries dipping and dodging past their heads to see again—the woman's smile had given her chills she couldn't explain—but when she does, the woman is gone.

When Madisyn turns again to head toward her team's designated rendezvous point, Marcie rushes up to her, grabbing her by the shoulders and jolting her back on impact. "I've been looking all over for you! What's wrong?"

Madisyn swivels her head, squinting her eyes in confusion. "I thought I just saw… never mind."

"Robbie's waiting for us outside. Let's get out of here," Marcie urges her, spotting a wandering Daniel McLean a few heads back in the crowd. The two of them push past the remaining crowd to leave the stadium.

Outside in a parked SUV, Robbie whips out his laptop and brings up a map matching the one on his phone. They both show a small blinking light inside the stadium. Robbie shows

Madisyn and Marcie, who sit on either side of him. "That's our guy. I've planted a bug in the device, so as long as he makes a phone call with it, the GPS will have a much stronger signal. We'll have his exact coordinates."

"What if he doesn't make the call?" Marcie inquires.

Madisyn smirks, her heavily mascaraed lashes fluttering over to her sister with an air of confidence. "He'll call."

Back inside the stadium at the bar, Daniel opens the phone screen, conveniently left without password protection, and scrolls through the fake message threads. He clicks on one for a contact that reads "Twin" with a kissy-face and pink heart emojis. Daniel smiles at this, scrolling to find a picture of the girl he just met with another girl who looked exactly identical to her, standing on a luxury boat in crystal clear waters—one of them in a fiery red bikini, and the other in powder blue.

"She has a twin?" Daniel grins widely. He *had* to see the girl in the yellow dress again, and at least now, he had something that guaranteed him another meeting with her. Without even considering the potential consequences, he clicks on the contact's information and dials the number.

CHAPTER 6

OUTSKIRTS OF LA

Much later that evening, a black SUV pulls up to an abandoned theater. The door opens, and out comes Senator McLean, dressed in his most casual blue jeans, a short-sleeve button-down, and a flesh-toned *Purge* mask with exaggerated features to hide his identity. His son follows closely behind, wearing his own plain white mask over his face. They make their way through the darkness of the starry night to the shabby old building's entrance, a seedy place in such a desolate area that it sent shivers down Daniel's spine. It didn't look quite like the type of place where men would die, but then again, he tried to keep an open mind. Only a single light hovers above them at the door as the senator lets his son through first, glancing around before going inside.

The round ceiling opens up grandly over a vast space that was quite clean compared to the theater's outward appearance. The cylinder-shaped room holds three sets of steps leading up to the second floor, overlooking the main floor with balconies. On the first floor, the senator and his son walk toward the center where eight money collectors in long black cloaks and *Scream* face masks sit at a long oak table counting stacks of bills from suitcases.

Daniel looks up to the second floor as The Players—a group of maskless men handcuffed together—are led down one of the staircases. Some of them appear completely shaken up, their bloodshot eyes perhaps more crazed from sleep deprivation and hysteria than fear. One of the men notices the masked boy staring at them and yells, a kind of pissed off roar that echoes up to the ceiling, causing Daniel to flinch. Pushed along by two men carrying assault rifles, the men are herded like cattle down the hall and through the double doors of the game room.

With a large gulp, Danny grabs his father's sleeve, his gaze lingering on the doors across the room. "Dad, should I be nervous?"

Senator McLean laughs and looks at him, baffled by such a question. "Son, if you're nervous, then you're not really my son, are you?" Daniel's head snaps over to his father, his mouth hanging open under his mask as he stammers to take it back. The senator gestures for his son to follow. "Come on, I want to show you something. It might cheer you up a bit."

They approach the table where the money collectors flip bills into new stacks. The senator snaps his fingers, and the men stop their count, revealing neatly stacked rows of cash. "Whoa," Daniel breathes, both taken aback by the large stacks of money as well as by the line of gentlemen dressed like characters from a slasher movie. He was grateful for his own mask right then, which hid just how freaked out he actually was.

McLean picks up a wad of cash and hands it to his son. "Take it all in, Danny! Go ahead, take a whiff of it. That's ten million dollars in cold hard cash." Daniel slightly lifts his mask to sniff the dollar bills, his mouth forming a grimace that causes his father to sigh.

"Look, son," McLean continues, his tone a little softer as he pulls Daniel a few feet away from the men. "I was nervous my first couple of times, too. But I need you to be strong and step up to the plate. Your old man's gotten himself into this thing so deep, I couldn't back out now even if I tried; none of these guys would let me. And to be quite honest, that scares that shit out of me. That's why I need *you* here with me. When I've trained you up enough to take over this operation completely, I can finally get out. It's simply too risky being a senator involved in this, you understand, right?" Daniel nods. "Plus, the money is just too good to *not* keep in the family." McLean chuckles, starting to walk away.

"Wait, Dad," Daniel stops him. "Can I ask you just one question?" McLean turns back to face him. "Why do we have to wear these scary masks? I mean, everyone here already knows each other, right?"

McLean laughs, his own distorted face already twisted into an amused smirk of pure evilness. "It's all part of the theatrics, Danny. You'll see real soon."

The senator heads toward the doors across the room. Daniel watches him disappear inside before turning back to the money collectors. He goes to set down the cash back inside the suitcase, but the man behind it swats his hand and gestures for him to set it down on the table to be counted instead.

"But you saw us with it? We didn't take anything," he protests. The man remains stern and unamused underneath his mask, to which Daniel purses his lips and sets the bills down on the table. He spins on his heels to face the theater doors, taking a deep breath and shoving his hands in his pockets before heading through them.

On the roof of the abandoned building, wickedness brewing just below them, a group of UCOCA agents dressed in black and toting semiautomatics scurry toward an opening that leads inside just above the stage. Ollie McAdam, the lead boy of Ghost Team—a group from UCOCA Seattle appointed to stealthily infiltrate the theater first and take out any bad guys with weapons—points and motions for his agents to get into position. They sneak across the beams that line the ceiling to the catwalk, sitting thirty feet above the stage and completely shrouded in darkness.

In the front of the building, the last of The Gamblers disappear inside through the front doors, their drivers taking off down the dark road. Soon after, two UCOCA agents drop from their hiding position above the entrance. They grab a heavy metal bar hidden nearby. Shoving the bar through the door's handles first, they kick the ends with their boots to bend it upward, locking the main entrance to prevent anyone from escaping.

Back inside, hidden on the second floor, Marcie and Robbie crouch behind the balcony walls, having come in from a nearby window with the rest of the team. They hold handguns with silencers at the low-ready position. Madisyn, with Heidi right behind her, motions for James, Drake, and a few others to go further past her sister's position. Peeking around the wall first to make sure the few stragglers mingling below are oblivious to their movement, the agents creep past the staircase to the other wall.

"All teams in position," Madisyn says into her earpiece. She sets a timer on her watch to ensure they didn't remain in the building for more than an hour. She nods at her sister, who nods back in acknowledgment.

Heidi and Madisyn back up and crouch-run in the opposite direction. They disappear down a hallway to clear the back way, also leading downstairs to the main level.

Robbie counts down into his earpiece for his team's signal. "Five… four… three… two…"

In unison, all the agents positioned behind the second-floor balconies jump up and shoot over the walls, killing each of their targets on the first floor—the sounds of each shot muffled by the silencers. Some of the team take the stairs down, and others hop onto the ledge and jump down to the main floor, chasing after a couple of the money collectors who weren't immediately killed and knocking them out before shooting them.

Meeting them downstairs, Madisyn points to the *Scream* masks on the faces of the dead money collectors. "Take those," she says to a couple of nearby agents. She removes one herself and puts it on, throwing another up to her sister.

"Guess we didn't get the memo this was a costume party," Robbie chimes, grabbing his own long-faced, ghoulish mask.

"The rest of you, black ski masks," Madisyn orders.

Marcie calls down from the second floor to James and Drake, who grab two masks for themselves. "Let's go." She takes off down a hallway upstairs, and the two boys run back up the stairs to follow her.

On the first floor, Robbie directs his team to secure the suitcases of money, stuffing the rest into bags. He motions for them to finish up and exit the building. Robbie stays inside and catches up with Madisyn and Heidi's team, who have surrounded the doors to the theater.

Upstairs, Marcie, James, and Drake locate the security room. Marcie kicks in the door to reveal four security guards inside, who scramble from their seats.

"Hey, what the fuck—" one of them says, choking on a mouthful of chips at the sight of the masked assailants.

The men struggle to find their weapons as Marcie lunges at them. She kicks the gun from one man's hands and knees him in the groin, swinging him around to take out the second guy. She roundhouse kicks the third guy in the face and punches the fourth in the throat. When all four are unconscious and lying in a pile on the floor, Marcie steps over the men to get to the computer to figure out the system. Meanwhile, James and Drake drag the four security guards from the room and into the storage closet across the hall.

Inside the theater—and oblivious to the happenings right outside its doors—The Gamblers, in casual attire and an assortment of masks, chat with one another as their coerced players are herded onto the stage and into a cluster in the middle, their grips shaky on the empty revolvers in their hands. In one of the aisles below, McLean and Daniel are engrossed in a playful yet heated discussion with Giovanni Sacchi—who wears a white *Phantom of the Opera* mask— about the soccer game earlier. Jay Saunders comes up to them from across the room.

"Jesus Christ, Jay! I said to wear something scary and conspicuous," McLean exclaims, referring to his companion's black lace masquerade mask, which only seems to cover his eyes and is held in place by the little handle in Jay's hand, keeping it upright.

Jay whisks the mask away from his face. "This was all my wife had!" he retorts. "I told you we should have never changed the theme!"

"Just put it back up before they see you," McLean hisses, looking back over his shoulder to the stage.

On the balcony above them, a couple of unmasked tough guys, more macho than the four security guards hired to stay put in the security room, pace back and forth, toting guns as big as their muscles and keeping a close eye on the men on stage. On the ground floor, a few more tough guys with guns line both walls on the left and right sides of the room. The announcer for the game—also unmasked and positioned on the far-left side of the stage—stands behind a podium with a microphone. He stares at his watch, waiting.

A few rows up, Alfie Morgan approaches the senators—McLean immediately gesturing for Daniel to move his conversation with Sacchi somewhere else. Even with the gruesome events that lie ahead, the senator was still wary of his son being around criminals as dangerous as Alfie Morgan. The man comes to stand a few feet away from McLean and Saunders, his own men at each of his sides and all of them wearing strangely different masks as if they were meant to be the heavy metal band Slipknot. Morgan himself wears a long metallic mask, with four slits just over the mouth area, and a long black wig; one of his guys wears a dark clown mask with a big nose and shaggy red hair; another dons a full helmet with long metal spikes like that of a porcupine protruding from it; another wears a gas mask; the last one wears a more ghoulish looking mask with a zipper across the mouth and a long Pinocchio nose. McLean's lips quiver under his mask, though he tries to play it off.

"Mr. Morgan!" McLean greets him. "Great to have you." He reaches out a hand. The crime lord doesn't shake it but instead points across the room to Ian Day, who wears a gold and white Venetian mask that only covers half of his face—the other half painted red. The second crime boss grimaces at the gesture, seeming to take it as a threat.

"You didn't tell me *that* son of a bitch was going to be here," Morgan growls through his mask.

McLean turns to Saunders, who stammers as Day comes over to join them, braced for a fight. "I—is that gonna be a problem?" McLean asks carefully so as not to offend anyone.

Day stops feet away, eyes locked with Morgan's, both parties with hands on their hips ready to draw guns for a shoot-out. Saunders puts his hands up—having to remove his handheld mask to do so—and steps in. "Now, now, hang on a minute, gentlemen! Remember, we're not here to kill each other. We're here to watch *those* men kill each other… for a lot of money, may I remind you." He laughs hesitantly as the two men let their hands drop from their guns.

"This doesn't mean anything's over," Ian says. "Morgan and I have some unfinished business."

"Well, settle it another time and be civilized tonight, damn it!" McLean demands, starting to lose his patience.

Ian Day holds his chin up, backing away as Alfie Morgan and his men move to stand on the other side of the room, keeping a shrewd eye on him.

McLean leans in close to Saunders. "What the fuck, Jay? You brought in two criminals who want to kill each other?"

"I swear I had no idea!" Saunders defends himself. "I saw maybe one mention in the file of Day's dead godbrother getting mixed up with one of Morgan's men, but I'm sure it was nothing."

McLean stares at him in disbelief. "V is for *Vendetta*, Jay! What the hell is wrong with you?" He catches a glance of his son sitting in one of the aisles by himself and scrolling on a phone. McLean shakes his head at his friend and moves over to Daniel. "Put that phone away. It's time for the boys to become men," he says, gesturing for his son to move a few rows up with him for a better view.

The announcer at the podium taps on his microphone. "Gentlemen, it's time. Let's begin the games."

In the security room, now tuned into the cameras and microphone inside the theater, Marcie narrows her eyes. "Yes, *gentlemen*, let the games begin." James and Drake smirk on either side of her braced for action.

Just outside of the theater in the hallway, Heidi speaks into her earpiece. "Ghost Team, we're in position. Take them out when you have eyes on the target."

"Roger that," Ollie says, crouched down at one end of the catwalk. Half of his team stand on-line, with the barrels of their guns pointing through the thin openings in the ceiling that allowed them to look straight over to the balcony. The other half lie down on the catwalk at an angle with eyes on the security below. Ollie peers carefully through the scope on his gun, lining up his aim on the announcer thirty feet below him.

Back in the hallway, Madisyn adds into her earpiece. "I want the senators alive. I repeat, do *not* shoot McLean or Saunders."

"What about Daniel?" Robbie asks, leaned back on the wall.

After a short pause, Madisyn looks at him. "He's fair game," she says, cocking her semiautomatic.

CHAPTER 7

———

Inside the theater, The Gamblers crowd in front of the stage, where The Players stand in a circle above them. "Players," the announcer begins, looking over to the men on stage with him. "Welcome! All of you have been brought here today for various reasons. Some of you are here for a chance to become rich, some of you are here to repay a debt, perhaps others were simply just looking for a beacon of hope in their sorry lives and happened to be in the right place at the right time—or I guess you could say the 'wrong' place depending on your perspective!" He looks down to The Gamblers, who let out a few chuckles. "Either way, no matter how or why you were brought here, you are here today because one of these fine gentlemen saw something special in you that convinced them to bet a lot of money on your life. No one came here to lose. None of these men brought you here intending for you to die. However, there can only be one winner." The announcer pauses, that line to hang in the air for a moment.

In the midst of the silent tension, one of The Players immediately breaks down crying and falls to his knees, his revolver sliding across the stage. "Please! I take it back! I don't want to do this anymore. I have a *kid*." He presses his hands together as if praying, looking to Ian Day below, the man who had brought him there.

"Get your ass back up there, you sorry son of a bitch!" Day spits at him, the rest of The Gamblers laughing hysterically at the man's outburst.

"Please, Mr. Day! I swear I'll get your money. I swear on my son's life—"

A gunshot goes off, the man's blood splattering across Day's face as he lowers the pistol he had just unloaded into his own player. The man's body falls over and topples off the stage, some of The Gamblers backing up to let him fall to the floor. From the middle of the group, Daniel lifts his mask to see better, unable to believe what he had just witnessed. McLean immediately forces his son's mask back down.

"Well, it looks like someone was eager to get the game started!" the announcer exclaims as more laughs echo around the room. "Unfortunately, Mr. Day, that's not how the game works." The announcer wiggles his finger in a lighthearted chastise, gaining more laughter from his audience. Two of the security guards off to the right side of the room move in and drag the dead man out of the way. The announcer looks over to The Players on stage with him. "Any more last words before we begin?" He chuckles softly, seeing that none of the men were willing to risk a sure death when they still had a chance to walk away from this alive and a very rich man at that.

Saunders pats Ian Day on his back. "Maybe next time, huh? Stick around though, I think watching the rest will cheer you up a bit. Always does for me." He laughs as Day only grunts in return and uses his sleeve to wipe some of the blood off his face, the red paint coming off with it.

"Shall I continue?" the announcer chimes, receiving positive roars from The Gamblers below. "Only *one* will live. This winner and his sponsor will take home ten million dollars in cold... hard... cash. So, Players... are you ready to play?" he pronounces each word, his eyes pressed on them as he gives a toothy grin. "The rules are as follows. You will take all commands from the tower. Upon receiving your bullets, you will load your revolvers for the first round. You will spin the cylinder of your weapon and take aim at the man to your right. And at the end of my countdown, starting from three... you will pull the trigger. We will repeat until there is one man remaining. Unless you're all just unlucky bastards, and no one ends up alive at the end!" The Gamblers burst out in laughter at the joke, though the men on stage shrink back at this possibility. "Oh, I'm only kidding," the announcer adds, sensing their uneasiness. "We've never experienced odds like that before, but it would be quite the spectacle." One of the tough guys below comes on stage, his rifle slung over his back as he begins to pass out one bullet to each of the men on stage.

"Let's start the first round," the announcer continues. "Players, load your weapon."

The men on stage begin to open the cylinders of their revolvers to place their bullets into their chambers. Several of the men load their revolvers quickly from experience—as if they had practiced prior to the game at hand—though others fumble, having never held a gun or a bullet before. Some of The Gamblers below laugh, noticing one man near the front of the circle who struggles to load his bullet. His hands shake feverishly, a trickle of sweat rolling down the side of his face. As he gets the cylinder open, he attempts to push the bullet inside, but his unsteady hand causes him to drop it, the bullet landing at his feet and rolling across the stage. Hesitantly, the man looks to the announcer, too afraid to move, his bottom lip quivering.

"Pick it up," the announcer says to him as if spelling out instructions to a child. The man darts across the stage to the bullet and brings it back to his spot in the circle before loading it. Below, McLean chuckles and nudges Saunders with his elbow, the latter shaking his head in the ripe disappointment of his choice of player. "Now," the announcer continues. "Spin the cylinder of your gun and take aim at the man to your right." The Players do as they're told, some of them sneaking glances at the muscled armed security above and below them, waiting to take out anyone who didn't cooperate.

From the cluster of onlooking men, Daniel stumbles backward, suddenly feeling lightheaded. McLean scolds him with a stern glance. "Dad," he says weakly. "I—I don't think I can watch."

The senator grabs his son by the sleeve, yanking him close. "Danny, don't you fucking embarrass me."

The announcer continues, "I will count down from three, and you will pull the trigger after 'one.' If you do not pull the trigger…" he pauses for effect, leaning over the podium to stare down The Players. "You will be left wishing you had."

Some of The Gamblers chuckle, the men in the circle barely able to hold their guns steady in their sweaty, shaky palms. Amped up, Sacchi repeatedly pounds his fist on the stage floor as if drumming to an anticipatory beat, slowly at first and gradually picking up speed as others closest to the stage join him. "Three…" the announcer begins his countdown. "Two…"

Daniel yanks his sleeve from his father's grip and pushes through the masked men, moving through the aisle toward the exit. As he passes, some of The Gamblers jokingly chide him for his reluctance to watch, McLean, sucking on his teeth but keeping his gaze forward. There was too much money at stake to let his son distract him from the matters at hand. He would deal with him later.

The announcer chuckles ominously into the microphone, noticing the commotion below and the fleeing young boy as the drumming dies off, Sacchi throwing his hands in the air and groaning. "Why don't we restart our count?"

As Daniel comes pushing through the double doors bent over and holding his stomach as if about to retch, the UCOCA agents freeze in the darkness of the hallway. The doors closing behind him, Daniel stumbles over to a wall and finally pukes.

"Tsk, tsk, tsk. Oh, Daniel..." Madisyn says, truly disappointed in his behavior. She pulls off her mask.

Wiping his mouth and spinning around weakly, Daniel's eyes grow as they adjust to the darkness, noticing the agents around him all toting guns. "Jenna?" he says, looking at her with large eyes.

From the side, Robbie jabs Daniel in the head with the buttstock of his gun, making him fall to the floor. Two agents drag his body away from the theater doors and into the lobby.

Back inside the room, the announcer goes on. "If everyone is ready again?" The men below hoot and holler for him to begin. "Places, people!" he shouts to The Players, who snap into their positions again, many of them sweating profusely. "Three..." he begins the countdown again. "Two..."

The room is silent with growing anticipation as everyone awaits the last number, the announcer grinning down at his puppets. As his lips begin to uncurl with "one," the announcer is struck in the head by a single bullet and falls over on stage. The heavily armed men on the balconies and on the ground level all spin around, looking for a target to shoot at. One by one, though, before they can identify the source of deadly silent shots, each of them is struck down by the snipers hidden high up on the catwalk.

Below the stage, The Gamblers twist and turn in confusion. The Players remain in their circle for a moment but then cautiously lower their guns, realizing their sudden freedom from their puppeteer. Alfie Morgan, Ian Day, and their posse of men all draw guns, unsure of where to aim.

From the security office, Marcie types in a combination of keys to control the light panel, switching off all the lights inside the theater. Every man inside the room freezes as darkness enshrouds them.

Breaking the stiff silence, Alfie yells with rage and shoots blindly at the balcony above them, his men following suit. Ian Day and his guys join in, shooting up into the ceiling.

When there is a pause in the gunshots below, the entire UCOCA Ghost Team use ropes fastened securely to the catwalk to sneak down, wearing night vision goggles and practically invisible in their black attire. They sweep through the room like a vapor, creeping past the men on stage and down to the ground floor with ease. Half the team moves to the right side of the room, taking out Alfie Morgan and his guys with quiet stabs to the abdomen before snatching their loaded weapons away. The other half move over to Ian Day, doing the same to him and his men. All that can be heard in the darkness are the muffled grunts of those being taken out and the thuds of their bodies falling to the ground. Ghost Team quickly creeps back onto the stage and uses their advanced rope-climbing techniques to quickly get back up to the catwalk, moving across the high beams and out the opening in the ceiling before shutting it behind them.

The lights in the theater switch on, and the men gasp at the sight of the two dead crime lords and their henchmen. Some of The Gamblers, having already removed their masks in the darkness, dash to the exits, refusing to wait around for the same uncertain death, though they soon find the doors all locked.

The sound of interference screeches throughout the room as a distorted, computerized voice comes over the intercom. Marcie speaks through a mic in the security room. "Players, remove the bullet from your guns." Hesitantly, The Players do as they're told. The Gamblers look around wildly as the booming voice seems to surround them. "Place the bullets and your guns on the floor in front of you," the voice commands. Marcie holds her hand over the microphone inside the security room to mute James' and Drake's snickers. They watch The Players on camera obey.

Drake speaks into his earpiece to the team surrounding the theater. "All weapons down, I repeat, all weapons down. You've got the green light."

Unsettled by the turn of events, McLean turns to Saunders, lowering his voice and mask in his hand as he continues to look around the room with apprehension. "Jay, what the fuck is going on? Is this your doing?"

Suddenly, the doors burst open from every entrance, and the men spin around as UCOCA agents flood inside. Several of them were flaunting the stolen *Scream* masks of the dead money collectors and the rest with black ski masks hiding their faces. Half the team swarmed The Gamblers while the others herd The Players off stage to stand against a wall on the right side of the room. In the back of the room, Heidi follows Madisyn up the stairs to better direct from the balcony. Robbie moves down the aisle toward the front.

"Gentlemen," Robbie says as he passes The Gamblers, their eyes widened at the obvious fact that their money collectors had been hijacked. "Thank you for cooperating with us today. I can assure you if you continue to do so, this will all be over very quickly." He beams at them under his mask and heads up the stage stairs to the podium, turning it to better face the middle of the stage.

As the room quiets down, Marcie struts through the double doors with James and Drake behind her, the three of them wearing their white, long-faced masks as well. Marcie joins her sister upstairs, and the two boys stay down below with the rest of the team.

"This is outrageous!" McLean shouts, having taken in the overwhelming presence of what he assumed to be a group of terrorists. The Gamblers all begin to murmur, both outraged and confused. "Tell us who you are! Who do you work for—"

"You will speak when you are spoken to!" Madisyn booms, leaning over the railing above with vicious eyes under her mask. The room falls silent at the thunderous order, all The Gamblers swiveling around to face the balcony above them. "Now," she begins, softer, "all you prim and proper tossers will go stand on that stage."

McLean holds up a subtle hand to the others, and none of the men move—paralyzed by the overall situation anyway but also infuriated and wanting to stand their ground.

Her ego slightly bruised at their reluctance to obey, Madisyn raises her rifle to the ceiling and fires it on burst. "I said *move!*" The Gamblers scramble to get on stage, being pushed along and herded more forcefully now by the agents below.

Marcie smirks down at them, amused, moving her finger in a circular motion. "In a circle, that's right," she coos. "You know how to play this game."

The men huddle in a cluster, hesitant to move. "Come on!" one of the men yells. "What is this, really?"

James hops on stage and pulls the outspoken man from the bunch, punching him in the stomach and then in the face. The man falls to the ground, and James takes out a pistol and shoots him. The men gasp, jumping at the echoing of the blast throughout the room.

Giovanni Sacchi, panicking at the sight of blood, puts his hands up. "Please! There has to be a way for us to figure this out. We can all pay you a lot of money. Let's just talk about this."

"Ooh," Heidi teases from the balcony. "Someone thinks they can speak out of turn because they're 'famous.'" The room erupts with cackles from the UCOCA agents, causing the terrified men on stage to shrink closer together.

More politely than before, Madisyn adds, "We've already got your money, haven't we? All ten million of it? So, I guess that offer is off the table." She beams at them under her mask.

"Proper game, though, mate," Robbie adds to Sacchi. "You lot killed it on the field today. Too bad they'll need another coach." From the podium, Robbie shoots his pistol at Sacchi with perfect aim, striking him once in the shoulder and once in the leg. Sacchi howls in pain and falls to the floor, clutching his wounds as his comrades look on helplessly. Two agents move in to grab the famous coach, dragging him up the aisle and out of the theater.

"Wh-where are they taking him?" McLean stammers, his gaze following the man out of the room.

"Let's proceed, shall we?" Madisyn says, ignoring his question. "With our *new* set of players! We have a rather fun twist to your little game of Russian roulette. You'll be using *our* guns!"

A few agents below move onto the stage. They each cradle a bag and pull out golden handguns with long barrels and aluminum alloy frames, each one with 'UCOCA' inscribed at the front of the barrel. The agents hand each of the men on stage a handgun, shoving them into a circle as they move along.

McLean peeks back at Saunders, whispering, "We have to make a run for it."

"Where?" Saunders says in a strained whisper. "There's nowhere for us to go!"

An agent shoves Saunders hard to move him into the right spot and hands him a gun.

"Half of these special weapons of ours are already loaded with a highly lethal serum that we made ourselves," Madisyn informs them. "And that's because we want to reduce the amount of blood that needs to be mopped up afterward." Madisyn's words are met with laughter from a few of the agents below.

Swallowing to muster some bravery, Saunders asks hesitantly, "How do we know you didn't just load all of them?"

"Now, now, Senator," Marcie says. "Why on earth would we ever lie to you?" More laughter erupts throughout the room.

Saunders cautiously steps forward, McLean's eyes widening at his friend's humongous balls. "We can make some kind of deal with you," he says. "Myself, and Senator McLean. We know it's us you're here for, right? After all, we're the ones with the most power. We can get you whatever it is you want." McLean forces a big smile as Saunders motions to him.

Madisyn's smirk disappears, glaring down at them under her mask—her hidden expression conveyed through her tone of voice. "You politicians make me sick. It's always the people who put on the most innocent, honest image, which you should trust the least. You think it's funny, don't you? You think it's *entertainment* to force vulnerable people to kill each other? Well, then... let's just see how funny it actually is. Let's see if you can make me laugh."

Saunders scoffs at this. "Absolutely not! You... terrorists, whatever the hell you are. You're meddling with things you don't understand, and I can promise you, you will regret this if you go through with this." He tosses his gun down defiantly.

McLean leans into his friend. "Are you crazy?" he asks in a strained whisper. "I didn't tell you to do *that*!"

Turning to McLean and laughing, Saunders loudly retorts for everyone to hear, "They can't hurt us! They obviously want something we can give them. So, come on already, what is it then?"

Fed up with his haughty attitude, Madisyn grabs her pistol from her hip and shoots down at Saunders, striking him in the knee. The senator hollers as he falls to the ground. McLean looks on in horror as a nearby agent on stage hunched over and punches Saunders in the face. Two others move in to drag him from the stage and out the theater. Silence falls around the room as the men take in the realization that they are, in fact, screwed. If the senators weren't even safe, the rest of them surely didn't stand a chance.

"Well, thank God we got rid of *him*, am I right?" McLean exclaims, laughing hesitantly and looking around for a similar reaction from the UCOCA agents, but only receiving stonelike masked faces. His smile disappears quickly, sweat dripping down his face as he starts to realize this could very well be the end for him. McLean takes a deep breath and then another until he starts to hyperventilate. He hunches over, placing his hands on his knees to breathe easier.

Robbie shakes his head and moves over to the senator, placing a careful hand on his back. He leans down to whisper into his ear, his pistol pressed to the man's side. "You can either choose a certain execution by not cooperating, or you can play our game and have a chance to live and see that sorry son of yours. What's it gonna be, hm Pat?"

McLean's breathing slows, and he looks over to see that terrifying *Scream* mask inches from his face. "I'll play. I'll play," he assures Robbie, nodding his head as if to convince himself.

"Okay, good," Robbie says, patting him on the back and moving back to the podium.

"Players!" Madisyn begins as everyone gets back in their places. "Are you ready to play?" she poses the iconic question once asked by the announcer. A few of the agent's smirk. "All commands will come from the tower—me! Hold up your weapons. And do *not* make me repeat myself again..." The men do as they're told this time. McLean swallows hard and is the last to follow suit, bringing his arm up.

"Hey guys!" Heidi calls down to the men standing against the far wall, who have been looking on at the turn of events with a quiet vengeance. "Why don't you help us count?"

The men burst out into excited hoots and hollers, causing the UCOCA agents to laugh.

Madisyn begins the countdown, "Three..."

Everyone else joins in unison, "Two... one..."

Squeezing their eyes closed, the men on stage pull their triggers, and every man except Patrick McLean falls to the floor. After a moment, the bodies on the ground begin to writhe in agony, foaming at the mouth and choking on their own bile. From above, Marcie puts a hand over her mouth and looks away briefly, disgusted by their reaction to the serum. Below, Senator McLean pants, his chest rising and falling as he watches his friends around him die, though his face soon distorts into a wicked smile as he comes to realize his incredible luck. He lets out a wheezy laugh at the sudden miracle, the rest of the room silently in awe.

"Well, I'll be damned..." Heidi breathes.

"I—I won!" McLean shouts, his voice echoing off the ceiling. "I *won*! Sweet baby Jesus! I *won*!" He drops his gun and clutches the hair on his head. "Jesus, this is fucking great! You know, I knew this would happen. Where's my son? I told him we'd be leaving here with ten million dollars, and look at that! Wahhh-hooo!" He cackles insanely, looking around at the eyes on him. "Hell, you 'terrorists' sure had me fooled with this little act of yours. Danny put you up to this, didn't he? He was getting back at me, wasn't he? Jesus, that kid—"

"*Shut up!*" Madisyn bellows. The cocky smile drawn on the senator's face dissipates. The room remains quiet as Madisyn makes her way down the stairs of the balcony and up the aisle toward the stage. McLean grimaces down at her.

"The person who survives wins the prize, *that's* the rules," he says flatly. "I survived, so where is my freaking money?"

"Did you actually think we'd let you win?" Madisyn says, stepping over a dead body and approaching him on stage.

McLean raises a threatening finger to her, lowering his voice. "Now you listen to me, you little bitch. I will sue the *shit* out of your ass if you touch one—" Madisyn drives her fist into his gut, McLean hunching over and groaning. She leaps into the air, and roundhouse kicks him in the head, knocking him unconscious.

Bending over the senator, Madisyn pulls out a needle filled with a strong tranquilizer and stabs it into his neck. The theater is silent for another long moment as the men against the wall stare at the teenagers, wondering what awful fate could be in store for them next.

"Hey, you lot," Robbie calls over, grabbing their attention. "There's one million dollars left in the lobby for you to split... *evenly.*" He smirks at his own joke, the men remaining paralyzed against the wall.

"We're done here," Madisyn says to her agents, standing up. "Move out!" The UCOCA agents dissipate from the room en route to their rides.

In the lobby outside of the theater, Madisyn and the others—having already taken off their masks and tossed them onto the floor—head toward the exit and pass a tied-up Daniel McLean, who stirs awake. "Jenna! Jenna, wait!" he pleads. "Don't leave me here. Please." Sighing, Madisyn walks over to him, the others waiting by the door to watch. "Take me with you! I—I can help!" He struggles to get out of the ropes wound tightly around his wrists and ankles.

Robbie laughs, nudging Marcie. "Is he serious? Pathetic little weasel."

"No, really," Daniel retorts, his voice cracking. "I thought I could be like my father, but... I'm just not cut out for it. *Please.* I'm a good person. If the police find me here like this, I'm going to prison!"

Madisyn tilts her head, curling her lip at his pleading eyes and scruffy hair. She turns back to the others, almost pouting.

"Oh, *no!*" Marcie says. "Are you mad?"

"You were the one who said we were heroes, and frankly, it got to my soft side!" Madisyn fibs, pulling out any excuse she could think of to justify her desire for a plaything of her own. "We should help him!"

"Right, like *you* have a soft side," Robbie says, unamused at her behavior. Madisyn ignores them and begins untying Daniel's feet.

"We can't just keep him!" Marcie protests. "He's not a dog. He can't be trained, for Christ's sake! Not to mention, we just screwed over his dad. He has no loyalty to us!"

"N—no, *screw* my dad!" Daniel cuts in, defending himself.

"Maybe he can stay with me!" Heidi says. "I mean, with our West Coast location. I can look after him! He is *American*, after all."

"Oh, fuck off, Heidi. I saw him first."

"All of you, shut up," Robbie says firmly, sick of their babbling. He turns to Madisyn. "Are you seriously willing to compromise our mission and entire operation for some silly frat boy who pukes at the mere thought of blood? I thought even you could do better than that, hmm?"

Shaking his head, Robbie pushes through the door and heads outside, unable to continue entertaining her foolishness.

The others follow, Heidi pursing her lips, slightly disappointed. Marcie lingers behind for a moment, seeing her twin remain frozen, staring at the door. She senses something in Madisyn that she wasn't used to seeing—maybe Madisyn *did* want a boy to be close to, and maybe she was slightly jealous of Marcie for that reason. So much that she was willing to risk befriending a total stranger to fill the void. Marcie hesitates to move forward, wanting to comfort her sister but decides to leave instead, giving her time alone with Daniel.

Madisyn turns around and kneels, bringing her face inches away from his. She leans in to kiss him. As he pulled slightly away, her lips brush his cheek with a sigh. "Danny…"

He pulls back to look at her, his eyes twinkling. "I knew from the moment I saw you there was something between us.

Come on, Jenna. We could be doing a lot more than kissing if you just untie me." Madisyn leans in to kiss his forehead, resting her head against his for a moment. "So, what do you say?"

Madisyn sighs again. "I hope Mummy has a good lawyer." Pulling away, Madisyn elbows him in the face, knocking Daniel unconscious before leaving.

CHAPTER 8

———

Inside their private jet, Robbie tosses down two duffel bags of stolen cash from their mission, one of them falling half-opened on the couch next to Madisyn. He sits across the aisle from Marcie.

With all three of them on their phones, one could almost mistake the trio for ordinary teenagers. Robbie tuned into his Spotify with earbuds, and Marcie scrolls through the latest articles on BBC News. Her legs propped up on the couch, Madisyn moves her thumbs across the screen at lightning speed as she kills a round of Candy Crush, one of her only outlets for teenage normalcy. Exhausted, all of them remain oblivious to the sudden turbulence that gently rocks the plane.

In the cockpit, the pilot slouches over in his seat, knocked out cold, a mysterious pinprick in his neck. A woman's hand reaches past him to the control panel, setting the plane on autopilot. She moves out of the cockpit and through the dim upper cabin.

As the woman's face comes further into the light, Madisyn looks up from her phone and screams, making the others jump in their seats.

"Valentina!" she shrieks. "What are you doing here?" Madisyn's phone drops to the floor as she scrambles to zip the duffel bag next to her closed. Valentina crosses her arms.

"Shit…" Robbie breathes, ripping out his earbuds. Marcie only bites her lip, turned around in her seat toward their mysterious tutor. Valentina's gaze travels to her first.

"Bravo," Valentina begins. "Job… well… done." Her eyes meet each of theirs with her words.

"It—it's not what you think—" Robbie stammers.

"Save it, Robbie," Marcie says, sighing. "She knows everything." Marcie gets up and rips open the duffel, showing Valentina the cash. Madisyn and Robbie exchanged baffled glances, horrified and utterly shocked by Marcie's apparent betrayal. "We took home ten million. And you should have seen us in there. Those guys never stood a chance. I mean the men we took down—"

"Were cowards," Valentina finishes. "But nonetheless, the time has come for you to know."

"Wait…" Madisyn shakes her head. "Stop, stop! What is going on here?" she demands, looking back and forth from her twin to Valentina, her gaze finally landing on the latter. "I thought we were the ones hiding a huge secret from *you*?" She turns back to Marcie, her eyes squinting as a vein forms on her forehead. "This was your doing, wasn't it? You told her everything. Just couldn't handle the pressure as usual."

"For your information," Marcie starts, balling her fists at her sister's accusation. "I had nothing to do with this—"

"Hush," Valentina says. "Both of you!" She looks to Marcie. "Sit." Marcie obeys, dropping the duffle bag at her feet. Valentina moves to the other side of Madisyn to sit as well, all their faces pressed on her. "There is a reason for why I am in your lives, why I sought out your parents ten years ago and begged them to let me teach you. You, Madisyn," she turns to face her. "I knew you were the one to take the lead. That is why I planted the idea in *your* head," she says, referring back to all those times as children when she had held Madisyn later than the other two for more "advanced" lessons. "So that when you were ready—when you felt you were too intelligent and too powerful to continue leading such a simple life—you would take those skills and become the mastermind you are today."

Robbie scoffs, his brows furrowed and his mouth hanging open. "So, all those little fucked up killing games you made us complete as lessons… I knew they were much too sinister for child's play!"

Madisyn looks back and forth from Valentina to her sister as if she had just found out her entire life's work was a lie. "So, y—you were just brainwashing us? Using *me*? Making me think I came up with UCOCA on my own!" She should have known better. She had always sensed Valentina's methods of teaching were anything *but* traditional. Looking back on it, Madisyn had always wondered why Valentina had deterred them from meaningless childhood games and books, pre-ferring to feed them mature content of a criminal nature instead. She could distinctly remember Marcie desperately wanting to take up golf or tennis, but Valentina had banned such activities, saying that they always had to be focused and prepared. Her excuse had been that children from powerful and influential families were often targeted by enemies. As children, this had made complete sense to them, though now they were seeing just how naive they had been.

"You still did," Valentina retorts. "I simply pushed you in the right direction. I may have taken you on trips around the world, but *I* was not the one who told you to befriend other teenagers of similar means, not to mention even going as far as recruiting orphans to run your entire operation!"

"So, why?" Marcie interjects. "How does this help *you*? Making us clever enough to do something like this? It doesn't make sense."

Madisyn laughs amused now more than anything at how absolutely absurd the situation seemed. "It's almost like we don't even know you at all, V. Who are you, *really*?"

Valentina sighs. "Look, I was preparing you," she says.

"Preparing us..." Robbie restates, his brows furrowing. "For what exactly?"

Valentina stares each one of them in the eyes, her volume dropping. "I was raised in a small town in Russia. My parents were very poor. My father was a drunk who spent most of our family's money on prostitutes half his age. But my mother loved him, worshipped him even—more than she had ever loved her own children. They wanted nothing to do with us, and I was more their slave than a daughter. So, when they heard about a boarding school called The Trinity that would take us in for free, they sent my little brother and me away without question the first chance they had—"

"You have a brother?" Madisyn interrupts. "What?"

"Quiet," Valentina orders, scolding her with a look. Madisyn shrinks back. Valentina's glance moves to the others to continue. "I was sent to this place as a teenager, but my brother Luka was sent not long after he was born. This was not a normal school, though. The Trinity is a spy academy. It trains orphans and neglected children of poor families to become killers until they are old enough to leave the school and commit evil doings for the headmaster—like infiltrating the government systems of Russia's enemies to spread hatred and the idea of Pan-Russianism along with it. We were allowed visitors sometimes to maintain a friendly appearance to outsiders who actually cared about their children, but my parents never came to see us. Our only visitor was our aunt..."

CHAPTER 9

KRASNODAR, RUSSIA

Eleven years ago, inside a school tucked far away from civilization, seventeen-year-old Valentina holds the hand of her five-year-old brother Luka, guiding him through a sparse visiting room. Their Aunt, Inna—a woman in her forties with chestnut hair and years of inconceivable stress etched on her face—follows closely with her head down as they leave.

Turning a corner down the dim hall, Boris Egorov—a boy a couple of years older than Valentina—stops them abruptly, using his stocky figure to block their way. "No visitors outside the visiting room," he says in Russian.

"Please. My aunt is pregnant and sick," Valentina lies. Aunt Inna hunches over, grabbing her stomach.

"Then take her outside," Boris says firmly. "No exceptions." He shoves her back.

"*Davay,*" Valentina says to her brother and aunt, obeying his order. She turns to wrap her arms around their shoulders. "Quickly." She leads them in the opposite direction and looks back to Boris, who keeps his eyes fixed on her.

They get to an outside corridor that lines the front courtyard of the school. Valentina lifts Luka to sit in an opening in the cement wall. Aunt Inna looks around her, the vast brick castle bringing back memories she wished she could forget. Her gaze drifts to the tall brick wall that wraps around the school, overlooked by watchtowers where the school's guards patrol. They were high up enough to see over the wall and out into the dense forest that isolated them from the rest of the world, save the one dirt road that served as the single point of entry to the exclusive school grounds. Aunt Inna purses her lips and glances around them once more to make sure they are alone, then leans in close to her niece and nephew.

"Children, I wanted to see you privately today to discuss your futures," she begins. "They are training each of you to become monsters here, to live with no souls and no emotions—"

"She lies!" Luka shrieks, turning to his sister. Valentina shushes him, patting his head and holding him in her arms.

"Luka," Aunt Inna says delicately, brushing the hair out of his eyes. "I know the dark secrets that lie within the walls of this school because I used to go here as well." His eyes grow at her confession.

Valentina knew her aunt's story well after so many years of their secret visits, though it was one they had chosen to withhold from Luka until he was old enough to understand. Aunt Inna was seven years younger than their mother Anita, a cruel woman who hated her adopted younger sister for stealing their parents' adoration. So, when their parents suddenly died of illness, nineteen-year-old Anita swiftly ran off to marry the first man she met drunk in a bar, abandoning her sister. A child orphan, Aunt Inna had been placed in a home, where she had been scouted one day by a man tender enough to be her father. He promised her a decent home where she would go to school with other children her age and never suffer an empty life again. She didn't have much choice in the matter, but she would be obedient and grateful to her new father—at least that's what she was told was expected of her. Inna went with this man to The Trinity, where she soon learned of the horrifying events she would have to endure for the rest of her childhood… until she managed to escape.

"When I escaped," Aunt Inna continues to her nephew, hoping to fill him in on everything his sister already knew. "I changed my name, my appearance—everything. That's how I am able to visit you. You're old enough to know the truth now." She takes a deep breath, looking at both of them. "I love you both so much. I only wish I could say the same of your parents… but there is a world out there, children, outside these walls. One where you are truly free."

Two students walk by, and Aunt Inna and Valentina snap their heads in their direction. The students glare at the odd trio with squinted eyes. Once the pupils are out of earshot, Aunt Inna and Valentina share a sigh of relief. No one at the school was to be trusted, and this was advice Aunt Inna had drilled Valentina on years ago, as well as a lesson Valentina had learned early on herself.

"They have deprived you of your freedom here for the headmaster's own selfish reasons—"

Luka shakes his head. "The headmaster is always right. His command—"

"Is the only command?" Aunt Inna finishes. Luka nods robotically, eyeing his aunt suspiciously, who shakes her head with another deep breath. "He is only brainwashing you to think so. Right, Valentina?"

Luka twists in his sister's arms to look up at her, wrinkling his forehead as Valentina nods in agreement. "But Valentina—"

"I know you are young and don't quite understand, but you will," their aunt assures him. "You have to trust me. There's a better life waiting for you, with me. That is why, this time next week, I'm getting you both out of here."

Luka shakes his head. Valentina hugs him tighter, but he pulls away. "I don't like what you're saying. Father said outsiders might try to lead us astray. That's what you're doing!" Wrestling from his sister's grasp, Luka hops down from the ledge and runs down the corridor back inside.

Valentina looks back to her aunt. "I will convince him, Aunt Inna. I just need some time."

Aunt Inna's gaze lingers after Luka. "You must be quick, Valentina. He's so young, so easily influenced…" She trails off and turns back to her niece.

She wraps her arms around Valentina, holding her tightly, before finishing her thought.

"I just hope we're not too late."

Later that night, Luka bolts upright in his bed, startled from a nearby noise. He stares at the wall, willing his eyes to adjust to the darkness. One of his roommates, a boy twice his age named Dima Gorky, walks inside the room and moves past Luka's bed, heading to his dresser. He looks back at the young boy while rummaging through his clothes.

"You okay, there?" Dima asks.

Luka nods, still facing the wall. "Just tired…" he answers weakly.

Dima grabs something hidden amongst his underwear and closes the dresser. He gives Luka a friendly shove on the head as he walks past him. "Go to sleep then."

Luka whips his head around to watch his roommate leave, his tiny fists balled, but instead, he turns back to the wall. The Trinity was his home, a place where he felt loved and safe, where he had friends and a real family. He did not want all that to end, and it made him question just how well he knew his aunt. She had disobeyed the headmaster once by fleeing—so how could he trust her now? He sighs deeply and lies down in his bed, switching off the lamp. If Valentina was foolish enough to follow in Aunt Inna's sordid footsteps, he would have to be the one to stop her—to protect them both.

A WEEK LATER

Inna waits by herself in the visiting room, surrounded by other visitors with their own students, when Valentina appears in the doorway holding Luka's hand. She looks up at her niece and nephew and faintly smiles. As Luka sees his aunt, he yanks his sister back. Valentina looks down at him, bending over so he can whisper something in her ear before tugging his hand away to leave. Valentina watches him go, then moves over to her aunt, who brings her hand to her cheek with worry.

"*Ne volnuysya*," Valentina assures her not to worry. "He just had to use the bathroom." She sits next to her aunt, holding her hand. Valentina's glance drops slightly, looking over her shoulder before lowering her voice. "Everything is in place. We're both packed and ready. Luka *promised* me he would cooperate."

Wanting to believe her, Inna forces a smile, her frail hands squeezing Valentina's. Her palms are cold and pale.

The blood has gone from them. She looks toward the doorway again, feeling the heavy absence of her nephew and sensing a sudden urgency to leave—the same feeling she had felt before her own escape so many years ago.

In another part of the school, Luka pushes through two grand doors, leading into the headmaster's vast office and living quarters. Peeping behind the doorway from the foyer, Luka cautiously approaches the man talking with an older male student—the appointed commandant over the student body. The headmaster, whose wrinkled face makes him appear old and withered, dawns a deep-violet velvet cloak to shroud his frail bones.

Luka lightly tugs on the headmaster's sleeve, looking up at the seemingly massive presence of the only paternal figure he had ever known. The man bends over to let him whisper into his ear. Straightening up again, the headmaster turns to face his student commandant.

"Gather everyone into the Great Hall," he commands, his voice feeble. "Tell the visitors we are ending visitation early and that they should leave immediately. *Idi seychas zhe.*" He flicks his hand, dismissing the commandant to carry out his orders.

The stern older boy nods only once, turning on his heels and swinging his arms like an obedient soldier as he exits the room. Luka watches him go. The headmaster pats him tenderly on the head.

"You've done well, my son," the old man says to him. He holds out his hand, and Luka kisses his ring—a gold engraved band holding an enormous sparkling ruby. He takes Luka's small hand into his, and they walk from the room together.

Back inside the visiting room, Valentina's and Inna's heads snap up as the firm voice of the commandant comes over the intercom. "Visitation hours have been cut early due to the headmaster's orders. All visitors must exit the building."

Others get up to leave, but Inna pulls Valentina close. "I need to see Luka first," she says, panic in her voice. "I have to be sure. What's keeping him so long?" Valentina looks over her shoulder as the room empties, wondering where her brother had run off to.

A group of older students, austere in manner, march into the room straight toward Valentina and her aunt. Boris, the same callous boy manning last week's visiting hours, leads the pack and apprehends Inna, grabbing her by the arm and yanking her to her feet.

"Unhand her!" Valentina yells, jumping up from her seat. "She's with me."

"Yes, we can see that, Valentina," Boris spits. "Headmaster's orders." He shoves Valentina further back, still holding on to the woman with his other hand. Valentina slaps his hand away, ready to fight, but another boy pushes her back harder, causing her to stumble backward onto the floor.

"Do not resist the headmaster's orders," the boy hisses, towering over her. "Get to the Great Hall immediately."

The group exit the room, dragging Inna along with them while Valentina watches them go helplessly, terrified for her aunt's safety. She looks up as the intercom comes on for a second time, "All students report to the Great Hall immediately. All students report…"

Inside the Great Hall, a rounded space with a high ceiling, the headmaster stands at the front of the room on a raised platform in front of his chair—a seat made of gold, covered in blood-red velvet. Luka stands next to him, holding the old man's hand as they wait. A few older students stand lined up on both sides of the headmaster, their hands behind their backs like chess pieces waiting for their master's next move.

Entering with a struggling Aunt Inna, Boris throws her to her knees in the center of the room, facing the headmaster. All the students in the school, ranging from as young as three years old all the way up to twenty, crowd into the Great Hall behind them, forming a semicircle of hundreds of bodies around the pathetic-looking woman. They buzz with excitement, shoving each other to see better and speculating what might happen to their new guest. Boris takes his place in the throng of students, pushing some of them back who long to get closer to see. Throughout the student body, there are a select few holding long swords in their hands with snarls etched on their faces, the other students pointing to them and whispering with wonder. The Great Hall was only reserved for special ceremonies and had not been used since the last slaying of a prisoner—a former student who had gone insane and poisoned the appointed commandant several years ago. For many of the younger students, such stories were just rumors, for they had not seen it with their own eyes. They pushed their way to the front, excited to witness their first execution.

Valentina pushes through the back of the crowd as one of her peers grabs her by the arm and pulls her along. "You," the girl says. "Go stand by the headmaster. Now."

Stumbling through the outskirts of the circle, Valentina gets to the front and sees her little brother. She rushes to him, but Luka pulls away, moving closer into the protective wings of the headmaster's cloak. Luka turns to face the middle again, and Valentina's gaze follows his. She covers her mouth and gasps, seeing her aunt so vulnerable and frightened. She looks back to the innocent face of her baby brother, who is blissfully unaware of the consequences his actions have manifested.

Silence enshrouds the hall as the headmaster holds up his hand. He lets go of Luka to greet the woman in the middle with outstretched arms. "Liliya!" he breathes, the room's acoustics allowing his weak voice to be heard by all. "Your return was not anticipated."

Aunt Inna's eyes dart to both sides, her body shaking uncontrollably as she takes in her surroundings—all eyes glued to her, making any escape impossible. She hesitates to speak, shaking her head. "No, sir—Headmaster, sir. My name is Inna. Inna Kovaleski."

The headmaster gives a breathy laugh. "I may be old, Liliya, but one does not forget his children… especially those who betray our family."

Aunt Inna lowers her head, still shaking it from side to side as if to debate the acknowledgment of her past identity. She squeezes her eyes shut to stop crying.

Valentina stands wide-eyed, anxious to do something but knowing it would be pointless; she would have a much worse fate if she were to help her aunt. She looks down to see her brother, his face blank, with a knot in his small brow. Valentina swallows the lump forming in her throat as her mind races with thoughts of hatred and blame toward the little boy she hardly wanted to claim as kin anymore.

A student from the crowd named Ruslan Orlov walks to the middle of the room, wielding a sword and tossing it from hand to hand as if to taunt his prey. Valentina's head flickers up to watch, her body tensed. Ruslan moves to stand right in front of Aunt Inna, blocking her view of the headmaster and her niece and nephew with a nasty snarl pasted across his face.

"Those who betray our family must be punished, Liliya," the headmaster continues. "You know this more than anyone in this room, don't you?"

Raising the weapon, Ruslan yells and brings his sword down, stopping inches from her neck, causing Aunt Inna to gasp aloud. Valentina jumps slightly, her mouth hanging slightly open as if to dare speak. The headmaster laughs thunderously, his entire frail body heaving under his cloak.

"You didn't think I would let you go that easily, did you, Liliya?" The headmaster shakes his head at her. "My, how much we forget when we are away from home for too long…"

Aunt Inna looks up hesitantly at the boy in front of her, who removes his sword and backs away slowly, holding fixed eyes and a smirk that terrifies her to her core.

The old man looks around at his students. "Children, let us teach sister Liliya a lesson, so this does not happen again!" He snaps his fingers to cue his minions into action.

Suddenly, a student steps forth from the crowd, holding a sword. A few more follow suit, clinging to their own weapons and swarming Inna like piranhas. She cries out with each painful slit, her clothes and face bloodied and torn apart.

Finally starting to take in the scene before him, Luka whimpers, tears running down his cheeks as fast as the blood from his aunt's body. Inna attempts to shield herself, throwing her arms up, but they are quickly shredded to pieces. The headmaster puts a hand on Luka's shoulder to comfort him through his first loss. He lets Luka cry—a wailing shrill shaking his entire body. Valentina squeezes her mouth shut to stop her quivering lip. She was not ignorant to the headmaster's evil. She had seen this coming, but she knew what she had to do now. She would wait. She would wait until the time was right, years even, to thoroughly plan her revenge. It would have to be something so incredibly shocking so that wicked old man would feel the same torment that she did.

The piranhas disperse, swarming back into the crowd. The entire room quivers in silence as the students and headmaster take in the ghastly image of a tattered woman bleeding and broken down. Breaking the stale silence, Ruslan—the first boy with the sword—approaches Inna, standing in front of her again. Except for this time, he does not hesitate to slice off her head, her disfigured body slumping over to the floor.

"No!" Luka wails, his shrieking the only sound echoing through the hall. The headmaster lets go of the boy, letting him fall into his pale sister's arms as he walks to the center.

"This is how those who betray our family die—at the hands of their family," the old man preaches. "Let this be a warning to you who have any will to go against my word, the word of your father."

He approaches Luka and Valentina, the entire room watching as he holds out his hand. Hesitating at first, Valentina kisses his ring. She shoves her resistant brother forward to do the same. Luka looks up at the old man with spiteful reddened eyes. Valentina can tell by the look on his face that this was not what he had wanted. He had thought he was doing the right thing reporting his aunt, but he had had no idea how awful the punishment would actually be. A person didn't need to die to be taught a lesson.

The headmaster pats Luka's head, clicking his tongue. "You have done nothing wrong, dear Luka. Your Aunt Liliya brought this horrible fate upon herself. You will come to understand that one day." He turns to Valentina, who is too filled with raw emotion to look the old man in the eyes. "Lead your brother back to his room. Reality can be brutal for a young child. Also... I trust after seeing such consequences, you will not behave the same. Do not disappoint me."

Valentina lowers her head further and guides her brother away, feeling hundreds of eyes on them as they pass. The headmaster's gaze lingers on her as if he could tell she was at risk of retaliating. He summons one of his pawns lined up on the platform, Oleg Tarkovsky, who moves closer to the headmaster.

"Keep an eye on them," he nods after Valentina and Luka. "Her in particularly. I fear she did not learn her lesson today, and she poses a possible flight risk. Do what you must to stop her." The boy nods and kisses the man's ring before leaving. The headmaster faces the eager, murmuring faces in the crowd, some of them finding their appetite for maliciousness satisfied fully, and others too petrified by the recent slaughtering to make their disapproval known. "Come now, children. Prove your loyalty!"

The old man sits on his throne as students all run to get in line, the older students skipping to the front and shoving the younger ones out of their way. One by one, they each bow to kiss the headmaster's ring before leaving the hall.

Valentina slams the door shut after dragging her little brother into his room, pushing him onto the bed. She slaps him across the face, and Luka shrieks, holding his cheek and lying face down on his bed crying.

"Do you see what you have done?" Valentina screams at him. "She loved us! She was our only hope! And now she's gone, and she..."

Valentina chokes back a sob, her desire to hurt him subsiding as she takes in his already fragile state. He was too young to be at fault. He had not known better like she did. Taking a deep breath, Valentina sits on the bed next to him. She strokes his hair, cooing softly at him until he sits up to let her hold him in her arms. His crying eventually dwindles to hushed sobs, and she moves him further onto the bed, cradling him as she softly sings a traditional folk song, "Good Night," the lullaby her aunt used to sing to her when she was little.

Skoro noch priydet, uspokoev solnze.
Soon night will come, qui-et-ing the sun.

Uspokoet zvuk prihodyashchey nochi.
Silent the sound of the night coming through.

Uslyshesh veter shepochet tebe.
Hear the wind whis-per-ing, whis-per-ing to you.

Spi, spi, spi. Spokoynoy nochi, moya sladkaya.
Sleep, sleep, sleep. Good night my sweet one.

Spokoynoy nochi, moya sladkaya.
Good night my dear one.

Spokoynoy nochi, moya sladkaya, spokoynoy nochi.
Good night my swe-et one to you good night.

Luka weeps, his face buried into his sister's chest until he falls asleep. Valentina moves his head onto the pillow and moves to the window. She sits on its ledge and stares outside at the dark, unforgiving sky, a single tear running down her cheek. It was just the two of them now. There was no time for tears, and there was simply no other option: she would have to find a way to escape.

Later that night, Valentina sits in the downstairs lounge on a sofa, staring at the burning fire crackling inside the fireplace, its flames reflecting off her glossy red eyes. This had been one of her favorite spaces to come to compared to the rest of the cold, cement walls of the prison they called a school. The spot was almost worthy of the label "cozy," though now, she felt uncomfortable even here. Nothing would give her solace anymore, except leaving. Luka comes down the steps from the bedchambers in his pajamas, standing by the doorway. Valentina's head snaps over her shoulder, anxious and a bit on edge, now that she knows she is being watched carefully by the headmaster's most loyal students. Seeing her brother, though, she breathes easier. Valentina moves to him, hugging his small body before kneeling in front of him.

"It was not right of him, Luka," she says, swallowing the lump forming in her throat. "She cared for us, you know that. She loved us and only wanted what was best. It was not right of him."

Luka looks down and slightly pulls away from her embrace. "But Valentina, *Otchim* is always right..." he says weakly, using the name many of the children had come to call the old man: stepfather.

She shakes her head solemnly. "No. Not this time. I'm getting us out of here, just as Aunt I—Aunt Liliya had tried to do." She pulls him in, but Luka breaks away more forcefully.

"We can't. You saw what happened. They'll do that to us!"

Valentina grabs him by his tiny arms, yanking him close. "Now, you listen to me. The only reason she was killed was that she came back. But she came back for *us*, Luka."

For a boy as young as Luka, who had grown up in The Trinity all his life, Valentina knew it was natural for him to not understand the concept of genuine love, let alone receiving that from a warm, stable nuclear family. She, too, had not known this early on until her aunt came along, having tracked her down after three years of being confined to the school. Before her aunt, Valentina had come to believe it ordinary for parents to be distant and cruel and for children to be shoved inside a new home without so much as a letter or a visit or even a goodbye. After all, she was surrounded by other children who had grown up the same way, many not even knowing their birth parents.

"The headmaster is unkind and controlling, Luka," she says. "We're getting out of this place. We're leaving, and we'll never look back." Luka refuses to look up at his sister, his face wrinkling as if in pain—the same face he had made when their aunt told him she would get them out. "*Tonight*, Luka. I have a plan," Valentina urges, sensing his reluctance. She grabs his chin, forcing him to look her in the eyes to see her seriousness. "You *will* listen to me. I'm your big sister, by blood. That should still mean something to you." She stands up and heads to the door without so much as looking back at her brother.

Sneaking down a dim hallway, Valentina stays close to the slightly damp, grimy wall. As she approaches her destination, she peeks over her shoulder and tiptoes to the door of a dark classroom. Grabbing the brass handle and pushing through it, Valentina moves between the old wooden desks to reach the back cabinet. She rummages through its contents of school supplies and pulls out an old map, setting it aside on a nearby table. Digging a bit further down, Valentina finds a metal box with a lock on it, her eyes lighting up at the sight of this. She quickly grabs it from beneath the junk in the cabinet and puts it on the table next to the map.

Valentina's eyes scan the room, looking for something that could help her. She dashes toward the front of the classroom and pulls open the drawers of a large wooden desk in front of the chalkboard. Valentina frowns, not finding the set of keys that would be her entry into the locked box, but as she pulls open the bottom drawer, her breath quickens.

"Yes," she breathes, pulling a small hammer from among a stack of sharp tools stained with blood. It seemed every teacher had a similar collection used for punishing students at every opportunity. Valentina herself had gotten quite familiar with a pair of pliers that one of her teachers was fond of using to break fingers. Not that Valentina had ever been outspoken or disrespectful to her teachers, but in a school full of what seemed like contagious wickedness, people had a way of noticing when someone was good-hearted. And the punishment for being soft or moral was much worse than for acting out. The headmaster himself, in fact, had encouraged students to break in their peers who needed a little more guidance on what it meant to be barbaric. Once students found themselves beaten and bruised enough by their teachers or peers, they were thrown into the underground prison to be starved and to suffer for a few days, only then being taken to the infirmary to have their wounds treated, which could take weeks to months to recover.

Valentina's nostrils flare, breaking her train of thought from the heinous memories of torture she had endured one too many times. She grips the hammer in her palm and struts toward the back table, not wasting even a moment before slamming down its metal head on the front of the box, the lock splitting in two and falling to the floor. Valentina tosses the hammer aside, and pries open the box to reveal neatly stacked rows of olive-green compasses. She grabs three, just in case, stuffing one in each of her two pockets and wrapping the other around her neck with its string. For a long time, Valentina never knew the reasoning behind keeping the compasses secured from students, but now she understood. A map alone would never be enough to get you through the forest outside.

Moving over to the outdated, bulky computer sitting along the side of the room, she logs on using the secret password she had acquired from years of snooping. Computer use was only authorized for student leadership, including division leaders and the commandant, as well as anyone eighteen or older. Valentina formerly assumed this was for the same reason they kept compasses locked up. She now knew the logic behind this was that student leaders were rightfully the most loyal and cruel students under the headmaster. And for the others, by the time students reached the age of eighteen, they were likely fully brainwashed with little intention of escaping two years before their graduation. Valentina, however, had no intentions of waiting another year to see if it was, in fact, possible to turn into one of the old man's puppets or be killed before that happened.

When the computer fully finishes booting up, Valentina pulls up a detailed map of the school and its surroundings and grabs the paper map and a nearby pencil. She pinpoints directions on the computer to the nearest town, miles away on the other side of the forest. Valentina sighs at this as she begins marking key spots on the paper map to help her remember. It would be a long journey for them, even longer if Luka refused to cooperate. And it would be treacherous in ways she couldn't imagine. She didn't know her bearing that far into the forest. During her four years at the school, she had only been invited to one game last year with some of the older students outside the school grounds. They had snuck over the school's thirty-foot wall, having hammered holes in it to allow them to scale it with ease. They headed out to the forest to play a deadly version of hide-and-go-seek—a game of eleven players where three never made it back, though these particular students had not been taken out by chance.

Valentina had been let in on a very dark secret by an older girl whose trust she had gained: the headmaster allowed the commandant to select three of the weakest eighteen-year-old students, invite them to a hunting game with eight others, and have those eight individuals break off into three small groups to hunt and kill these three students. It was a method of "trimming the fat" that the headmaster agreed was necessary but wanted to keep on the down low to prevent targeted students from ever finding out its true purpose. So, those who led the game spread rumors around that this was a top secret and very exclusive activity for selected older students to have fun, something the headmaster could never find out about, they would say.

Valentina remembered from her experience out there in the forest that they had never gone out past the creek that ran through the dense vegetation. Some of the older students had always teased that something horrible lurked that far back into the woods and that if you weren't careful, you could easily get turned around. A person could get lost for days, perhaps dying of starvation or hypothermia, if not from a carnivorous creature like a wild boar or a wolf.

Brushing the thoughts from her head, Valentina goes back to marking up her map before quickly logging off the computer. She would have to brave whatever was out there in the forest if she wanted a better life for herself and Luka. And she would rather die having tried than to stay with the wretched people who had killed her aunt and were so eager to kill each other. Valentina folds the map and slips it inside the waist of her pants. She puts the box of compasses back in the cabinet and grabs a clean map as a decoy before closing the cabinet. Grabbing the hammer off the back table, Valentina slinks to the front of the classroom.

Checking her surroundings first, she moves out the door and sneaks back down the hallway, her head turned over her shoulder as she turns a dark corner and bumps into Oleg, the older boy appointed by the headmaster to keep an eye on her. She hides the hammer in her right hand behind her back.

Oleg grabs her tightly by her left wrist, Valentina wincing in pain as he pries the rolled paper from her palm. "Where do you think you're going with this?" The boy unfolds it to reveal the decoy map. "Did you not learn anything from your stupid aunt? *Glupyy blyad'*," he curses. He snatches the compass dangling from her neck with a snarl.

Valentina releases her right hand from her back and wields the hammer in the air, but Oleg—a force much bigger and stronger than her—blocks the strike and grabs it, tossing the hammer to the floor. He pushes her back against the wall and wraps his large hand around her neck, choking her. A smile spreads across his lips as Valentina gasps for air, scratching at his hand desperately.

He releases his chokehold but grabs Valentina by the arm, jerking her down the hallway. She twists to escape his grasp, but Oleg quickly overpowers her, grabbing her shoulders and shoving her through a door into another dark classroom. He forces her over to the desk. She tries to push back, but he grabs her by the hair and slams her face down into the wood, pressing his body against hers and breathing down her neck, laughing into her ear. Valentina screams and elbows him in the face, causing his lip to bleed. Oleg groans and punches her, bruising and bloodying her face. Valentina whimpers from the blow, covering her face from his continuous punches.

Oleg grabs Valentina and tosses her backward, sending her toppling over one of the small student desks. She scrambles over to a corner and uses her arms to shield her head, but as Oleg walks over to her, he does not hit her. He bends down in front of her, Valentina's crying bringing a smile to his face.

"Now be a good girl and get back to your room," he hisses. "I'll be back for more later until you learn to behave yourself." He stands back up and leaves.

Valentina is left sobbing alone in the dark, too broken down and weak to move just yet.

Having made it back to her room, wiping tears from her face and still sniffling from her horrid encounter with Oleg, Valentina hurries and packs a small bag with her belongings. She retrieves the map hidden in her waistline and holds it up to examine it. The sight of it allows her to release a deep breath, knowing she and Luka still had a chance to make it through the forest to whatever destination lies beyond it. Valentina tucks it back inside her jacket next to one of the compasses she had stolen for safekeeping.

Grabbing a kerosene lantern from the dresser and turning to head downstairs, Valentina halts as one of her roommates, Anna Sharapova, comes into the room and stops at the doorway. She was a year younger than Valentina and had always been an utter pain in her ass. Anna had tried desperately to be the most competitive younger sister Valentina had never wanted. She followed her everywhere, though Valentina was beginning to wonder if this was because Anna had grown suspicious of her more than anything else, and she was constantly wanting to show Valentina up in everything they did.

"Where are you off to?" she asks in a tone that sounded more like a demand. Anna's gaze moves up and down, taking in Valentina's injuries.

Valentina stammers caught off guard. "M—me and a few older students are holding a hunting game outside."

Anna's forehead wrinkles. "That's not permitted, plus it's after curfew… What happened to your face?" She folds her arms, waiting for an answer.

Valentina straightens, narrowing her reddened eyes at the girl. She takes a step forward, lowering her voice. "You're too young to know what's permitted."

The girl scoffs. "I'm only a year younger." Her face softens a bit, her eyes darting to the ground and back up at Valentina as she uncrosses her arms. "Take me with you!"

"Like hell, I will."

Clenching her jaw, Anna squints, examining Valentina suspiciously as a smirk sneaks across her face. "Take me, or I tell the headmaster. Then it'll be more than just that pretty little face of yours that's ruined."

Valentina's nostrils flare. She sucks on her teeth, feeling trapped. "Fine," she snarls. Anna's smirk grows as Valentina walks toward her. She stops in the doorway next to the younger girl. "But don't blame me if you don't come back."

Anna loses her smile quickly, and Valentina shoves her with her bag while leaving. "I *will* make it back. You'll see!" she calls after her. The girl rushes over to grab a jacket from her bed and races from the room to follow Valentina at a safe distance.

Both girls head down the stairs into the lounge, where Luka waits with his bag on the couch. Anna raises her eyebrow, scoffing in protest.

"Why's he here?" she demands.

"He's my brother, that's why."

"You're kidding! He's *much* too young." Anna looks back and forth between the siblings, raising her chin slightly as she comes to. "You're not going hunting, are you? What are you up to then? Why do you both have bags packed like you're going somewhere?"

Valentina licks her lips and shakes her head to herself with a deep sigh, knowing what she had to do. She drops her bag and lunges at the girl, tackling and pinning her to the ground. Anna screams as Valentina grabs her by her hair, bashing her head repeatedly on the floor until the girl appears to be unconscious, her nose broken and her face bloodied. Valentina stands up, her pulse racing.

"What have you done?" Luka shouts. "She's our sister!"

Valentina spins to grab Luka by the arm. "Be quiet! *I* am your sister. The *only* one, do you understand me? These people are not our family." His eyes widen, just now seeing her bruised face up close.

Letting him go, Valentina grabs a blanket and pillow from the couch, positioning Anna to look as though she is sleeping on her side in front of the fireplace. Valentina grabs her bag and Luka, and they run from the room.

Running down the hallway with their bags in hand, Valentina pulls Luka behind a wall as two students, Grigoriy Menshov and Yuri Sokoloff, walk by on night patrol. As they pass, the two siblings continue moving down a stairway into another hallway, Luka slowing until he finally pulls free.

"Valentina, we can't!" he pleads.

"Luka, we're almost there!"

He drops his bag, his face distorting into a whine. "I'm scared!"

Valentina shushes his crying, trying to cover his mouth, his chest heaving with the threat of tears. "Pick up your bag. *Davay!*" she orders. "*Now,* let's go."

"I won't go! You'll get us killed! We'll die out there!" Luka shouts. "The headmaster is always right! His command is the only command!" Luka covers his ears and shuts his eyes, shouting at the top of his lungs, Valentina failing to quiet him and starting to panic.

Grigoriy and Yuri run down the stairs and come around the corner. "What's going on here?" Yuri demands.

"They're going to make a run for it!" Grigoriy answers, recognizing the Dementiev siblings. The boys sprint down the hallway toward them, Luka abandoning his sister to run in the opposite direction.

"Luka!" Valentina shouts after him. As the boys get to her, she whips her bag at Yuri and kicks Grigoriy in the face. As Yuri gets up, she pulls a pocket knife out and stabs him in the stomach, the boy falling to the floor, clutching his abdomen. She leaps in the air to spin-kick Grigoriy again, knocking him over. Valentina comes to stand over him, her knife in hand, ready to slash him, as Grigoriy throws his hands up in defeat.

"Please!" he begs, glancing over at his friend, whose blood pools underneath his body on the floor. Valentina's breath slows, also watching Yuri cry out in pain. She swallows the lump forming in her throat as she realizes this was the first time she had ever killed someone. As much as she wanted it to feel good, to feel some sort of vengeance for her aunt, she felt like a monster instead. Valentina backs away from

Grigoriy, deciding to spare his life as she grabs her bag and runs further down the hall.

Seeing a large stained glass window up ahead, Valentina takes her bag and uses the force of her body to break through it. She falls ten feet to the ground, the bag breaking her fall. Knowing there wasn't much time until her escape was made known to the school, Valentina gets to her feet quickly. She runs over to the wall surrounding the school grounds, tossing the bag over her shoulder first and then using the same jagged holes the students had shown her during their hunting game to climb up and over it.

The alarms of the school go off behind her, lighting up the guard towers in bright red, but Valentina keeps running through the thick layers of snow on the ground, her bag sliding further down her back. The guards high above the school's walls start to shoot down at her, but one of the guards holds up his hand to command the others not to waste their bullets. She would likely be dead in less than a day anyway. Russian winters were unforgiving like that.

Valentina knew that freedom was ahead for her, though, and that her determination would keep her as warm as she needed to be to stay alive. As she reaches the edge of the forest, she heaves her bag higher onto her shoulder—running away from the only place she had ever called home and never looking back.

CHAPTER 10

PRESENT DAY

The twins and Robbie remain paralyzed as Valentina finishes revealing her disturbing past. "Luka was in so deep back then. Eleven years later, I'm afraid to see what he has become. But he's my brother…" She trails off, feeling a ping in her chest as she imagines what her brother must be like now, only a year younger than she was when she ran away. She places a hand over her chest, unable to speak for a moment.

After a few moments, Valentina continues, "I made contact with someone on the inside, who has supposedly been working as some kind of double agent. He assured me that Luka is still alive. You three—UCOCA—you're my only hope of getting him back and giving that wretched old man what he deserves. I have waited for so long." Valentina pauses and frowns as if choking back tears. Marcie's eyes widen, never having seen her tutor convey more emotion than a frown. Valentina clenches her teeth in anger as a single tear manages to escape her eyelid. "I have put *everything*, my entire life, into making sure you are ready. You *will* help me with this," she says. The teens swallow the lumps in their throats, exchanging glances, the blood drained from their faces.

"V…" Marcie starts carefully. "If he's been in there for eleven years…" She shakes her head slowly to express her doubt. "Rescuing a victim who actually *wants* our help is one thing, but this…"

"Sounds like you want us to kidnap a trained assassin," Robbie says, more furious than surprised that she would ever demand such a favor. "Marcie's right. Even if we did manage to get in, he'd probably want to kill us the second we do."

"Exactly," Marcie agrees. "We steal from greedy, *gutless* businessmen! We've never faced a target that has the same set of skills that we have."

"Don't forget the ravenous, bloodthirsty, *emotion*less mindset they brainwash them into having," Robbie adds.

Amid the discussion, Madisyn—whose gaze had previously drifted to the floor—snaps her head over to Valentina. "We'll do it," she says firmly, the others turning to her with their mouths open.

"You've really hit a new level of psycho, haven't you?" Robbie breathes.

She ignores him and turns to her sister. "Marcelle, *you* were all for helping her at the beginning of this!"

"That was before I knew her silly plan to rescue her psychotic brother!" Valentina sucks on her teeth at this statement. "No offense, V, but even you know he's probably a *complete* nutter by now."

Madisyn stands, sick of the excuses. The others look up at her. "What's the point of running UCOCA, feeling high and mighty when we never actually put ourselves in any *real* danger?" she asks them. "V has been there for us our whole lives. We can't abandon her!"

"She just admitted she was using us all that time for her own twisted needs!" Robbie reminds them as if Valentina is not sitting right next to him. "Why should we help her with anything?"

Valentina's gaze falls to the floor, the emotion wiped from her face. Madisyn turns to face her. "Because she *gave* us a purpose in life. That's why," she says softly, Valentina's head slightly coming back up to look at Madisyn.

"Oh, yeah?" Robbie asks, breaking their tender moment. "Who's *she* to decide that?"

Madisyn only keeps her eyes on Valentina. "We'll help you get your brother back. And we'll destroy that wretched school. Even if it kills us." Valentina's eyes sparkle with gratitude.

Robbie scoffs in disbelief. He gets up, heading to the back of the plane, where he locks himself inside the bathroom. Marcie's gaze lingers in his direction. She sighs heavily, looking down at her fingers, her eyebrows furrowing. Valentina notices Marcie's refusal to look at her and moves to the cockpit of the plane. Madisyn watches her go. She looks back down at her twin adamantly, at a loss for words to persuade her.

"This is stupid, Madisyn," Marcie says, shaking her head. "Even for you... This mission is a death sentence."

Madisyn rolls her eyes. Marcie and Robbie had always been afraid of real challenges. Sometimes Madisyn wished she wasn't alone on the road less traveled, and it wasn't enough for her that UCOCA coasted through most of their missions. She needed someone who could really keep up with her, or at least to experience the thrill of brushing death's grip—that would be a real challenge for once. Having made up her mind, Madisyn turns away from her twin to go after Valentina.

Upon entering the cockpit, her eyes initially grow at the unconscious pilot next to Valentina, who looks up at her from her own seat. "They don't see the bigger picture," Madisyn says. "But I guess that's why you chose me." She smiles a little, feeling special for someone to finally see her full potential.

Valentina doesn't speak, though, likely discouraged by the others' reluctance to come around even though time was of the essence. Madisyn purses her lips, thinking of a solution. She then moves the pilot over to sit in his seat. Valentina watches her curiously as Madisyn puts on a headset and takes over the autopilot on the control panel.

"We're getting your brother back," she says firmly.

"We need time to prepare," Valentina insists, leaning forward. "And they need time to think about all of this. They're right. It's dangerous."

Madisyn continues pressing buttons on the dashboard, choosing to ignore the rare apprehension in Valentina's voice. "UCOCA Rule number five: Never abandon a fellow agent, no matter how risky the mission." Madisyn winks at her tutor. "They'll change their minds by the time we get to Kiev," she assures her. "We have a UCOCA headquarters there. And like you said, we've been preparing for this since we were six years old. How much more time do we really need?"

CHAPTER 11

———

Seventeen-year-old Vasyl Franko—appointed leader of UCOCA Ukraine and heir to Franko Corporation, an energy and oil company headquartered in Kiev—pulls up a hologram blueprint of The Trinity. A few of his Ukrainian agents gather around the table across from the twins, Robbie, and Valentina, all braced to hear Vasyl's newly collected intel for their seemingly impossible rescue mission.

"This was all I could find," Vasyl says flatly, clearly sensing their disappointment in the lack of information as Madisyn raises a questionable eyebrow at him.

Two years ago, the twins had met Vasyl during a family trip. Their father was attending a summit in Kiev to fulfill his obligations as a nonexecutive director on the board of Franko Corporation. Before the start of that meeting, the Montevega family had mingled in a room among other international officials, including Egor Franko with his son Vasyl, who had appeared displeased to be there. Bill had always taught his daughters how resourceful summits were to network with top investors, and it proved to be just the right opportunity for the girls. They had already been in the early stages of their operation and looking to open another headquarters under their mother's dealership in the city. After its establishment, though, UCOCA Ukraine did not always run operations as frequently as other locations, being given an exception to the "one mission a month" rule. As the son of one of the few wealthy families in his country, Vasyl's family was under constant public scrutiny for his father's controversial business practices, making it hard to get away to his underground life of crime. He often let one of his top agents take the lead in his absence, only making a significant effort to show up when the twins made contact every so often.

This lack of involvement slightly worried Madisyn. A line was forming on her forehead. She had never expected their UCOCA missions to ever take them to Russia of all places, and if she had, perhaps they would have held the Ukrainian headquarters to a much higher standard.

Vasyl zooms in on the hologram for all of them to examine the intricate channels running through the school. "We'd be foolish to think these are accurate," he says.

"There are a few secret tunnels missing," Valentina confirms.

"Exactly. We cannot go in blind."

Madisyn bites her lip, thinking. "Maybe we don't have to. V, do you remember any of the secret passages?"

Valentina scans the blueprints, squinting as if trying to recall them in her mind. She moves the hologram from the table to float in front of her and then closes her eyes for a moment. "I knew all of them when I was there…" Opening her eyes, she uses her fingertips to draw in the passages on the hologram. "There could be more, though, by now."

"It's been eleven years…" Marcie reminds them. "Of course, there are new ones!"

"You mentioned that friend on the inside," Madisyn says to Valentina, ignoring her sister's worry and eager to find a solution. "Can't we just ask them for help?"

Valentina shakes her head. "He's not a friend. Even connecting with them was by chance, and it'd be too risky to make contact again. We're on our own."

Robbie sighs, pursing his lips. Marcie stands beside him with folded arms, both of them united in their unenthusiastic manner. Neither one of them wanted any part in this, but they also didn't want the guilt of having Valentina or Madisyn killed when they could have been there to prevent it.

"Before we start drafting this elaborate plan," Robbie says, redirecting their focus, "maybe we should think about how we're going to get *inside* the damn school first."

Vasyl turns to Valentina. "How did you escape when you were there? Maybe that's our key inside." Everyone looks to her as well, Valentina's gaze drifting off to her past.

"The system wasn't all that hard to beat. There were only a few guards on the outside because, well... no one had ever tried to sneak *inside* the school before."

Robbie laughs. "Probably because anyone crazy enough to sneak in would surely face a terrible fate, something like death, I would imagine, and possibly being chopped into tiny little pieces by a thousand bloodsucking Russians," he spits.

Valentina sighs, unable to disagree with him. Robbie's tense jawline softens a bit, and he sets aside his jokes as he sees her distress. He didn't have siblings, but he knew that he would easily be doing the same thing if it were Marcie trapped somewhere—and maybe even for Madisyn too. Robbie sighs aloud in frustration, everyone turning to him with expectance.

"Okay," he says. "If we're going to do this—even though it's *nuts*—we need to do this right." Marcie squints her eyes at him, seeming to wonder where this sudden motivation was coming from. "We go in heavy, locked, and loaded. Machine guns, grenades, the works."

A smile grows on Madisyn's face, intrigued by Robbie's new macho attitude. She was impressed, but also, she needed him. As much as she wanted to take on this mission alone purely for the thrill, the reality was they would need as much unity and manpower as possible to come out of this alive.

"We're not taking any chances in there," Madisyn continues, taking back over. "Everyone in that school dies, understood? Except for the boy, of course."

"Whoa, let's not get totally carried away," Marcie warns, scolding her with a look. "We're not just going to kill *everyone*... right, V?" She turns to look at her, but Valentina only refuses to look up, her silence communicating that her response would not be one Marcie cared for.

"Guess that answers it," Madisyn says firmly, shrugging.

"Absolutely not." Marcie crosses her arms, staring her sister down. "We take out only those necessary—those who get in our way." Robbie lifts an eyebrow, wondering if Madisyn would budge when even he was eager to make sure everyone in that awful school didn't live to see another day. How could they risk letting those animals loose out into the real world?

Madisyn groans and rolls her eyes. There were very few instances when Marcie would actually stand up for something she believed in, and Madisyn knew this was one of those moments. "Fine," she sighs, not wanting to waste another minute arguing when they had to prepare. "Let's move people. We have shit to get done!"

They scatter in different directions, Madisyn heading straight to the weapons room to find the biggest guns she can carry. Marcie heads to the underground garage with Robbie to load gear into bulletproof black jeeps, their transportation to the private jet waiting for them at the airport. Back in the main room, Valentina stays with Vasyl to plan a route on the map, in front of which she would stay for the next twenty-four hours to ensure she accounted for every detail that could go wrong.

CHAPTER 12

———

Across the Ukraine-Russia border and deep inside The Trinity boarding school, sixteen-year-old Luka Dementiev sits in the library of his division's living quarters. Flickering lights from the ceiling illuminate the Cyrillic carved into spines of dusty old books stacked neatly on shelves in the rows around him. He flips open the velvet-red covering of a book propped up on his lap. Three words scribbled in bold red ink across the first page reflect in his eyes:

Yesli ty posmeyesh.
If you dare.

He rips to the next page, intrigued by what lies ahead, but averts his gaze when he hears a faint noise echoing from somewhere within the library. Luka ducks behind one of the aisles, setting the book in an empty space on one of the shelves. It was past curfew, and he knew he couldn't take the risk of being seen, fearing the consequences of another violation.

At the end of the aisle, a sharpened sword sits in the palm of a statue as part of an art display. Luka bounds toward it—his bare feet landing softly on the carpeted flooring with every swift motion. He snatches the sword from its home. Wielding the shiny weapon in a tight grip, he moves down another row of books with a honed, quiet grace resembling that of an Iga ninja—trained and perfected in the art of concealment as he had learned over so many years in the school's martial arts gym. He sees the outline of a woman's head through the spaces between the books and stops to observe her, his piercing gray eyes squinting and fixed on her figure like a laser sight. The woman's head cocks to the side as if she can sense another presence in the room. Luka moves behind an encyclopedia collection so as not to compromise his position.

As both of them approach the end of their aisles, parallel in movement, Luka watches the woman through the shelves. She glances over her shoulder again in obvious paranoia. Luka turns on his heels, gliding around the end of the row like a ghost. As the woman turns her head back around, Luka is poised in front of her with his sword nestled in the crook of her neck. He raises an eyebrow, surprised and a bit disappointed in the stranger's initial reaction of such coolness as if she had been expecting him after all.

"Bringing a knife to a gunfight I see…" The woman smirks. Luka's eyes lock on the foreign AP-9 pistol strapped to her hip. Her Russian was flawless, though he suspected she did not belong there. She had to be at least ten years his elder— much too old to be a student. The rage inside of Luka simmers in his chest as he concludes: *intruder.*

"Move, and I'll slit your throat," he says to her in his native tongue.

The woman laughs but holds her hands up with caution. Luka inches his sword into her neck, grazing her skin and causing blood to bead down her neck. A shadow behind the woman's figure catches Luka's attention. A girl from his division, Sveta Pantaeva, who he had known was awake on quarter's guard duty, passes through the door of the library and approaches the intruder from behind. She snatches the strange woman's pistol from her hip and presses the muzzle to the back of her head. The girl nods to Luka, and he lowers his sword with a smirk.

"Sveta," he greets the girl, returning her nod.

The strange woman clears her throat, raising her hands to her head. "Are you going to tell the headmaster?" She smiles ever so slightly at Luka. "Come on, you're not the only one who likes to sneak around at night."

Luka scowls at her. "You're not a student here," he says, calling her bluff. He grabs the woman by the shoulder and shoves her through the library door and out into the main lounge of *Vipera* division's sleeping quarters. Sveta keeps the gun pressed to her head as they move.

"Yes, I am," the woman argues. "Just because I'm not in your division—"

"Shut up!" Luka thrusts the sword in his hand back up to her neck to silence her. "*Pozovi na pomoshch'! Seychas*," he mutters in a growl to Sveta, who nods and takes off running from the room. "I don't know who you are, but you'll be punished for this... severely."

The woman lowers her hands in a deliberate, careful motion, distress washing over her face. "Please..." She speaks in a pleading whisper as if she were going to tell him a secret. She looks over her shoulder to make sure they're alone. "Luka, you must listen to me," she says with haste. "I need you to cooperate this time! Luka, it's me." The ring of his name voiced with such familiarity from a seemingly total stranger makes him flinch. He withdraws slightly from her, taking a step back on his heel but keeping the sword up. He swallows hard. The woman reaches out with a tender hand, trying to touch his face. Luka starts to pant and grabs her by the wrist with his free hand as she screams at him. *"Luka! Luka!"*

The woman's voice still ringing in his ear, a bucket of freezing-cold water splashes Luka in the face, jerking him awake with a loud gasp. Coming to consciousness, Luka shouts as two older boys grab each of his arms and drag him from his bed, his roommates jolting awake and watching, terrified from their own beds. The boys pull Luka from the room, throwing a potato sack over his head. Luka struggles and screams for someone to help him. He'd had the same dream about his older sister for the third time that month, and he couldn't help wondering if the headmaster had somehow tapped into his brain and whether this was his punishment for such thoughts.

"I didn't do anything!" Luka shouts. "I swear it!"

"Shut up! Or you'll really be in trouble," one of the boys snarls, the other laughing darkly.

The boys drag Luka through the dark halls of the east wing, forcing him to his feet as they reach a flight of stairs. Luka calms his breathing, letting them guide him down what seems like an endless spiral staircase. They walk down another hallway until Luka hears a wall shift and a door creak open to what he assumed was some kind of secret room. The boys push him inside and onto his knees, then rip the bag from his head.

Luka blinks. As suspected, the headmaster stands before him. A glance to his right and left reveal eleven division leaders of the school—all males between the ages of sixteen and nineteen, wearing black cloaks and each with a candle in their hands. Luka squints, knowing there were, in fact, supposed to be twelve division leaders, four for the three divisions. He wondered what horrid things could have happened for the fourth leader of *Vipera* division—Maxim Shkurat, who had been over his quarter—to not be there. Had he been the one to report him?

The room remains mostly dark, only lit by three candles on the wall and a burning fire in the far corner. Luka could tell by the dankness of the air and the water spots on the cement walls that they were in the lowest level of the school—a place rumored to be forbidden to students.

"Luka," the headmaster crows. Luka braces himself for punishment. "We have brought you here today for a very special occasion." The old man moves to the front of the room and rips a white cloth from a raised platform to reveal a blood-streaked altar behind him.

Swallowing hard, Luka shudders uncontrollably. He blinks several times, hoping to still be dreaming. "Headmaster," he begins, his voice trembling. "I swear I meant no—"

The old man motions for Grisha Yurkov, his appointed student commandant and the most vicious boy Luka had ever known, to step forward. The nineteen-year-old approaches Luka, a black hood was shrouding his head as he carries a tattered black book with both hands. "Place your right hand on the book," Grisha orders, squinting at his junior as if to influence his obedience.

Luka carefully raises his hand to set it atop the book, swallowing hard again as Grisha's eyes flicker down momentarily. Luka's nostrils flare. He had never been this close to the commandant before, and at the moment, all he could hope for was that the rumors about him weren't true. Luka braced himself for the worst.

Suddenly, the division leaders around him move in with their candles, enclosing Luka within a tight circle as they chant.

Nash velikiy otets, my teper' proiznosim etogo muzhchinu
By our great father, we now pronounce this male

Dostoynyy svyatoy sily.
Worthy of holy power.

My naznachayem etogo mal'chika glavoy svoikh sverstnikov,
We ordain this boy head of his peers,

Nadziratel' divizii vipera.
Overseer of *Vipera* division.

Pust' on vedet s bol'shim vliyaniem,
May he lead with great authority,

Neumolimyy i besposhchadnyy.
Unforgiving and merciless.

Chtoby on ne raskayalsya v etom svyashchennom obeshchanii
Lest he repent this sacred promise

Proklyani yego krov' i yego dushu navsegda.
Damn his blood and curse his soul eternally.

When the chanting concludes, Luka moves his gaze back around to Grisha. The older boy states, "If you agree, say 'I do,' and it will be so."

Luka hesitates at first, knowing he did not have much choice either way. "I do."

Immediately blowing out their candles, two of the division leaders lift Luka by his armpits and carry him to the altar. Luka's breathing picks up again as he is forced onto his stomach. The headmaster moves to stand in front of his new recruit, his hands linked in front of him as he watches his leaders preparing for the ritual's finale.

"All the greats before you have gone through this initiation as well. You are one of us now," the old man breathes. Luka didn't understand. He was already a student at the school—hadn't he already *been* one of them? "And Luka… you will speak to absolutely no one regarding the ongoings of this night." Luka's brows furrow, and he swallows hard as the headmaster drops his chin to stare a little more intently.

Breaking his gaze away, Luka turns his head as one of the leaders pulls his shirt up, revealing Luka's bare back. Luka watches as the division leaders pass around a large knife, each of them cutting a thin slice of their palms open and rubbing the blood on his back. He grimaces as one of them comes around to the head of the altar, pricks his own thumb, and strokes his blood across Luka's forehead in an X. Luka's gaze follows the boy as he moves behind the altar again to join the others. Another leader carries an elongated metal stake from the fire and hands it to the commandant. The hissing of burning coal causes Luka to stiffen. He struggles as the realization sets in, but the other leaders swarm to hold him in place. Grisha presses the sizzling metal into Luka's bare back, and he lets out a deafening shriek, writhing on the altar.

The following night, having recovered from what he had learned was the *Dogovor Krovi* ceremony—meaning Blood Pact—and finally feeling the full extent of mightiness from his promotion, Luka struts through the dimly lit corridor of *Vipera* division, his chest puffed out. Becoming a division leader had made great strides for his ego. The past was now the past: no more silly nightmares, no more feelings of worthlessness, feeling repressed and less than worthy. This was his opportunity to finally make a name for himself outside of his sister's wrongdoings and move past the shadow lingering over him. No one would dare question him with his new authority, and he would make sure of that.

Luka approaches double doors engraved with the head of a large serpent. Its blazing red eyes twinkle from the glow of the lanterns on the wall as he pushes the heavy doors apart, walking into his section's lounge. Three of his cohorts— Ivanna, Yakov, and Rurik—look up from their spots on the couch in front of the fireplace as he enters.

"Where have you been all day? We've been looking for you!" Ivanna says, leaned back on the couch, her arms and legs crossed. Rurik's easy expression twists into an uncomfortable scowl, unseen by the others.

"Shouldn't you all be in your rooms?" Luka asks.

"Not tired yet," Yakov says, shrugging his shoulders.

"We'll have a long day tomorrow," Luka reminds them, walking over to the couch. "You should all be getting some sleep soon."

Ivanna sits up taller on the couch, her eyes locked on him. "Don't ignore the question! Where were you? Your roommates told us what happened—that you were snatched out of your bed in the middle of the night! They said they haven't seen you all day."

"Heard you were with some of the older guys..." Rurik adds, raising a brow but trying not to seem too interested.

"Did the headmaster really summon you to the lower levels?" Yakov asks. "I thought no one was allowed down there. What happened?" Luka only shrugs, remembering the headmaster's last words to him.

The door to the lounge swings open, revealing Grisha standing in the doorway. Ivanna, Yakov, and Rurik immediately stand to face the older boy. Luka remains slumped on the couch.

"You three, out!" Grisha says, in his usual scowl.

The three students hurry from the room, keeping their heads down as they pass the commandant in the doorway. Grisha's daunting gaze follows them, his hands behind his back as he turns to Luka, his expression softening.

"Grisha," Luka says, acknowledging him from the couch. He sits up straighter, still a bit uneasy in the commandant's presence.

"You'll have to cut them loose if you're going to be in charge, Luka. Especially that girl," the older boy advises. Grisha tosses him a book, and Luka catches it, opening its pages to examine the content. He flips through its crinkly pages, torn and stained yellow with age—the type of book that must have been passed down for several generations. Grisha puts his hands behind his back again. "The headmaster wanted me to give you that personally—the rules of what it takes to lead along with his purpose for us. Study and memorize its content. In forty-eight hours, you will recite all the rules back to me, so I suggest getting started now. Questions?"

"I thought the other three *Vipera* division leaders were supposed to be my mentors?" Luka asks carefully.

Grisha lifts his chin, his jawline twitching. "Normally, that is how this process goes, but for some reason, the headmaster seems to think you're a little more special than the others. Therefore, I'll be keeping a close eye on you myself. That being said… don't screw up." Grisha turns on his heels, leaving Luka alone with the book.

Luka releases a deep breath, his attention moving to the book in his hands as he opens its pages. He had always been curious about what their futures had in store and whether the end goal would be worth all the waiting and preparation once he was sent "away" in four years, whatever that really meant. Luka wanted answers. Sometimes it felt as if they were being kept locked inside The Trinity with no clear guidance on their overall purpose. And surely, they would need some kind of exposure to the outside world to know what they were really up against, didn't they?

Luka's eyes dart to a few highlighted passages after flipping through the first couple of pages of dense writing, one reading the following:

"Students will be permitted release from the school upon reaching the age of twenty. Only then will they be fully ready to employ the headmaster's plan. Pan-Russianism is an immeasurable concept that takes much time to achieve. Each generation is merely a small phase forward in a gradual attack."

Luka's gaze trails over to a handwritten note beside the passage: "Patience is key." He shakes his head and snaps the book shut. He couldn't help feeling insignificant in a plan that could take decades, maybe more, to carry out. He was eager to be out in the world already. What were they waiting for?

Getting to his bedchambers, Luka closes the door behind him and tosses the book on his desk. After his promotion yesterday, he had been upgraded to a much larger suite by himself, a room twice as big as the others with a full-size desk in front of a large window that looked out into the courtyard, a king-size bed in the center of the room, a tall wooden wardrobe on one side of the bathroom and a closet on the other. Lukas couldn't be more grateful for having the luxury of a private space right then. His branding was killing him and had seemed to grow more painful the next day. Walking over to the bed, he peels off his shirt, wincing from the pain. Luka groans and stretches his body when the sudden creak of a door catches him by surprise. Luka spins around, pulling a knife from his pocket—a gift given to him by a fellow division leader—and chucks it across the room like a dart. Stepping out of the closet, Ivanna ducks just in time, the knife penetrating the wall instead of her head. She pants from her swift reaction.

"Shit," Luka breathes. "What the hell are you doing in here, Ivanna?"

She laughs, slightly out of breath. "Sorry for breaking in. I just wanted to check on you after your talk with Grisha. He can be so nasty, I've heard." She grabs the dagger from the wall and stabs it into the wooden desk.

Luka shrugs his shoulders. "He's like that with everyone, I guess."

Ivanna moves to sit on his bed, taking a good look around his room at first. "Nice upgrade." Luka doesn't answer, his gaze simply trailing hers as he admires his new room again.

"Whoa," she breathes, her gaze coming back around to catch the embellishments on his back. "What's that?"

Luka takes a step back as she moves closer. "It's nothing," he says quickly.

She furrows her brows. "That's what happened to you when you disappeared last night, wasn't it?" Sighing, Luka squeezes his eyes shut. Surely it didn't count as "telling" if Ivanna had discovered the branding first. "Let me see," she urges, already moving around to get a better view. Ivanna gasps at the sight of the ritual scarring which emblazed the skin of his back: a drawing of the Trinity symbol with its three main divisions of *Vipera*, *Borov,* and *Volk*, derived from three of Russia's deadliest predators—the Caucasus viper, the giant Russian boar, and the gray wolf. "How'd *you* get these?" Ivanna asks, tracing her fingers along the lines of the Trinity and through the blonde hair on Luka's back.

Luka turns around to face her. "He made me a division leader," he says, Ivanna's eyes growing. "But you can't tell *anybody* you saw this, Ivanna. I took an oath."

"So, what happened to Maxim?" she asks.

Luka huffs at her failure to acknowledge his secret. "I'm serious, Ivanna. You can't tell anyone! Swear it."

Ivanna shakes her head quickly. "I won't tell a soul. I swear!" Luka breathes a little easier. He grabs his shirt from the bed and puts it back on. "How are you holding up, though?"

He looks at her, his brows furrowing. He didn't understand why Ivanna was asking about his feelings, especially when he tried so hard to convince his peers he didn't have any. Ever since he could remember, half the students in the school seemed to coddle him, wondering if he remembered anything about his sister's escape and if he felt alone. The other half seemed reluctant to even speak to him, likely assuming he would mar the school's honorable history like his family did. Over the years, the unsolicited opinions seemed to subside, but there was always a random question or two from an inquisitive younger student longing to know more about events before their time. Luka just wanted to be rid of these perceptions overall. And he especially did not want to discuss his feelings.

"I'm fine, Ivanna," he says. "You shouldn't be in here. It's past lights-out." Female sleep quarters were on the opposite side of their quarter, and while Ivanna and other girls had often snuck over at night to hang out, Luka could no longer allow her to break the rules under his supervision.

Ivanna flops down on the bed. "I know... but as your friend, I'm obligated to make sure you're all right."

Luka holds her gaze, rolling his eyes. "Thanks, I guess. Now get out. You'll be in trouble for being here."

"But *you're* in charge now! I wouldn't get in too much trouble." She smirks, leaning back on her elbows.

Luka knew what Ivanna wanted. He could tell by the look in her eyes that she hoped he would take the time to really look at her, so he could see how beautiful she was. Luka was not supposed to encourage such things, though. Such things as lust were forbidden. Even knowing of several others in their division who were maintaining secret affairs, he could not allow her to think that would ever happen, at least not with him. Luka averts his gaze from her.

"Well... I guess if you're fine then, I'll just leave," she says. Ivanna sighs and gets up from the bed, a note falling from her pocket. Luka stares at it as she moves toward the door. She turns around to face him by the door, watching his face for a moment. "Do you still think about her?" she asks. Luka squints at her, but he doesn't speak. Ivanna looks down at the floor. "I won't come back here if you don't want me to." Luka turns away from her as her head comes back up. Ivanna nods only once, turning to go.

"Ivanna…" he calls. She spins around a little too quickly. Luka walks over to his bed and picks up the folded piece of paper she had dropped, holding it out to her. "You left this," he says flatly, and her shoulders seem to fall.

She walks back over to him. "It's for you, actually," she says.

"What is it?" Luka asks, already growing tired of his conversation with her. He kept thinking about what Grisha had just told him—to lose his old friends, especially the girls. Girls only seemed like trouble to Luka anyway. First his aunt, then his sister, and now Ivanna was trying to lead him astray. After all the work he had done to lose any connections from his traitorous family, he would not allow himself to engage in any more punishable offenses.

"Why don't you open it?" Ivanna suggests.

"Who is it from?" he demands. Ivanna looks away, fiddling her hands. "Is it from you?" he asks, more impatiently. She looks back up but doesn't say anything. "Here," he says. "*Take* it."

Ivanna just stands there, holding back any urge to convey feeling wounded. Luka grabs her wrist and forces her palm open, shoving the note into it. She looks down at her paper and swallows hard, averting her gaze further from him.

"Fraternization will get you punished," Luka says. "I took a vow to follow the rules. But I'll spare you—I'll let you off with a warning this time. I need to stay focused on the headmaster's plan, and so do you. He has great plans for us, for our nation, and it is our duty to serve him." Luka purses his lips, not even convincing himself as the words come out in a flat, robotic tone.

Ivanna keeps her eyes down. "I just care about you is all, Luka. I'm your friend—"

"We're not *friends*. You're my sister," he hisses, trying to ignore his history with the word. "In the way that we're all brothers and sisters here. Do you understand that?" He pauses, but she doesn't answer. "Maybe in another life, this could happen," Luka continues, more softly. "But not in this life." Ivanna brings her head up to look at him, her eyes glimmering and optimistic. Luka's chest puffs with frustration. "*Not* in this life," he spits, taking a step forward and making her flinch. "Now, get out." With her head down, Ivanna leaves his room.

Alone, Luka takes a deep breath before moving into his private bathroom. He flips on the light switch, a faint green glow lighting up his face in front of the mirror. He fills the sink with icy cold water. Bending over, he submerges his golden blond hair and face in the water for sixty seconds. Several other division leaders had told him to complete this nightly ritual before injecting a large dose of *Uspet'*—a special drug the academy had created and reserved only for the hierarchy to make them feel invincible, fearless, and ready to kill anyone at the headmaster's command. And at this point, Luka was finally ready to try any ritual that separated him from his peers.

He pulls his face from the water, staring at his pale reflection in the mirror. One of the new brandings on his shoulder glimmered red from the streaks of water dripping down from his hair. Luka reaches across his chest to touch it, reading its words aloud. "Brothers and sisters," he breathes. "Sister…"

His breathing seems to fail him as he repeats the word. He is paralyzed as his own face in the mirror seems to disappear, his mind swirling into a blur as his childhood floods his memory: standing in the crowded hall in tears, the headmaster next to him. His Aunt Liliya on her knees in the center of the floor, her clothing ripped and soaked with blood. Valentina by his side, holding him, shielding his eyes as they watch their aunt's gruesome beheading.

The headmaster's distorted words ring in his mind, "Those who betray our family die at the hands of their family." The words wash away the memory from the Great Hall, replacing it with another—the moment Valentina had dragged him down the hallway with packed bags, Luka dropping his to pull away from her grip, screaming at the top of his lungs.

"Luka!" The sound of his sister screaming his name for the last time echoes in his head, jerking him out of his memory. He gasps for air, his chest heaving as if a dagger had reopened the wound he had tried for so long to heal—to forget. Unable to contain the sudden flood of emotions, Luka breaks down sobbing. He desperately scoops handfuls of cold water from the sink and splashes his face to wash away the memories. He holds onto the sink's edges to steady himself, his sobs slowing as he regains control of his mental state.

Lukas looks up into the mirror, furious at himself. A newly branded division leader should never pity those who broke the rules and got what they deserved. He picks up the needle of *Uspet'* sitting on the edge of the sink and shoves it into a vein. His head drops back to stare into the ceiling, his mouth half opened as his eyes roll to the back of his head. He breathes deeply, feeling the fluid inside the needle inject into his veins. A single tear falls from his eye. Luka lets his head fall forward again to face himself in the mirror—eyes glazed over and the memory becoming hazy and distant.

"The headmaster is always right. His command is the only command," he chants under his breath. "The headmaster is *always* right. His command is the only command…" Luka pulls the needle from his arm, setting it back down on the sink to look at himself one last time. He scowls at his reflection as if his old, weakened persona was now trapped inside the mirror as he took on a new, unfamiliar one—one that was much more of a threat.

CHAPTER 13

In the cover of the night, four guards patrol the balconies that wrap around The Trinity, overlooking the wall that encloses the grounds. Suddenly, one by one, the guards fall to the ground, shot by a UCOCA sniper sitting high in the distant trees. The other three dead, one of the guards is struck only in the shoulder, the shot sending him backward over the balcony. Rolling over and groaning with the impact, the guard gets up and tries to make a run for it but is shot a second time in the back and falls to the ground.

Now clear, the UCOCA team moves through the darkness in all black. Having traveled a long way through the forest by foot, they haul only the bare minimum of weapons—two pistols on each hip, a waist belt of lethal gadgets and explosives, and backpacks containing extra firearms. Approaching the school grounds, they get to the wall and pull out their ropes and climbing tools for the ascent.

Inside the school's security room, a few guards play Durak at a table, oblivious to the events outside as their job typically required very little focus. One of the men slams his hand of cards down with delight. "I win again!" he shouts. The others groan and throw their hands down. He scoops his newly won coins toward his already towering stack.

"I quit!" another guard declares. "You're cheating." He stands up from his chair and moves to light a cigar in the corner. The others set up for another game, unaware of the sudden movement on the camera screens across the room—where the only guard put in charge of manning them is fast asleep and snoring loudly in his chair, drool dripping from his mouth. One of the guards at the table looks over and shakes his head. He slaps the guard to his left to get his attention, nodding his head in the direction of the man behind the camera screens.

"Looks like someone's wife has been keeping him up all night again," he says, referring to the man's pregnant spouse at home, whom he had frequently complained about waking him throughout the night. The others chuckle as the sleeping guard snores like a bear. "Check those cameras over there while you're up," he says to the smoking guard.

The man walks over to the screens. He squints, seeing the dark figures climbing down ropes on the wall. The guard laughs, puffing on his cigar. "Looks like some of those little brats must have snuck out earlier for a game in the forest… and now they're sneaking back in."

The others laugh, but one of the guards gets up to see for himself, flipping a coin in his hand as he watches the screens. "Exceptionally crafty, those buggers," he says. "Should we go bust 'em for breaking curfew?" He turns back to exchange looks with the others at the table.

"Nah!" they all sing in chorus. The men chuckle and go back to their game.

Back outside on the balconies, Vasyl motions for his team to get themselves in position as lookouts. They climb further up the castle's brick walls to the towers where the previous guards had been. Once in place, Vasyl swings over to another balcony, joining the twins, Robbie, and Valentina. Together, they scale to the top of the castle until they find a clear window large enough to sneak inside. Unlatching and pushing in the bottom of the window, Valentina pokes her head inside first, ensuring the dark hallway is empty before slipping inside. She unhooks herself from the rope and motions for the others to join her.

"We'll find the old guy and hold him for you while you find your brother," Marcie says to Valentina, shuffling out of her harness. "But hurry. We don't want to be sitting ducks."

Robbie whips out a small device from his backpack and holds it up. "No worries, I grabbed some of these to place around the school."

"No!" Valentina says quickly. "If we get trapped in here, the last thing we want are high explosives going off while we're still inside!"

"I'm not *stupid*, V!" Robbie retorts. "They're not timed. They're controlled by a detonator. I'll keep it safe and sound." He smiles sarcastically, insulted by her assumption that he would pull something so amateur. "And FYI, I don't plan on getting stuck in this shithole." Robbie tosses the device up in the air and catches it swiftly, grimacing at the grimy cement walls and wrinkling his nose as he gets a whiff of the faint musty odor around them.

"Let's get going," Madisyn says, pulling Valentina. She purses her lips and follows Madisyn. The two of them run down the dark hallway, and Marcie, Robbie, and Vasyl head in the opposite direction.

Madisyn and Valentina arrive at the doors of *Vipera* division, where Valentina had spent the bulk of her childhood. She holds up a hand to Madisyn, signaling her to wait outside as she clears the lower level. Valentina disappears inside, leaving Madisyn pressed against the wall, waiting.

Madisyn's head swings back and forth, surveying the dark corridor. It was just as creepy as she imagined it would be—lanterns lining the black cement walls, the fires inside them providing a faint eerie glow. She had seen a lot in her past, but this was otherworldly, like they had taken a trip back into medieval times. The doors crack open behind her again, and Valentina pulls her inside.

"I'll go upstairs to find him," Valentina says. "Stay hidden until I come back down."

"Do you have the serum?" Madisyn asks, referring to the needle she had suggested Valentina bring in case Luka refused to cooperate: a concoction that would knock him out just long enough to kidnap him and carry his unconscious body out of the school. Valentina nods, pulling it out to verify. She had no intention of using such methods to capture Luka, but she also realized he was not the innocent boy she had known all those years ago. And even back then, he had refused to obey her. It would be much harder now to convince him to leave behind everything he knew. Valentina squeezes the serum in her hand, and Madisyn nods reassuringly to her. "Good luck, then."

She watches Valentina ascend the staircase and slip behind a corner. She knew she wasn't supposed to, but Madisyn was dying to explore the quarters. She had never been the obedient girl who stayed put when others directed her to, and her twin was surely off doing something exciting in another part of the school. Madisyn had only volunteered to pair off with Valentina because she felt obligated to help her get her brother back. Not to mention, Marcie and Robbie had both refused to be the ones to kidnap the psychotic Russian boy and opted to stay together. Madisyn couldn't help but feel left out now, standing guard while they were ransacking the power-hungry old man who ran the school and getting to place explosives. She looks around the vast, somewhat homey lounge for something to pique her interest and soon noticed a door near the back.

Upstairs, Valentina skulks down the hallway of the boys' sleep quarters. A door creaks open behind her, catching her attention. She spins around to see a little boy, no older than five, standing in the doorway. He stares at her blankly, sucking his thumb. Valentina straightens and clears her throat, holding her chin higher.

"Where is Luka Dementiev?" she demands, willing authority into her voice. If she didn't show intimidation, maybe he would think she was an older student from a different division. The boy simply raises his free hand, pointing to the door at the very end of the hall. Valentina's gaze follows. She swallows hard, knowing the significance of the last room.

She turns back to the boy. "Go to bed, little one, and I will not report you for being awake." The little boy backs into his room and closes the door. Valentina turns to the end of the hall, staring at the door. "They made him a division leader…" she breathes. She takes a deep breath and continues slowly toward it. Frozen for a moment, her nose only inches from the door, she reaches for the knob and turns it to peek inside.

Not seeing anyone in bed, Valentina walks fully inside the room, surveying the space that is vastly bigger than the other bedrooms. A sudden chill comes over her, causing her to shiver. She had never been inside one of the division leaders' rooms before. During her time at The Trinity, Valentina wanted no part of anything related to the school's hierarchy. The division leaders worked directly under the commandant, who she knew had always been the most wicked individual in the school. The leaders under him—as the selected commandant had *always* been male—were sure to be no different. Her mind begins to race with all the disturbing things Luka must have done to get appointed as a leader. Had he been bullied into such a role or could her younger brother always have been inherently bad to begin with? Perhaps it was her doing—her escape that catapulted him into such behavior. Was he now as awful and cruel as some of the boys she had gone to school with? Did he have it in him to beat someone senseless—to even *kill* an innocent soul? Valentina covers her mouth with a hand, squeezing her eyes shut as she muffles her own crying. Could this really have all been her fault?

Valentina's head snaps to the left, breaking her train of thought when she hears a noise come from the bathroom. She wipes her face quickly and slinks over to the bathroom door, which is cracked wide enough for her to see through. Valentina peeks through the crack, and her reddened eyes widen at the sight of her brother standing in the middle of the floor wearing only pajama pants. Luka has his head down with his eyes closed. She spots the needle in the grip of his hand as he chants softly to himself. Valentina covers her mouth, remaining silent as she watches her brother's head roll back, absorbing the drugs.

In another part of the school, Robbie, Marcie, and Vasyl crouch behind a corner as they hear footsteps of students patrolling the hallway. Vasyl looks down at his watch to pull up a hologram of the school's blueprints. "Keep going that way," he whispers, nodding straight ahead. Behind the others, Robbie examines the designs engraved in the wall, running his hand over the exaggerated teeth of a snarling boar. He remembered the three divisions Valentina had told them about, which separated the students of The Trinity and assumed they must be within *Borov* territory. He grimaces at the creature as if snarling back with disgust.

Peeking around the corner, Marcie sees the two patrolling students turned away from them for a brief moment. She motions for the three of them to pick up again. They run across the hallway into another winding corridor, staying low to the ground. Robbie lingers behind to place an explosive on the wall before following.

Back in the *Vipera* division, inside a small library, Madisyn walks through its claustrophobic aisles, stopping to pull a book from a shelf. She opens it, reading through the pages written in Russian, not finding anything particularly interesting. She hated books, especially after so many years of being forced to read them cover to cover. Marcie was the brainy type, relishing in the hours of reading Valentina had ordered them to complete as children. Madisyn much preferred living her own stories, and maybe one day, when she was old and frail, she would have someone write about her and share her legacy of UCOCA with the world. Now *that* was a book she would actually read.

At the end of the aisle, a ghostlike shadow moves past, causing Madisyn to snap her head up in its direction. She shuts the book softly, setting it down before drawing her gun. Her heart flutters with excitement. This was exactly the kind of thrill she was seeking—meeting her combative match in a slightly less competent Russian spy. She creeps toward the end of the aisle, gun at the ready. Pausing first at the end, she steps quickly out into the open space but sees no one. She moves down the next aisle before halting to lower her gun. m very still, Madisyn cocks her head to listen, hoping the figure hadn't been a figment of her imagination.

As if responding to her doubt, a book comes flying off the shelf in front of her, hitting Madisyn straight in the face and jerking her head back. She groans aloud, instinctively bending over to clutch her now bleeding nose. Reminding herself to be vigilant, she whips back up but finds a sword pressed to her neck and a Russian girl standing in front of her. Madisyn laughs through her pinched nose, the hemorrhaging blood running down her face, making her look like a madwoman. Despite the sword to her neck and knowing she had the upper hand, she brings her pistol back up to her enemy—causing the girl to take just a slight step back with hesitance. Before Madisyn can pull the trigger, another book flies out from the shelf and knocks the gun to the floor.

Just as a third book comes flying out toward her head, Madisyn blocks it with her arm, leaping into the air to kick the girl's sword from her grasp to even the playing field. Madisyn lunges at her, but the girl is quick to react and grabs Madisyn by the shoulders with an unexpected strength, swinging her around and releasing her grasp so that Madisyn stumbles backward out of the aisle grunting as she slams into the wall near the library door. As Madisyn tries to get to her feet, a boy appears in front of her, holding her fallen gun and pointing it at her head. Madisyn laughs, tilting her head cutely.

"You don't know how to use that," she teases in Russian. Moving her hand to reach for a gadget in her belt, the boy cocks the gun with ease. Madisyn freezes, the smile disappeared from her face, realizing she had underestimated the modern training methods of the seemingly medieval school.

The girl picks up her sword, her nostrils flaring at Madisyn. She moves it back into the crook of Madisyn's neck. "Stand up," she orders, keeping the blade steady against Madisyn's windpipe as she slides up the wall. The girl moves in closer, shoving Madisyn out the door and back into the lounge.

The boy mutters something to the girl, who nods and hands him the sword before swiftly running from the room. Madisyn watches over the boy's shoulder as the girl pushes the double doors open. She turns back to the boy in front of her. Thinking quickly, Madisyn blurts out: "Are you going to tell the headmaster?"

The boy raises his chin, his eyes narrowing. "I know you're not a student here."

Madisyn scoffs. "Oh yeah?"

"Shut up!" He takes a defiant step forward. "You don't go here because I would know if you did. Do you think I'm stupid, foreigner?" Madisyn opens her mouth to respond but is cut off quickly. "I *said* shut up…" The boy whips the sword up to her neck. "Only high leadership of each division are allowed to carry weapons. And this gun of yours definitely does not belong to us. So, tell me, who are you, and why did you break into our home?"

Madisyn glares at him, trying to think up a quick reaction. Her eyes dart to the door to distract him, her gaze lingering there for a moment. "Called for backup, hm? You must be so scared."

Falling for her bluff, the boy calls over his shoulder, "Go wake up Luka!" When no one responds, he looks over his shoulder. Seeing an opening, Madisyn leaps into the air and kicks the sword from his grasp. She tumbles forward on the ground and snatches the gun from his other hand.

The boy pounces on her. He wraps both of his hands around her arms, moving the aim of her weapon above their heads before she can shoot. The two of them intertwined roll across the floor, Madisyn's earpiece falling out of place. She lets the gun drop from her grip to release his hands before rolling to her knees. On the ground in front of her, the boy kicks her in the face. He thrusts his body into the air to land on his feet. Madisyn struggles to pull herself up after the blow—blood from her nose running down her face more profusely from his kick. She lunges at him, and they flip over the couch together, nosily smashing into the glass table.

⚔

Upstairs, Valentina jerks herself just from out of her brother's view as he whips around at the earsplitting shatter coming from downstairs. Luka pulls the needle from his arm and struts from the bathroom. He snatches the dagger from his desk, not seeing Valentina crouched in the dark corner as he leaves his room.

Valentina begins to pant, sensing that something had to have gone wrong with Madisyn. She presses the button on her earpiece. "Madisyn, are you there? What's happening down there?" Not hearing a reply, Valentina swallows another lump forming in her throat. "Madisyn, I repeat, come in. What's going on?" She grabs a handful of her hair, wanting to scream out in frustration but knowing it would not be wise. She lets her head fall back against the wall, her face scrunched in pain.

⚔

Back downstairs, Madisyn scrambles across the floor to get to her earpiece as the bloodied Russian boy struggles to get up from the pile of broken glass. "We've been compromised!" she shouts into the device, panting.

Vipera division students flood down the stairs from their bedrooms, and the boy on the floor points to Madisyn. "Intruder! Grab her!"

On the other side of the school, Marcie, Robbie, and Vasyl hear Madisyn's distress call. Crouched behind a doorway, they break into a run down the dark hallway in the opposite direction toward Madisyn.

Valentina shouts through her earpiece at them. "Do *not* go after her! Hold your positions!"

"They're going to *kill* her, V!" Marcie protests, running ahead of the boys blindly and past the hallway with the two students on patrol. The students whip around and shout as they spot the intruders, immediately dashing in their direction, but as Robbie passes last, he shoots them both, striking each of the boys in the chest.

Still crouched in the corner of Luka's room, Valentina squeezes her eyes shut. "Shit…" she mutters to herself. This was exactly the scenario they had not planned for, assuming their plan had been rock-solid before leaving Ukraine. This was also the very outcome that scared her the most, especially because this time, she was not alone or just with her brother. She was now responsible for the lives of three teenagers she had spent most of her life raising. Valentina had never been a mother before, but this was the first time she truly felt the kind of worry only a mother can experience for her children's safety.

Upstairs, Valentina stares blankly ahead and presses her earpiece again, this time speaking to the Ukrainian agents left outside. "All teams, retreat and wait for further instructions." She swallows hard, stammering as the reality of the situation sinks in. "This may take days, maybe weeks. Do not try to contact us again on this frequency."

Getting to the double doors of the lounge, Marcie tries to push through but finds them locked. The three of them all push and kick at the doors, unaware of the flock of Russian students slowly surrounding them in the darkness of the hallway.

"Fuck," Robbie breathes, alerting Marcie and Vasyl of the situation. The three of them rest their backs against the doors as their hands instinctively reach for their utility belts.

Behind Marcie, Robbie, and Vasyl, the doors swing open. As they turn around, the students behind them shove them all inside the room. Luka, downstairs now, grabs Madisyn and pulls her into the center to stand with the rest of the intruders. Marcie gasps at Madisyn's bloody face.

Grisha and Leo Gorsky—one of the *Volk* division leaders—come pushing through the crowd. With everyone's faces turned to the older boys, Robbie slips the detonator for the emplaced explosives into his pants, wedging it carefully behind his belt buckle. The commandant and his best friend approach the encircled captives.

"What's going on here?" Grisha says to Luka.

"Like hell if I know," he retorts. Luka motions to some students nearby. "Go check the rest of the rooms." The students scatter, some going upstairs and several others checking the library.

The same thumb-sucking five-year-old boy who had run into Valentina upstairs takes a step forward in the crowd, still wearing his blue cotton nightgown. He tugs on Luka's shirt and looks up at him, taking his thumb out of his mouth.

"Aren't we going to execute them, Luka?" the boy asks, his voice ringing with innocence. A raggedy stuffed rabbit toy dangles by its ripped ear from his tiny palm. The twins, Robbie, and Vasyl exchange horrified glances and also look to Luka for his answer. So, *this* was Valentina's younger brother whom they had come to "rescue."

Luka ignores the boy. He looks to Grisha for guidance, who is staring down the intruders with wide eyes as if he were completely stunned by the spectacle. They never had unwanted visitors in this manner before. Grisha turns to some of the older students next to him. "Get them out of here," he orders. "Wake the headmaster. He must know outsiders have breached the school. And warn the other divisions. Have them check the rest of the perimeters."

Most of the crowd floods out of the room. Leo, followed by a group of older students, closes in on the intruders, yanking them from the room as well. The little boy stands next to Luka, sucking his thumb again as he watches them go. He looks up at Luka, pulling his thumb out just long enough to say, "There's another intruder looking for you. She was in our hallway upstairs." Luka looks down at the little boy, his brows furrowing.

Upstairs, Valentina gets to her feet and takes a deep sigh. She hated that she would have to escape this ungodly place, yet again. But she didn't have many options. Prepared to give herself up, she moves to the bedroom door, turning the knob to reveal a crowd of Russian students blocking the doorway, ready to apprehend her.

Here we go again, she thinks, before succumbing to the mob.

Below the school, in the prison, the group of Russians pushes their five intruders through the dark, empty room until they reach the last two cells. They grab the UCOCA agents' weapons and communication devices and pat them down. Robbie eyes the girl patting him down, holding his breath as she quickly brushes over his belt. They unlock the two cells to shove the spies inside.

"No, no. Not those two," Leo protests, gesturing to the twins. "Separate them." They lock Valentina, Marcie, and Vasyl in one cell and Robbie and Madisyn in the cell across from them, to Robbie's dismay. He grimaces over at Madisyn, whom he knew in his soul was the reason they were caught.

One of the Russian males crosses his arms, looking Robbie and Madisyn straight on. "I don't know why you entered our home," he begins, turning to face the other prisoners as well, "but you can trust me when I say you'll be in here for a very long time."

The only female in their group, an eighteen-year-old named Galyna Ivashova, leans against one of the cells, staring down the prisoners with a smirk. "Don't worry. We won't kill you right away. Instead, we will… *utilize* you—like lab rats. Most of us have never seen outsiders before. They'll be thrilled to receive some new toys." She turns her head to look into the other cell as well, holding her sly smile before pushing off the wall to head toward the stairs. Most of the others follow, but Leo lingers, staring into Valentina's cell with a strange smile as if trying to piece together a puzzle. The others notice his absence and stop on the first step.

"*You*," Leo breathes, his puzzled smile growing. "You have a familiar face, you do. How is that possible?" Leo laughs to himself, squinting his eyes and cocking his head. Valentina keeps her head down, away from his gaze.

"Quit your flirting," Galyna calls from the end of the prison. "That pathetic little thing will hardly be human after we're through with her." The others laugh, but Leo keeps his eyes on Valentina. He narrows them further before turning on his heel. Together, the Russians all leave the prison.

Valentina sinks to the floor, burying her face. Robbie sighs, holding on to the bars of the cell with both hands as he looks across to the others. "Valentina... now would be a great time to have that inside friend of yours magically appear to rescue us."

Vasyl shakes his head. "We'll be out of here in no time. My team will think of something back at headquarters. We've trained them all exceptionally well."

Robbie laughs in disbelief. "Have you?" he says to Vasyl. "You barely show up as it is, Mr. Franko. How would you even *know* if your team was trained well enough to handle something like this? You've been a piss poor leader to begin with, and everyone knows it!"

"Excuse me?" Vasyl snarls. "I'm more of a leader than *you* are, Ancens. Or maybe you just can't accept the fact that I'm more of a man than you." He glances at Marcie.

Madisyn clears her throat to dispel the tension, well aware of the feelings both Vasyl and Robbie felt for her sister. She had always sensed a simmering tension between the two and knew it had everything to do with the very brief moment Vasyl and Marcie had years ago upon first meeting. They had snuck away from their father's business meeting. Madisyn had come too, but there was a softness about Marcie, especially that seemed to attract a strong longing for her in Vasyl. He had pulled her into a nearby coat closet, insisting he wanted to show her something, and then he grabbed her face with both hands and kissed her more deeply than he had ever kissed any other girl. What he hadn't known, though, was that Madisyn had seen what she knew to be Marcie's first kiss and years later used the information to tell Robbie out of spite. It had been their justification for their secret affair, though, to Robbie, it still hit hard in his core to know another guy was after the girl of his dreams.

"Let's put this energy toward getting out of here, shall we?" Madisyn says weakly, lacking energy from the weight of the situation. Marcie shoots her a small look of gratitude, but Madisyn pulls her glance away quickly, knowing she didn't really deserve it.

Robbie pulls out the detonator from under his belt with a defiant look toward Vasyl. "How about I just blow us out of here, then? That's what a *man* would do, right?"

Marcie scoffs. "Don't you dare, Robbie! I saw you putting all those explosives out, you know. You shouldn't have done more than three! Are you trying to kill us?" Robbie rolls his eyes.

"She's right," Vasyl adds flatly, his narrowed eyes on Robbie. "We need a way out of here before that thing can do us any good. You'd think a 'man' like you would know that."

Robbie sucks on the inside of his cheek, stuffing the detonator into his pocket. Vasyl had never been so much of a threat for him, being all the way in Ukraine, but somehow it really bothered him now, seeing the two of them locked away in a cell together when he should have been with Marcie. Instead, Robbie found himself locked inside a small, unbearable space with the one person he often disliked the most, the same person he had betrayed Marcie with. It was his karma, and he would just have to accept it.

"I'm the reason we're in here, anyway..." Madisyn says quietly, drawing everyone's eyes. She stares at the ground, unable to meet their gazes. "I just… thought I could handle them. But then one after the other, they all started coming out of bloody nowhere." She shakes her head. "I got us into this mess. I'll find us a way out." In an action that seemed contrary to her promising words, Madisyn slinks over to the far dark corner of her cell and sits on the ground, wrapping her arms around her knees and burying her face hopelessly.

Robbie turns back to face Marcie and Vasyl, the only two who weren't sulking in the corners of their cells. He sucks in one side of his cheek again, unamused by the lack of confidence in Madisyn's last words. "Great," he says, his tone ringing of sarcasm.

CHAPTER 14

———

The following day, Luka sits among his peers before the start of class. A talkative boy named Stepan Petrov had been stirring the pot all morning in their other lectures and showed no sign of letting up now. "Place your bets," he says to the group huddled around him. "How long until the new prisoners are dead?"

"A week, tops," Ivanna answers confidently, sitting atop Luka's desk.

Pyotr Swierczynski sits on top of another desk across from them, flipping a coin in the air and catching it repeatedly. "No," he pronounces. "The headmaster is much more deliberate than that. A week isn't long enough."

"I agree," chimes in Katia Dashkova, below Pyotr in the desk's chair. She leans in as if revealing newfound gossip. "He'll want to know who's behind this and why. Nothing like this has ever happened before—people breaking *into* the building."

Lukas twinged at the possible reference to his sister's escape. Even after so many years of constant torment, he could still be wounded by such insignificant insults, and that enraged him. He balls his fists, an action that does not go unnoticed by the others.

"What's your deal?" Katia scoffs.

"Don't mind him," Ivanna says. "He's just pissy because those prisoners have been exposed to the outside world, unlike any of us. It's almost as if *we're* the prisoners actually…"

"Don't act like you know what I'm thinking, Ivanna," Luka adds quickly, giving her an icy glare. She was right, but he wasn't going to acknowledge that. She was already potentially tarnishing his reputation by sitting on *his* desk. He was a division leader! He couldn't be caught fraternizing—especially not with girls who were under his authority.

Luka slides out from his desk and walks to the front of the room, the others watching him. He says something to the teacher, who only nods, and Luka leaves the classroom. Ivanna's gaze falls the fastest.

"Someone's a bit strung out," Katia says.

"The process has started. He's beginning 'The Change'…" Stepan teases, his eyes flaring as if to entice the others further.

Ivanna whips around to him, furrowing her brows. "What are you talking about?"

"The Change?" Stepan repeats as if it were common knowledge. "You know how all the division leaders use, right? The headmaster gives them some kind of drug to brainwash them. Something they reserve for a select, *elite* few. Turns them into brainless puppets if you ask me." He and Katia laugh. "Trust me, The Change is real. I know because I saw it happen to one of my old roommates, Filipp. He's a *Borov* division leader now. I don't know how to explain it. He just became a completely different person…"

"You're wrong," Ivanna protests. "Luka doesn't use." Her entire body becomes rigid, braced for a fight. Stepan laughs at this and rolls his eyes at her naiveté.

"What do you think those prisoners were up to anyway?" Pyotr's older brother, Viktor Swierczynski, chimes in. He and his brother exchange careful glances, Pyotr still flipping his coin over and over in a metronomic tempo. He observes the others around him as if calculating their intentions.

Katia shakes her head. "Who knows…"

Pyotr conceals the sly smile etched across his lips toward his brother. His face becomes still and serious again as he tosses the coin higher up in the air this time, looking up at it from the edge of Katia's desk. "Guess it's only a matter of time before we all find out," he says. The coin lands on the back of his hand, and Pyotr slaps down his other palm to stop it, his gaze left on Ivanna, who shrinks back uncomfortably.

From the front of the class, Grisha clears his throat, eyeing the rowdy students who hurry back to their seats in his presence. As Ivanna comes back to her place in the front, Rurik leans over and grabs her by the arm. "Why do you always defend Luka?" he whispers accusingly.

Ivanna narrows her eyes, shoving his hand away. "What do you mean? He's our friend."

Rurik scoffs. "You still think he's your friend? He's one of *them* now," he says to her darkly. She shakes her head.

"We're all on the same team, Rurik."

"Don't be so naive," he says, raising his brows at her.

The teacher's eyes on them now, Ivanna turns back to the front, Rurik's glare lingering on her. A seat over, Aleksander Swierczynski—the youngest of the brothers—watches Rurik and Ivanna. He looks over his shoulder at Pyotr and Viktor, squinting his eyes and nodding once as if to signal something only known to them. Aleks spins back around as Grisha motions for the entire class to stand together, each student with their hands at their sides as they recite their midday pledge—another vow of allegiance to the headmaster and the school—before starting their lesson.

Inside a men's lavatory, Luka leans over one of the toilets and retches—now a common reaction to his persistent drug use. It was making him sick and often blurred his mind so much that he became prone to headaches. From the book Grisha had given him, Luka knew the daily injection of *Uspet'* was mandatory for division leaders, though, and he did not want to experience the consequences of disobeying.

Pulling himself together, Luka moves out of the stall to wash out his mouth in the sink. As he turns to leave, he slightly jumps at Grisha's presence, standing a few sinks down, his hands intertwined behind his back. "Grisha..." Luka greets him.

"Have you memorized the book?" the older boy asks. The flushing of a toilet echoes through the lavatory as a male student comes out of a stall. Both Grisha and Luka turn to face him, and as the boy sees the commandant, he quickly averts his gaze and makes haste for the exit.

Luka swallows as Grisha turns back to him, waiting for an answer. He purses his lips, reminding himself he was now a division leader and didn't have to fear the commandant as others in the school did. He clears his throat aloud. "Mostly," he lies, not wanting to admit he had, in fact, gotten through all its contents and was left disappointed more than enlightened.

Grisha squints. "Not good enough." Luka furrows his brows, not knowing what to say. "You're a division leader now. You have more responsibility, and you must start acting accordingly. You're held to a higher standard than the others." Grisha takes a step forward, and Luka lifts his chin slightly higher. "And you are not permitted to skip class when you feel like it," Grisha raises his voice, his eyes narrowing further. "If anything, you will stay in classes longer to thoroughly absorb the information better than your peers. Becoming a division leader is not a pass to slack off."

Luka's gaze falls to the floor. He still felt slightly queasy from the aftereffects of the *Uspet'*, but he knew if he wanted the commandant's respect, he would have to start acting the way Grisha expected his division leaders to act. Maybe he was being targeted because Grisha could smell his intimidation. Or perhaps he could sense the doubt lingering in the back of Luka's mind. Doubting the headmaster's wisdom was as good as treason at The Trinity, and it was certainly not a concept that other leaders displayed.

"Look at me when I am speaking to you," Grisha hisses. Luka's eyes shoot back up to the older boy just feet in front of him. "You will finish memorizing the book tonight before your forty-eight hours are up. It is the only way you will understand the art of being a division leader, thus preparing yourself to carry out the headmaster's plan the way he intends us to. And because of your recent behavior of skipping class, I want a report as well, two-thousand words, on what it means to be a leader and your action plan for how you will live up to these standards."

Luka narrows his eyes. He had read up on the headmaster's mission for them—a rather short blurb at the beginning of the book followed by fifty pages outlining different types of punishments they were allowed to use at their own discretion within their divisions. For the first time in his life, Luka had been given insight into what the headmaster wanted and expected of them, and because of this, it was the first time he also felt utterly foolish and ignorant. Their entire existence and all the preparation that went into it, it all seemed so trivial for a purpose that was rather vague and indefinite. The book had not outlined any exact person or target they were being taught to go after, and he didn't quite understand the importance of taking over other governments around the world. Even with his nonexistent exposure to the world outside their school, he knew it would be fairly impossible for them to complete their "mission" any time soon. Of course, he wouldn't dare speak out against the headmaster, especially not in front of the commandant, but was he really the only person who thought they were wasting their time?

Mustering his will to speak, Luka balls his fists at his side. "I don't have to listen to you anymore. I'm a division leader now, and I don't take orders—I give them."

Grisha's eyes widen, taken aback by Luka's reply. He takes a step forward, his glance narrowing again and his nostrils flaring. "Be careful how you talk to me," Grisha snarls. "I am still the commandant! No division leader talks to me that way, not ever. I hate to go against the headmaster's judgment, but I think he has mistaken choosing to promote you, and I shall let him know of it if you can't change your attitude." Luka holds his gaze. "Now, get to class before I have you reprimanded, Luka Dementiev."

Luka sucks on the inside of his cheek, attempting to suppress the growing fire within him. Without another word, he makes his way over to the doorway, his eyes darting to the side as he passes Grisha. He didn't know what the direct consequences might be for talking back to the commandant, but he had a feeling he had not heard the last of it.

After dinner, Pyotr walks through the dim halls and down a flight of stairs, stopping as he comes to a jagged wall bulging out subtly from the rest of the flat surface. Looking over his shoulder, he strokes the cool cement wall until he finds a weak spot that pushes in, releasing a secret door. He steps inside, and it closes behind him. In the darkness, he runs down a long, winding passage and steps out into the school's kitchen.

An old cook named Yelena and a young girl cut vegetables on the wooden counter. "Hello, Pyotr," the woman says. "What brings you?" The girl looks up shyly with a smile.

"Just up to no good, as usual," he jokes, kissing the old lady's hand and winking at the girl. Blushing, the girl snaps her head back down to the carrots and potatoes in front of her.

"Go on," Yelena says. "Your brother is waiting."

Pyotr nods thankfully and goes to the other side of the kitchen, moving the tall bag of flour to pull up a hidden trap door beneath it. He slides inside, closing the door behind him. Going down a tight staircase first, he follows the dark corridor underground until it leads to an opening above the prison. Pyotr drops to the floor from the ceiling's hidden door.

He walks over to his younger brother Aleks, who sits at the end of the prison on the floor, staring at the prisoners. "These people are so weird," Marcie whispers to Vasyl, knowing the boy can hear her. Aleks turns around at his brother's footsteps and stands.

"Did you bring it?" Pyotr asks him. Digging into his pockets, Aleks takes out some bread pieces for the prisoners. He gives his brother some, and they approach the cells together.

Aleks extends bread to Robbie first, who only scoffs with disgust, still standing toward the front of the cell, unafraid.

Valentina stands at the back of her cell. "We don't want that from you," she says firmly, speaking for the first time since they had been imprisoned.

Pyotr smirks at his brother. "No? You'll starve down here otherwise."

"Since when does the headmaster allow prisoners to have food?" Valentina asks.

The brothers exchanged looks again, Pyotr's smile growing. "So, then…"

"You must be the visitor we were expecting," Aleks finishes. The others all look to Valentina.

"What do you know?" she asks in a low, cautious tone.

"Several months ago, we received an encrypted transmission from an anonymous source inquiring about the sorry likes of Luka Dementiev," Pyotr informs her, Valentina's lips quivering. They were the ones she had been communicating with, after all. "I'm Pyotr," he says. "And this is my brother Aleks."

"I'm Valentina—Luka's sister," she adds quickly.

Pyotr and Aleks's eyes grow. "You're a legend," Pyotr says. "Your escape eleven years ago is what inspired our entire cause." Valentina shakes her head, confused.

"We've been keeping eyes on the radio channels for outside messages," Aleks says. "You are lucky our brother Viktor found it and not one of the headmaster's 'children.'" Madisyn stands up and moves to the front of her cell to hear better, intrigued now.

"Children?" Marcie asks, standing near Vasyl in the front of their cell too.

"The students loyal to the headmaster," Pyotr explains.

Robbie snorts at this. "You mean they're not *all* that way?"

Aleks snaps his head over. "Would we be down helping you if we were?" Robbie looks the boy up and down, realizing that he makes a good point.

"Over the years," Pyotr continues, "the school has changed. There's a large community of students who are against the headmaster, in secret. We know most of our fates end in certain death as sacrifices for our so-called father, which is bullshit. They claim they're teaching us, but they've kept us prisoners inside these walls. Your brother, though…" He turns to Valentina. "He's worked hard to shake your reputation from his name. He's struggling, but… he's not the boy you once knew. I'm afraid he might be a lost cause."

Valentina shakes her head quickly. "No. I can get him to come around."

"I don't think even *you* believe that statement, let alone the rest of us," Aleks says. "What did you think you were going to do? Waltz in here and rescue him?" The others are silent, looking around at one another with guilt from having thought exactly that.

"Look," Pyotr says, seeing their diminishing hope. "We don't care that much for your brother—especially now that he's been made a division leader. But it's not news to us that something needs to change at this school, and fast. If you want to 'save' Luka, we may have a way—"

"One that benefits *us*, as well," Aleks adds.

Valentina narrows her eyes. "What is it you want?"

The brothers exchanged glances, Pyotr looking back to Valentina to give her their answer. "Total destruction."

Walking into the school's main library, Pyotr sees his brother Viktor standing on a ladder, organizing books on a shelf. He hesitates as if reluctant to approach him straight on. While the Swierczynski brothers were always careful to keep their treasonous planning under the radar, others had not been so discreet. There had been two incidents already of rogue students who had been careless and anxious to make their opposition of the headmaster known. Both had been slain in their sleep by their peers, after which students were told to immediately report any displays of insubordination so that it could be handled "properly." To play it safe, the Swierczynski brothers insisted they keep their plotting to minimum face-to-face contact, as there were watchful eyes and keen ears everywhere.

Pyotr walks to the other side of the aisle and pulls a book off the shelf. He pretends to flip through its pages, keeping his head down. Viktor steps down a few rungs on the ladder from the other side until he sees his brother's head. "It's her," Pyotr tells his brother through the opening. "The Dementieva sister… can we use her identity as part of the plan?"

Viktor glances over to a group of students studying quietly at a nearby table. Seeing their faces all buried low in their books, Viktor faces the shelf again. "It's dangerous," he says, careful not to move his lips too much. "But we'll need to lure in an older student who would recognize her—someone reactive. Leave it to me."

Pyotr snaps the book shut, looking over his shoulder as he places it back on the shelf. He leaves the aisle and heads toward the other side of the library. Viktor watches his brother go, waiting a few moments before coming down the ladder. He looks over to the nearby table again, where a student glares at him. Viktor fully turns to face the student, holding a much more intimidating scowl on the younger boy, who looks away quickly, returning to his studies.

In the school's martial arts gymnasium, a circle of rowdy students cheers on two girls in the center mat, dueling in a vicious knife fight. The instructor watches grimly with crossed arms, in no rush to call their round until one of them just barely evades death.

In the corner of the room, a bruised Ivanna practices her sword-fighting skills with a dead boar hanging from the ceiling. Rurik approaches, but she continues slashing the animal, spilling its guts into a grated drain on the floor.

"You lost again?" Rurik asks, a hint of sympathy in his voice.

Ivanna roundhouse kicks and jabs her sword into the boar. She hated gym class and was always put in remedial fighting sessions for losing all her rounds. She was the worst fighter in their class and couldn't help but think that she wasn't good enough—for both the school and Luka. "What do you want?"

"I'm sorry, Ivanna," he presses, hoping she would at least look at him.

Ivanna rolls her eyes and sighs heavily. She finally turns around. "What's gotten into you?"

Rurik pulls her to the side, away from the carcass. "Ivanna... I came here to warn you. I'm worried. Luka is no longer acting like himself. Don't you see that? I heard him talking with Grisha. He's not even supposed to associate with us anymore."

Ivanna looks away from him. "You can't believe that," she says, though she had a feeling that maybe Rurik was on to something.

"It's true. I think he really is using those drugs Stepan was talking about. You haven't noticed how much he's distanced himself from us already? He and the other leaders want nothing to do with us."

Ivanna snaps her head up at this. "You heard the headmaster. We're a *family*! We take care of each other."

Rurik shakes his head. "It's all politics, Ivanna. The academy's changed. Or maybe it hasn't. Maybe it's always been like this, and we were just too young to notice. Either way, we're no more than disposable pawns to the higher-ups. *Especially* the girls." He looks over his shoulder to make sure the students across the room are still engaged with the ongoing bloodbath before leaning in closer to whisper to her. "You're not going to be safe here, Ivanna!"

Ivanna shoves him back hard. "Would you listen to yourself? You sound absolutely insane!" Unable to look at him, she goes back to beating the boar with her bare hands.

"The headmaster wants us to think all of us are important, but really—he'd sacrifice any of us. Luka knows he's safe with his new rank, and he's made of point of shoving it in our faces. Yakov sees it too…" Ivanna hesitates, her focus momentarily breaking away from the boar. "Don't you see? Luka doesn't care about any of us anymore, Ivanna. He doesn't care about *you*."

She fully snaps over to him, this time lowering her voice. "Shut up, Rurik. Or you'll pay."

"Threaten me all you want," he says, taking a step closer to her. "He's going to break your heart. And I'm just trying to protect you from following him down the wrong path. He's made his choice, but it's not too late for you! The Trinity isn't safe anymore." He looks over his shoulder again before looking back to her, their noses almost touching. "I've been talking with some of the others. There are two sides now, and I'm on the side that's going to keep me alive." Ivanna glares at him, flustered. "Ivanna, do you even *know* which side you're on?"

Ivanna shoves him backward. The Trinity was all she knew. What would she do if the very place she had spent practically her entire life was suddenly a place she wouldn't be safe in? What if everything was suddenly different and her peers were actually waging war against each other instead of against the supposed enemy outside the school's walls? Ivanna wasn't ready to face the possibility of something like that.

Instead of inquiring further like she wanted to, she grabs her sword from the boar and storms past Rurik. Watching her leave, Rurik suddenly remembers what Pyotr had once told him in secret: You can't save everyone, and you just might end up dead if you try.

Later that night, in a lounge within *Volk* division, Grisha sits on a couch with a few of his companions. Leo—being one of Grisha's closest friends and someone who had a similar reputation as a person not to be reckoned with—smokes on a cigar next to him. While Leo may have seemed soft around the edges—with his slick chestnut hair, a cool, relaxed attitude upon the first impression, and a devious smile—Leo was the filthiest kind of predator. Being praised for this macho "attribute" by his teachers and older male students in the school had landed him his current role as assistant to Master Ogiyevich. He was rumored to be The Trinity's most vile instructor. None of the younger students at the school knew exactly what class Master Ogiyevich taught, as it was rumored that his instruction was so heinous, students 'of age' were sworn to secrecy; this only added to Leo's aloofness and made him someone certainly meant to be feared, his friendship with Grisha forming quite naturally from that alone.

Adjacent to Grisha and Leo are their buddies Gavriil Baranov and Matvei Vasiliev, both pudgy with short buzz cuts and permanent snarls on their faces that resembled bulldogs. While the three divisions of The Trinity were meant to be equal in standing, *Volk* had always been held to the highest level of excellence. The last two commandants before Grisha had also come from his division, and it seemed that the most power hungry and competitive students were always wolves. They won the most rounds in their fights, they held the best grades in all their classes, and they even kept actual wolves they had captured from the forest and tamed for their own personal use in an outside shed right on school grounds. One of Grisha's favorite things about *Volk*, though, was that they possessed the fewest females—a factor he personally saw to upon his appointment to commandant, recruiting notable male candidates from other divisions to replace many of the girls in *Volk*. They were a brotherhood unlike any other, only fit for the toughest individuals mentally and physically, though Grisha still expected what was left of his division's females to meet their high standards if they wanted to remain a wolf.

Hiding behind a doorway, Viktor observes the group for a moment. Viktor had been at the school since he was ten—long enough to know how things worked in the hierarchy. He had originally been in *Borov* division with his two younger brothers, but five years ago, when they joined a small secret force with hopes of destroying the school and getting out of there for good, Viktor made it his life's work to get in with those who sat at the top of the school's food chain in *Volk* division. To do so, he did everything he could to befriend the commandant and gain his trust. Already physically larger than many his age, it took Viktor three years, excelling in his fighting and all his classes, to catch their attention. Matvei had originally recruited him for *Volk* at age seventeen, and Viktor had used the time since then to learn the ins and outs of the school's most loyal students. He had only been waiting to find the perfect moment for their group of rebel fighters to unleash their cause—and what better distraction was there than having a returned mutineer to The Trinity?

Narrowing his eyes, Viktor walks out from behind the doorway to join the guys on the couch. Gavriil offers him a cigar, and he takes it, pouring himself some of the Pertsovka vodka on the table. He always seemed to need alcohol to deal with the likes of Grisha, and he had become somewhat of an alcoholic to keep from exploding and blowing his cover whenever the boys did something heinous. And they were *always* doing something heinous.

"We were just saying how eager Luka will be to kill the new prisoners," Gavriil informs him. Viktor nods, quickly forcing a scoff and looking to Grisha for a reaction.

"Over my dead body," the commandant spits. "That little shit has deceived the headmaster somehow. But I don't trust him."

Matvei clears his throat, shifting in his seat. "Well... it *would* be a good way for him to prove his loyalty... right?"

The guys all look over to Grisha, waiting for a retort, but his face only sours at the suggestion. Even as his closest friends, they were always on edge with Grisha, never knowing if he might explode or banish them from the *Volk* division for speaking out against him. He had once stabbed another student when he was only fourteen for speaking lies against the headmaster, spreading rumors to others that he was a wretched old man with ill intentions. This act immediately propelled Grisha's advancement into the school's hierarchy, becoming the youngest division leader of *Vipera* when he was only fifteen and being quickly recruited over to *Volk* two years later. He had been promoted to commandant within a year.

"I don't think Luka has got it in him, anyway," Leo finally says, likely just saying what Grisha would want to hear. "He tries to be tougher than he actually is. You should have seen him in the class. I helped Ogiyevich with... squirming in his seat like a little pussy. Couldn't even keep his eyes up." The guys laugh, but Viktor sips on his drink to mask his distaste. He remembered Ogiyevich's class well, along with the excruciating blood oath he and his classmates had taken as a promise to keep what they had seen to themselves. It had been a day that fully solidified Viktor's opposition for both The Trinity and the headmaster and left a permanent repugnance in his stomach.

The door to the lounge opens as Galyna joins them, the boys immediately losing their smiles. She walks over to them and sits on the edge of the couch, seeming ignorant to their hostility or at least choosing to ignore it. She was eighteen and therefore should have known better, but as one of the few highly rated females in the *Volk* division and the entire school, Galyna liked to think of herself as one of the boys and had no problem flaunting that.

"Can I join you guys?" she asks. Without receiving a reply, she looks to Leo, whom she had grown close to over the years. Even with Leo's sordid reputation for the way he treated women, Galyna had thought it strategic and better for her image to pursue him first. "Hand me a cigar," she says to him, nodding at the box on the table closest to him.

Leo refuses to look at her and keeps a cautious side-glance on Grisha. Snarling at her offensive interruption, Grisha finally looks over to acknowledge her. "Get the fuck out of here," he says in a low scathing voice. "This is a private conversation."

Galyna glares at him, though not too boldly—as if she were hurt but also not naive when it came to the commandant's rage. She looks back to Leo, who simply turns his head and raises an eyebrow at her. Galyna scoffs and gets up to leave. Without so much as a snide remark in her own defense, she makes it all the way to the door about to turn the knob when—

"Filthy slut, that one," Leo mutters loud enough for her to hear. Gavriil and Matvei chuckle, letting out simultaneous "oohs." Galyna whips back around, clearly offended by the comment coming from Leo.

"What did you say?" she asks, daring him to repeat it as she stands her ground by the door.

Fed up with her and without so much as a smile from Leo's quip, Grisha gets up from his seat, cigar still in hand, and walks over to stand right in front of her. The boys watch silently from their spots on the couch, Leo clenching his jaw in a way that Viktor could tell was in anticipation for the commandant's wrath toward him afterward. Grisha inhales his cigar and blows the smoke right in her face, Galyna turning her head to keep from inhaling it. He steps closer and grabs her face with his free hand, whispering a threat only she can hear. Galyna, flustered red, snatches her face from his grip and leaves promptly.

Grisha returns to the couch. "These silly girls," he says. "They're starting to think they're one of us... it disgusts me."

"But Grisha," Viktor says. "If we're all expected to graduate and fulfill the headmaster's plans, shouldn't we be regarding them with more respect? You know, so they won't turn on us?"

Grisha sucks on his cigar and blows out a drag of smoke. "Don't be so naive, my friend. Once they're out of here, they'll mean even less to the world than they do now to us. And they'll be someone else's problem. They're not stupid enough to get killed and expose us. The only reason the head-master even takes them in is for more bodies." The others laugh deviously.

"Well, I think you're completely right," Leo adds. "I'll defi-nitely do my part to keep them in their place." He holds up his glass in a cheer, but Grisha only turns to him, grimacing.

"This is partially your fault," he accuses, Leo lowering his glass and swallowing hard. "Whatever silly little thing you and Galyna have going on—cut it out. *You* of all people should know better." Leo nods quickly, looking down into his lap.

Viktor shifts uncomfortably in his seat. "So, the prison-ers," he interrupts, changing the subject for everyone's sake. "One of them, the older girl, looked so... familiar?" The guys exchange glances. "I don't know," Viktor says, feigning an agitation to remember and hoping to jog their memories. "I just feel like I've seen her here before."

Grisha raises an eyebrow, squinting at Viktor. "*Here*, you say? That's impossible."

Leo sips his drink, obviously feeling a bit more comfort-able again with the turn in their conversation. "Oh, yeah," he says, nodding. "I took the prisoners down there. I did think I recognized that girl. I just couldn't remember where from."

Grisha squints his eyes at Leo and then back to Vik-tor. "Hm. We'll have to look into it. Not sure who she could *possibly* be. But it's unlikely coincidental two of you would recognize her when none of us have been exposed to people outside this school. That's certainly something…"

"Why don't we go down there?" Viktor suggests eagerly when a knock comes from the door. The boys all look over. Grisha puffs on his cigar once more, holding a finger up to Viktor, who purses his lips and slumps back in his seat.

"Come in," Grisha says. Galyna steps inside hesitantly at first and then pulls her fifteen-year-old sister Zenya through the doors, who is too shy to look up. "Leave us. I'll deal with you later." Fuming and puffy-eyed, Galyna obeys and leaves the room, her little sister still standing by the door. "What are you waiting for? Grab me one of those and get over here," he says, nodding in the direction of the fireplace where three long metal stakes lie on the edge, roasting in its blue flames.

Zenya moves from the door and slowly picks up one of the stakes with a wide flat head, the metal seeming to shake in her trembling hand as she carefully makes her way over to the boys on the couches. As she approaches Grisha, she steps on one of her loosely tied shoelaces and falls to the floor at his feet, the stake still gripped tightly in her hand. Matvei and Gavriil burst out in laughter.

Grisha rolls his eyes and groans in obvious annoyance. "Stand up, you twit." Zenya does not move, seeming too afraid to do as she is told and unable to look up at them, her long blonde hair shielding her face from the others around her.

"This is the commandant," Leo hisses down at her in what seemed like an attempt to get back on Grisha's good side. "Don't just lie there."

The girl flinches at his tone. Slowly, she gets to her knees first, and as she lifts one of them in preparation to stand, Grisha lunges forward and wraps his body around hers, shoving her sideways to lean over on the table in front of them. He presses his cigar into her face, causing her to shriek and drop the metal stake on the table. Leo follows suit and grabs both of her wrists from the opposite side of the table, holding her in place as Grisha takes the metal stake and presses it down on one of her outstretched arms. Zenya lets out an earsplitting scream, writhing beneath him.

Viktor shakes his head, infuriated, looking to Matvei and Gavriil for any sign of opposition, but seeing them grin with their usual snarls. "Grisha," he argues. "She's only fifteen—"

Grisha lifts his gaze slightly. "Like I said before, it's never too early to start preparing them for the real world." The guys laugh. Grisha looks across the table to Leo. "On her stomach," he orders. Leo pulls her forward across the table, holding her in place. Grisha lifts the back of her shirt, bringing down the hot flat end of the metal stake and pressing it into her bare skin.

Zenya shrieks—the noise, coming from her throat, bloodcurdling. She twists and turns in their grip, and Matvei pushes off the couch to help them hold her legs down. Gavriil looks over to Viktor, chuckling obliviously to the latter's complete opposition for such acts. Viktor brings his drink up below his face, tempted to take a sip, but instead, his eyes flicker down just above the glass, narrowed and locked in on Grisha.

Inside UCOCA's Ukraine headquarters, Yaryna Borisova stands from her desk, moving briskly through the room. She runs up the stairs and enters the main office, gripping a hard drive in her hand. The lead agent in Vasyl's absence, Borysko Chernetsky, looks up from his work as Yaryna struts up to him.

"We have a problem," she says, holding out the device to him. "We just received a transmission from the team in Russia. They say it's urgent."

Borysko stands from his desk, snatching the device from her. "Why haven't we heard from them sooner?"

The two run down the stairs to Yaryna's desk, where they connect the hard drive to a computer and pull up the transmission. Before they can play it, the doors to the main room burst open, the Ukrainian team that had been stranded in Russia coming inside, led by Pavlo Avramenko.

"The mission was compromised!" Pavlo, Vasyl's right-hand man, blurts out. "They're being held captive and told us to retreat." His team throws down their equipment, exhausted from the long trek through the forest.

"When were they captured?" Yaryna asks.

Pavlo shrugs his shoulder. "At least twenty-four hours ago. Only took us so damn long to get here because the jet pilot was absolutely *nowhere* to be found! Then, when we *did* find him, he was drunk off his ass. Had to wait until he sobered up before we could get out of there!" He shimmies off the vest with his gun holsters and throws it on the desk. "That man *needs* to be fired."

"No matter," Borysko interrupts his whining. "You're just in time."

Everyone gathers in, agents flocking from their desks as Borysko pulls up the video transmission onto a large screen. A recorded video of Madisyn plays—sent from a secret transmitter device disguised as a plain silver band around her wrist:

"Greetings UCOCA team. Our rescue mission has taken a rather ironic turn. We're being held in a prison under the

academy, but we have managed to link up with some Russians who are willing to aid in our escape. It would be foolish to trust them entirely, so we'll need your help. Have your team prepared, heavily loaded, and in the nearby town of Krasnodar in less than forty-eight hours. You'll wait there for further instructions. Hopefully, we'll see you soon."

The room remains quiet, all of their gazes stuck on Madisyn's face. Breaking the stiff tension, Yaryna slams down her laptop and the screen flickers off, everyone turning to her expectantly.

"Well…" she says. "You all heard her! Let's move! Let's go!"

Immediately following her lead, Borysko adds, "Gather all the weapons and gear up, people! Get a move on!"

The agents scatter in different directions, except for Pavlo. Borysko turns to him as Pavlo groans in exhaustion. "I just got back from that God-awful place…" Borysko puts a hand on his friend's shoulder.

"Our endurance is shit, I know," he laughs. "But you know how this goes. If we quit now, UCOCA Ukraine will never again see the light of day. *Davay, brate!* We need you."

Pavlo sighs but nods his head, putting his hand on Borysko's shoulder in unity for their cause. "Let's do this." Borysko slaps him on the back and races off to the weapons room, overwrought like a kid on Christmas morning and eager to shoot something big.

CHAPTER 15

In a dark office of New Scotland Yard's Criminal Investigation Department in London, Detective James Harding pecks on his laptop's keyboard inside a cubicle while simultaneously fingering through files in a manila envelope. A nearby television on the wall lights up the room with vivid "Breaking News" flashers, catching his attention. A reporter tunes in from outside Number 10, the headquarters for the Government of the UK and residence of the Prime Minister:

"US President Blair Montgomery has just reportedly canceled an important meeting with Prime Minister Hagley Kinnard to look further into the incident involving US Senators Jay Saunders and Patrick McLean of Texas. Both men were found alive and are recovering but will face hefty jail time for leading an organized game of Russian roulette in the US, which sources are saying has possibly been going on for years right under the government's noses. Answers are still being sought to uncover who killed others involved in this heinous game and where the money has disappeared to. Investigators presume this was the work of an inside man. Ultimately, this is a huge embarrassment for the US government at such a critical time.

Prime Minister Kinnard said he had been looking forward to renewing ties with the president after a spat that left the two country's relationship 'questionable.' We hope to have more details for you on the matter soon."

Detective Harding's gaze drifts to the floor. Coming to his senses, he flicks off the television and scurries through the pages on his desk to find a specific document relating to the report. Ripping the page out from under one of his files, he skims the detailed news story on the Russian roulette game. He spots the circled words "Los Angeles" and "abandoned theater" and "organized crime group affiliation," then reads his own scribbled handwriting next to the last word cluster: *Possible UCOCA involvement?* He picks up another page with headshots of Madisyn and Marcelle Montevega, his eyes narrowing on the girls.

A door across the office opens as Detective Art Wilson peeks inside, spotting his friend in the dark. "Harding!" he calls, walking inside. "I thought that was you. I saw the light coming from your cubicle."

Harding hurries to pack his files away, stuffing them in a briefcase as Wilson comes over. "You know that group I was looking into? This is them," Harding says, waving the headshots of the girls. Wilson laughs nervously.

"The Montevega twins? The daughters of *billionaires* William and Theresa Montevega?" he says, using what he assumed to be Reese Montevega's full name. "You're being absurd!" Wilson looks over his shoulder, lowering his voice and becoming serious. "Come on, Harding. Even with their mother's innocence remaining questionable in the death of her ex-husband, the department cannot keep pursuing cases against that family! They'll have us shut down in a minute.

And even with the press on our side, the public deems any shot against Theresa 'institutional racism,' the babbling idiots. We can't risk our image."

Harding slams his brief shut and locks it, shutting down his computer next, having taken in hardly a word said by his coworker. "They call the group UCOCA: the Unorthodox Capitalists Organized Crime Association. They target some of the richest businessmen all over the world—the Netherlands, Italy, the US, that incident not long ago down in South America—killing them and stealing everything."

He had been studying the group for years now and had only recently come across clues linking the young Montevega girls to its origin. It had happened by accident that he stumbled across two different tabloids showing the twins on holiday suspiciously close to the scenes of two major robberies and murders of big businessmen, one in New York City and the other near the South of France. The timing was too close to be merely coincidental, and while most people brushed off the tacky articles as purely tainted gossip, Harding took the lead and ran with it. He was later able to track down more of their undocumented trips through the private jet service the Montevega family frequently used before losing his only inside connection. Even so, there was enough intel to convince him he had a case on his hands. And with ten uneventful years in the CID, after a long probation from a case of mistaken identity involving a French diplomat, he was adamant about getting back out there and making a name for himself.

Wilson scoffs and shakes his head. "Yes, I do know the group well. We actually found a lead for the man we're *sure* is behind it. Although, I admit I understand your intrigue. The Montevega kids are more than just kids. They're assets—geniuses. Did you hear Bill and Theresa had their genes customized before they were born? Customized! Brilliant, really. Don't know if I'd want my kids that smart, though. Just think when they're old enough to really think for themselves… Can you imagine? They could be the next Denise Coates, *easily*." Without looking up, Harding finishes tightening up his desk. Wilson notices Harding's inattentiveness. "Oh, come on. Forget that hogwash. There's no way that teenage girls are savvy enough to pull something off like this. Organized crime groups are simply not led by children."

Harding's head snaps around to face Wilson, holding a quick finger up. "Not children—intelligent billionaire heiresses who are bored and have been provided every single possible resource they could ever need or want," he methodically recites as if he had rehearsed the answer. Wilson sighs with concern as Harding grabs his briefcase and slaps his coat across his arm before brushing past him.

Hearing the doorbell ring throughout her luxurious villa, Reese Montevega—impeccably dressed in a pin-striped, black suit with red-bottom Louboutin's—struts through the front corridor muttering under her breath after a long day at the office.

"Where the hell is that, Valentina?" she spits, irritated at the absence of her housekeeper. Reese was the head woman of a mansion so vast she needed at least ten maids on-call on a normal day. The last thing she expected herself to be doing was a task as menial as answering the front door of her own home. The doorbell continues to ring, and Reese whips open the front door to reveal an eager Detective Harding. "My God, I do apologize for the delay," Reese says quickly, in her usual unfriendly, straight-faced tone. "I have absolutely no bloody clue where all the help is around here." She forces an unamused smirk that somehow almost comes across as a frown.

Detective Harding smiles warmly at her, forcing a laugh. "No matter, Mrs. Montevega. I'm Detective James Harding. May I?"

Reese hesitates, looking over her shoulder as she sees one of her maids poking her nosy head around the corner. "I actually am rather busy—" she says to him. "*Magdalin!*" she snaps at the maid, who immediately jumps and shuffles over to her boss.

Detective Harding clears his throat and stammers, trying his best to remain patient while also making his sense of urgency known. "If I—if I could just have a moment…"

Reese ignores him, turning to look at the maid in front of her. "Where the hell have you been? Didn't you hear me calling? And where is Valentina?"

Magdalin stammers, looking down at her feet. Reese snaps her fingers at the mousy woman to get her attention, Magdalin's head snapping back up. "Never mind that, handle this." Reese begins to walk away from the door, Magdalin looking helplessly at the detective.

"Wait, Mrs. Montevega!" he calls after her. "I am actually here to see *you*. And your husband." He squeezes past Magdalin, who steps aside. Reese squints her eyes at him curiously, stopped by the stairs. "If I may?" he asks politely before stepping further inside. Magdalin closes the door behind him. "I just need a minute of your time. It's about your children—"

"I don't *have* children. I have teenagers," Reese corrects him, giving him a once-over. "Do you know the difference, detective?"

Harding stammers, and Reese rolls her eyes with an impatient sigh, sensing that he didn't. "Magdalin, go fetch William and tell him we have a guest in the receiving room." Magdalin nods and eagerly scurries away.

Reese forces a smile at the detective, gesturing him into the room by the doorway. Twenty-year-old Mackenzie Montevega comes down the front stairs. "What's going on here?" she asks her mother. Reese does a double take on her eldest daughter, forgetting she had been inside the villa.

"My God, I thought you were away at school," Reese says, placing a hand dramatically over her heart. "Have you really been here all this time?"

Mackenzie scoffs, slightly offended her own mother would forget her circumstance, but also not that surprised. Reese was not the kind of mother who constantly worried or probed about her daughters' whereabouts. In fact, she hardly seemed to care at all, which had only been ideal for Mackenzie's social life. "Mother, *honestly?* I've been on a gap year for, like, the last six months. What's with the detective?"

Reese rolls her eyes and sighs. "Something about your sisters."

"No shocker there," Mackenzie adds. "They're total heathens." She follows her mother into the room, Bill coming out of his home office soon after to join them.

Inside the receiving room, Bill and Reese sit across from the detective, Mackenzie lying on the couch on the far side of the room, half-listening and half-diddling on her phone. She was interested in any gossip about the twins, but only because she was bored and didn't have much else planned at the moment.

"How is it you say you know our girls?" Bill asks.

Detective Harding sits up straighter, clearing his throat. "They hired me, actually," he lies. "They wanted more freedom on their trips than what you two were giving them with their escorts. They said they 'were always too flashy and would restrain them from participating in normal teenage activities.'" He laughs uneasily, hoping his story was convincing. "So instead, they had me keep an eye on them." Harding had done his research prior to this visit with Reese and Bill and had discovered that while they usually only allowed the twins to go away on trips with escorts, Madisyn and Marcelle were always quick to pay off these guys substantially—probably with stolen money, he assumed—so that they had complete freedom from chaperones... or rather "witnesses," he liked to think.

"But that doesn't make sense," Reese says. "Why would Madisyn and Marcie want security outside of our family network? They wouldn't just trust somebody we don't know."

Harding shifts in his chair, thinking how to best approach her concern. "Um... Theresa—is it?" he starts.

Reese squints her eyes at this, and Harding immediately senses he had chosen the wrong thing to say. "It's *just* Reese," she corrects him, almost seething yet still in a ladylike fashion. She often used the same face when talking with annoying wives of her husband's friends at the Wentworth Golf Club, a place she despised for its fake snobbery—though she too could play the part quite well. "I'm no Saint Theresa, detective." She smiles at him, her eyes narrowed.

Detective Harding clears his throat uncomfortably, and Mackenzie giggles at his brutal mistake from the couch. Harding makes a mental note to reprimand himself later for taking after Wilson. "My apologies. Reese, I believe your daughters are involved in some... dangerous activity. You see, up until a few weeks ago, I was in contact with them. They simply fell off the grid." Reese and Bill squint at the detective. Harding leans in closer to them, speaking slowly. "Do you have any idea where your daughters are? Did they even tell you?"

Reese's chin slightly sinks, taken aback. "We don't *micromanage* our teenage daughters, detective," she hisses. Mackenzie rolls her eyes as if anyone would ever mistake her mother for micromanaging.

"No, of course not," Detective Harding adds quickly, tapping his fingertips together nervously. "I don't mean that offensively. I just meant—"

"Didn't they say they were going somewhere in the States?" Bill asks his wife, her eyes rolling to the back of her head as if coming to a realization.

"God! That explains where Valentina is!" she says. "We *must* remember to have her hire extra help before she disappears like that again. I was this close to firing her." Ever since the twins became old enough to travel "alone" at age twelve, she had become used to having Valentina around the house to help with chores. Reese had even dragged her a few times to the Rossi dealership as if she were her personal assistant. She liked most that Valentina only spoke when spoken to, was a diligent worker, and always brought her coffee before she asked for it. There was also something mysteriously dangerous about Valentina that she could never quite pinpoint. It made Reese feel like her own version of O-Ren Ishii—from her favorite American film *Kill Bill: Vol. 1*—with a personal bodyguard as deadly and badass as the young Gogo Yubari.

Bill turns back to the detective. "Are you trying to say that our daughters are *missing*?" Mackenzie fully turns toward them from the couch, curious to hear the detective's answer. Harding clears his throat again, sitting up in his chair.

"Oh please!" Reese interrupts before he can answer. "It's only been a couple of weeks. The twins are notorious for behaving this way."

Harding sighs. "I know you two are *very* busy people. Very important people too. But if I may say, that is quite a long time actually for parents to not have had any contact with their children… I mean, *teenagers*," he corrects himself.

Bill and Reese draw back at this. Bill purses his lips and glances at his wife, who looks at him too. Reese scoffs, turning back at the detective. "Do you even have children?" she asks, somewhat accusingly.

"Well, no, but I—"

"We're not bad parents, detective," she says firmly.

"No, no. Of course not Mrs. Montevega—"

"But what exactly… do you suggest we do?" Reese says, without her usual air of confidence, a slight frown across her face. She hated being called out by someone for her hands-off parenting style, but if the man was offering his services, surely the right thing for any parent to do was to take his suggestions and be done with it.

"As two intelligent businesspeople like yourselves," Harding begins. "I would think perhaps you have some other way to 'keep tabs' on your daughters and their whereabouts?"

They sit quietly, pondering, when Bill finally clears his throat, sitting up taller. "We had tracking devices placed in the girls' teeth when they were children." Mackenzie's eyes widen, and her hand flies up to touch her own cheek.

Reese tilts her head at her husband. "We did?" she asks in a whisper, attempting to conceal her surprise from the judgmental stranger in the room.

"Does this mean I have a tracking device in my teeth, too?" Mackenzie blurts out, her parents looking over, both somewhat distracted by her question but also refusing to answer.

Harding laughs in delight, ignoring the eldest sibling as well. "Well, that certainly helps! We'll just have to get the information on those, and I'll handle the rest."

Reese forces a big smile and sits up straight. "All right, well, that settles it then!" she says quickly, ready for their conversation to be over. She stands abruptly, and the two men follow suit.

Bill shakes the detective's hand. "Jolly good, detective. We have no doubt you'll find them."

Harding smiles warmly again. "Yes, and I will certainly let you know when—"

"Thank you for stopping by," Reese adds, cutting him off once again. She shakes his hand and guides the detective out.

Back inside the room, Mackenzie stays on the couch and lets her hand slowly fall from her cheek. Her forehead wrinkles and her eyes trail off as wild thoughts fill her mind. She had always wondered what kind of weird things her younger sisters were getting into. As homeschooled freaks, she believed what the detective had said about the twins possibly being involved in dangerous activity. And now that she was home and had nothing else to do, this newly presented scandal would surely prove to be quite the entertainment.

CHAPTER 16

───

In a hotel room in Krasnodar, Detective Harding sits on a couch in front of a small, muted television, typing on his laptop. He had wasted no time getting the tracking information on the twins' location, and when he did, he was on the first flight out to Russia. He pulls up the map tracker, which shows two red blinking dots, representing both girls somewhere in a remote location, miles outside the city. He could see they were inside a boarding school called The Trinity, which may have looked innocent to the naive, but Harding hadn't a naive bone in his body. He knew there had to be something particularly ominous happening there for Madisyn and Marcelle to be at a boarding school, and it didn't involve them pursuing degrees in Russian studies. He squints his eyes at the map.

"Why aren't you moving?" he says as if talking to the girls directly. Their location hadn't seemed to change since he had first discovered it, and it was typically unlikely for criminals to remain at a site for so long…unless they truly weren't up to something suspicious. He longed to go inside the school, but it could be dangerous for a lone detective with no backup, and he was in no position to call for backup. He wasn't even supposed to be looking into the Montevega family in the first place. His boss had warned him to drop such accusations when he had first presented what he considered to be substantial evidence linking the twins with UCOCA. Their department was simply too afraid of dealing with the hefty lawsuit that would surely result from an accusation like that against powerful people like the Montevegas. So, he was on his own.

Harding pulls up a program to record the live map and its locations and sets the laptop aside. He grabs a box of take-out food from the nearby table and turns on the small stereo across the room, leaning back on the couch. "And now we wait…"

He takes a bite of freshly baked pirozhki as the stereo plays one of his favorite classical pieces—"Playing at Swans and Peacocks," the second movement from Josef Suk's orchestral suite "Fairy Tale/Pohadka." It had just the metronomic melody he needed to set the mood for his next couple of hours of mindless, insufferable waiting…

MINUTES LATER

Harding lies on the bed fully clothed, drinking a bottle of Baltika Premium Lager—his eyes glued to the laptop, now sitting on the desk inside the bedroom. The first couple of minutes was always the hardest for this kind of game of drawn-out anticipation. But he was an expert at playing the waiting game, as good as any experienced detective on a slow mission.

FIFTEEN MINUTES LATER

Still laying in bed, Detective Harding tosses a rubber ball in the air and catches it, unamused but still quite patient in the early phase of passing the time. Every now and then, he looks over to his laptop, seeing the unmoving dots still blinking inside the lines of the boarding school.

THIRTY MINUTES LATER

The detective sits in the large cushion chair in the corner of his bedroom reading a book, his gaze sneaking up over his reading glasses to peak at the laptop and the dots—still stationary.

FORTY-FIVE MINUTES LATER

On the floor, Harding pumps out some pushups, sweat dripping down his body as he pushes himself harder, almost reaching two hundred. Every time he pushed up, he couldn't help looking over to the laptop, but to no avail. The dots had still not moved! What were they doing, for Christ's sake? Physically exhausted but determined not to give up on the trackers, he collapses on the floor and flips onto his back to catch his breath.

A FULL HOUR LATER

Detective Harding practices karate moves, wielding a hand knife, the couch pushed over to the side to give him space. The laptop sits on the kitchen counter, where he peers over to periodically.

After kicking and slashing the air for a good three episodes of a Russian soap opera on the small television, Harding looks over to the laptop one last time. Seeing the dots unmoved, he yells at the top of his lungs in frustration, throwing the knife into the air and leaping up to spin-kick it with the back of his bare foot across the room and into the wall.

He moves to the couch and slumps over, his head resting against the wall. He knew it would be a slow day, but Russia was far from his favorite place, and he had no intention of leaving his suite. He had promised himself no distractions on this very crucial trip that could vindicate his career and, God willing, bring justice to the world, but perhaps there was a better way to kill time than being alone in his hotel room. Either way, he would have to think of something fast before he drove himself utterly insane.

CHAPTER 17

———

Far outside of the city, within The Trinity, Rurik storms through the empty halls during study period, having acquired a pass to the bathroom to confront a newly decided enemy. He gets to a dimly lit room with students sitting at long wooden tables, looking over maps and marking locations. From the doorway, he spots Luka in the middle, who looks over to the flustered boy. Just from Rurik's adamant face, Luka could tell he was about to discover the reasoning behind his strange and sudden hostility toward him over the last few days. The teacher at the front looks up briefly, but aware of Luka's leadership status, he turns away as Luka gets up to exit the room.

"Shouldn't you be in class?" Luka says.

Rurik balled his fists by his sides. "I just came to warn you. There's a storm coming."

Luka smirks at the threat. "A storm, hmm? I've noticed you've been acting a bit odd lately. You're jealous the headmaster chose me as a division leader."

"Don't think everyone 'below' you are ignorant to the fact that you're screwing us all over," Rurik spits.

Luka shakes his head, disappointed in his would-be friend. They had never been all that close, but Luka had once considered Rurik and Yakov two of his only friends. He wished he could say the same of Ivanna still, who had been there for him for as long as he could remember, but he refused to acknowledge any kind of relationship with her now. It didn't matter what he wanted to think or feel anyway, or what his emotions told him was right versus wrong: Luka had taken an oath to obey his father and to lead with merciless fury, and that was exactly what he planned to do. "Go to class, Rurik. I don't have time for you." As Luka turns to leave, Rurik grabs him by the arm, yanking him back around.

"You'll stop leading Ivanna on," Rurik demands. "You don't love her!"

Bursting out in laughter, Luka removes Rurik's hand from his arm. "So *that's* what all this is about? See, that's your problem—caring about the girls here like they're equals. You have so much to learn," he says, not that he completely agreed with the statement, but he knew it was knowledge he had over Rurik's lack thereof. "And what would you know about love, hmm? Why don't you tell me what love is, Rurik?" he taunts, taking a step closer and lowering his voice in the same way he often saw Grisha use with his subordinates. "No one's ever loved you before, and no one ever will."

"And *you* would know?" Rurik questions. "Your parents hated you and wanted nothing to do with you, and neither did your sister! She knew she was better without you. That's why she abandoned you. *Ty nictozhestvo.*" He wrinkles his nose, his lips twisting in a satisfied grin, knowing he had hit a soft spot with his insult. "You are nothing."

At the mention of his sister, Luka shoves Rurik back against the wall and drives his fist into the boy's face, causing

Rurik's nose to bleed. Not quite satisfied, Luka pins him in place with one hand and uses the other to punch Rurik in the stomach. Rurik groans, unable to protect himself from his stronger opponent. Seeing the spat from the door, the teacher comes running out of the classroom and pulls Luka off the younger boy.

"Enough of your foolishness, *idioty*!" the teacher hisses to both of them.

Luka whips around to face the man. "*He's* under *my* division! I can do whatever I want with him!"

The teacher leans closer to Luka's face. "You will not disrespect me. Now get back in the classroom." He shoves Luka in the head toward the door, and Luka spits in Rurik's direction before going inside. The teacher shakes his head. "*Neblagodarnyy,*" he mutters under his breath in obvious frustration before turning around to Rurik. "Clean your face up," he snarls, motioning his head for the boy to leave. The man goes back inside the classroom and slams the door in Rurik's face.

Below the school, the UCOCA prisoners and Valentina mill about in their cells—the latter sitting in the back corner. Marcie lies on her back in front of Valentina, and Vasyl sits toward the front against the bars to the door. Across from them, Madisyn paces as if trying to hatch a crafty plan to get them out of there. Robbie watches her, seeming unamused from his spot on the floor at the front of their cell as he twirls the detonator in his hand. If it started to seem like they weren't going to make it out of their current situation alive, he would make sure those filthy Russians were on the same ride down to hell with them.

The five of them look up as they hear nearby voices coming from the prison doors. Leo, Gavriil, and Matvei come inside, Viktor trailing them quietly like a shadow. Robbie quickly hides the detonator under his belt buckle just as the boys get to the end of the prison, gawking at their new prisoners as if taunting animals at the zoo. A stern-faced Grisha arrives moments later, pushing his friends aside to have a serious look. Valentina drops her gaze as she feels Grisha's glare turn on her.

Leo nods his head toward Valentina. "That's her—that one," he says, confirming what Grisha appeared to have already discovered for himself.

"Pretty little thing is shy," Matvei says. "Let's see your face, sweetheart," he coos at Valentina, trying to get her attention.

Leo gestures to Marcie. "I like this one better. I want *her*." He smiles deviously, and Marcie shrinks back, her nostrils flaring.

Robbie jumps to his feet. "Filthy Russian prick!" he spits. The boys only laugh, turning around toward the other cell, but ignoring Robbie completely and looking straight over to Madisyn instead.

"*Smotri*," Gavriil points out. "There are two pretty ones. Except her face is a little more fucked up."

"She's a fighter, that one," Leo teases, seeming impressed by the damage Madisyn had done earlier to the other boy before getting caught. "I say we take the girls out one at a time, you know, to interview them. What do you think, Grisha?" Gavriil and Matvei laugh, though Grisha hasn't seemed to move, let alone take his eyes off Valentina for even a second.

"*Vstan'*," Grisha orders her. Valentina remains in place, her jaw clenching shut. He may have been too young for her to remember, but she could tell he must be the commandant, as he reeked of toxic masculinity.

"*Stand up!*" Grisha roars. The other Russian boys quit their goofing, obviously sensing that playtime was over. Viktor watches Grisha closely.

Valentina keeps still, with her eyes down, and swallows hard. She balls her fists, trying to keep her cool. There was nothing she wanted to do more than break through that cell and wrap her hands around his neck until he couldn't breathe. A boiling rage sat inside her heart as Grisha's presence brings back moments of horror from her past: they flicker through her mind like wildfire, causing her to wince and making her body shake uncontrollably. Grisha was obviously just as wicked as the guys before him and had probably done equally terrible things, if not worse. This must have been the boy who had been grooming Luka as a division leader and had surely tainted his mind. For that, Valentina wished she could show Grisha and the others that she was not that same weak, silly girl people had once thought her to be during her time at The Trinity. Given a chance, she would fight her heart out, even if it meant giving her last breath to ensure this boy—who was so much like the tormentors of her past—and that wretched old man upstairs never got to see the light of day beyond those dreadful walls.

Fuming, Grisha takes a step closer and grips the cold metal bars tightly within his palm, almost as if he might rip the door from its very hinges. Vasyl moves back slightly with a look of disgust.

"If I have to say it one more time," Grisha threatens in a low voice, his chest heaving like he might explode.

Uninterested in Grisha's temper, Leo's gaze flutters over to Madisyn again, giving her a once-over. She glares at him but raises an eyebrow, seeming amused slightly by the Russian boy whom she might have considered attractive if it weren't for his obvious threat to their livelihood. Her eyes flicker over to the other cell again as Valentina slowly stands. Valentina only slightly raises her head but stays safely in the back corner.

Grisha's eyes grow as the light hits her face, steam seeming to pour from his ears like the relentless hiss of a locomotive. He pounds the cell bars with his fists and yells. Fed up with hiding any longer, Valentina finally dares to look up at him with piercing eyes, her nose wrinkling.

"*You*," he snarls, spit dribbling from his quivering lip. "You will pay." Shoving past his friends, Grisha storms from the room. Valentina holds her chin high, her body still trembling with anger. In a subtle fashion among the dissipating tension, Viktor catches Marcie's eye and quickly winks at her before following Grisha out. Gavriil and Matvei trail behind without another word.

Lingering behind, Leo bites his bottom lip, clearly still fascinated by Madisyn. Her face softens just a touch at his impaling eyes, almost as if she were lost in a dark fantasy of the exciting ill intentions he must have held for her in his mind. Valentina narrows her eyes on Leo from her cell, knowing the reality of what boys like him were capable of, despite his somewhat desirable face. Madisyn was young and obviously too naive from her privileged upbringing to understand what was *actually* going through his mind. Before Valentina can interrupt, Robbie breaks their moment with a scoff, glaring at Madisyn. She purses her lips at him, only slightly embarrassed.

"*Otvratitel'naya svin'ya*," Valentina mutters. Leo turns his gaze from Madisyn and smirks at Valentina's insult. He eyes her coolly one last time before slinking away. After the last of the Russians are gone, Valentina sinks back down to the floor, arms wrapped around her knees.

"Can someone *please* tell me what the fuck just happened?" Vasyl demands.

"They know…" Valentina answers quietly, keeping her eyes down.

"That guy…" Marcie says. "The quiet one. He winked at me. Before following the crazy guy."

Robbie snorts, seemingly bothered by Madisyn's overall presence still. "Yeah, well, your sister was eye-fucking that sleazy Russian prick, so you're two for two." Madisyn scoffs loudly at Robbie's announcement of her private moment.

Marcie dismisses the claim with a shake of her head. "No, I mean, he winked at me as if he was trying to tell me something. Like maybe he was on our side?"

"Maybe that was their brother," Vasyl adds. "Pyotr's and Aleks's?"

Valentina looks up to face them. "Whoever he was, let's hope he's part of whatever plan those boys have to take down the headmaster. That other one, the mean one… that was Grisha Yurkov. He was here before I escaped. He must have been very young, though I am surprised none of them recognized me sooner." As Pyotr had said earlier, Valentina was the legendary traitor who got away, and she was sure the headmaster knew she would be back for what she left behind, just like her aunt. She had only hoped she could find some way to have a private moment with Luka before anything drastic happened—that he would at least come down there to see for himself. It bothered her that he had not seen her face since she had had the opportunity to see him from inside his bedroom. Eleven years later, Valentina couldn't help thinking that when the time came for them to meet, Luka might not recognize her.

⚔

Pressed by his appalling discovery of the returned Dementieva girl, Grisha moves through the hallway with fury. Students fly out of his way to avoid becoming roadkill under his merciless strides. He approaches a classroom and halts at the doorway, spotting Luka, who looks up from his work to the door. Grisha shoots daggers at him, his clenched fists shaking.

Luka stands but does not move. "What's up, Grisha?" he asks, shrugging his shoulders.

Grisha wanted so badly to pull the boy from his chair and bludgeon his brain into mush before Luka had the chance to do something horrendous, like rescue his sister from prison and escape with her. But he knew he had to be patient, as his master would want justice for the girl's betrayal. At least *then,* he could have the pleasure of killing them both with an audience to cheer him on.

An evil smirk slithers across Grisha's lips. Students look back and forth between the two, likely wondering if their stand-off would transition into something more. Grisha breaks away his glare to throw a dirty look toward the teacher, who only purses his lips in defeat. Having displayed a fear-induced influence in more ways than one, Grisha rips away from the door, eager to share his news with the headmaster. Moving through the vast school, he gets to the west wing and flies up a flight of spiral stairs until he reaches double doors. He pushes through them without so much as a knock.

Inside a lounge space adjacent to his office, the headmaster stands upon a platform with his arms raised as two tailors take his measurements around his thick red cloak. Grisha struts through the doorway to approach the man, who immediately bids the tailors to leave. As the old man steps off the platform, Grisha kneels before him and kisses his ring. He stands up straight, hands behind his back as a faithful servant.

"It seems we have a returned visitor, Headmaster," he informs him. "One of the prisoners. I think you'll remember her well… Valentina Dementieva." Grisha's nostrils flare while saying her name. The man's eyebrows rise, though he smiles slightly, chuckling.

"I have been waiting for her return. It has been many years now that I had almost thought she had given up. Our school has gone through so much trouble with that bloodline, it seems," the old man breathes. "Does her brother know?"

Grisha takes a deep breath, clenching and unclenching his jaw at the thought of Luka. "I'm not sure. But I don't trust him, *Otchim*. I have always been suspicious of him. He is too rebellious. And now that she's back…" He looks away for a moment, sensing the heat rising quickly in his chest. Closing his eyes, Grisha sucks in a deep breath through his nostrils and lets it out slowly—an attempt to calm himself out of respect for his superior. The headmaster had warned him about losing his temper and how it could be used as a weakness against him as a mechanism of control if he wasn't too careful. It was the only piece of criticism he had ever gotten from the headmaster, and so he made a point to show he was working on it every day. The headmaster had even gone through the lengths of assigning him daily breathing practices that he was to complete at least twice a day and whenever he found himself getting too worked up. He could still be the ruthless brute he had always been praised and promoted for, but as commandant over the entire school, he had to act with grace and remain in absolute control. Grisha turns his back to the man, having regained his composure.

"I don't think we should kill him, though." The headmaster tilts his head for Grisha to continue. "Let's test his loyalty to us—to *you*. Make him kill her. In front of the entire school, just like his wretched aunt." A smile creeps across the old man's face, and he laughs, seeming impressed. "I would feel a lot better about him if he did. And we would finally know what side he is on, because like you said, his blood has been *nothing* but trouble."

The old man nods, stroking his chin in deep thought. "Yes, yes… let's make a point of this once and for all. Very good, Grisha. Bring everyone to the Great Hall. We will let the events unfold in front of us. And if there is any hesitance from Luka, we will kill him as well."

A snarky smile fills Grisha's face. "And I will *gladly* do the honors," he spits, spinning on his heels to exit the room with spewing satisfaction.

Not even an hour later, a different group of students storms the prison, displaying a more serious urgency than the first group's entrance. They promptly move in to open the first cell, two of them swarming inside to grab Valentina. She fights back, thrusting one guy back into the wall and spinning around to whack the other in the face with her balled fist. As two more students burst through the cell door, Marcie and Vasyl lunge at them. Vasyl punches the first guy, but the stocky boy recovers quickly and drives Vasyl back into the wall with his head pressed into his chest. Marcie knees her opponent in the groin and uses all her strength to swing him around, throwing the student on top of one of Valentina's guys.

From the opposite cell, Robbie and Madisyn yell, banging on the cell door and wishing they could do something to help. "Watch your back, Marcelle!" Robbie warns.

Marcie uses the heads up to twist around and punch another student in the face, but he overpowers her quickly and thrusts her back into the wall. Marcie groans from the impact but manages to kick him in the stomach and thrust him backward with just enough time to flick out a small pocketknife hidden in the sleeve of her shirt. As the boy yells and lunges back at her, Marcie drives the knife into his abdomen. Pulling her weapon out, she lets the boy fall to the floor. Just as she moves forward to help Valentina with her two guys, one of the Russians still standing outside of the cell pulls out one of UCOCA's confiscated guns, pointing it right at Marcie's head. Two more pull theirs out, too, aiming their weapons at Madisyn and Robbie in the opposite cell, immediately quieting the room.

"*Glupaya suka!*" the boy with the weapon pointed on Marcie yells at her, moving forward quickly and ready to pull the trigger. Marcie takes a step back, panting.

"No!" one of the Russian girls yells, dropping her aim on Robbie to pull back her eager companion. "We must keep them alive for now. The headmaster will want to see their execution himself, remember?"

"She murdered Daniil!" he spits back, keeping a wide-eyed snarl on Marcie.

The Russian girl moves inside the cell and snatches Marcie's knife from her hand, scowling in her face before turning around. "Leave him," she orders, gesturing to the boy lying on the floor and choking up blood. "Let's go."

The three students still inside the cell pull Valentina out with ease, one of them going back briefly to drag Daniil's body to rest just outside the cell, away from the prisoners. They lock the door behind them, only then lowering their pointed guns before leaving.

"Bastards!" Madisyn calls out to them. "You'll pay for this!"

Robbie punches the cell. "Shit! What are we going to do now?" They all become quiet, looking at one another.

"They're going to kill her," Vasyl states, glancing at the dead Russian boy on the ground—one of their own whom the Russian students didn't even have enough decency to take with them. "Aren't they?" The others look over to him with worry, all of them unable to speak.

Marcie sinks down to the floor, tears flooding out of her. Vasyl immediately sinks down next to her, gently taking her hand into his palms to soothe her. He buries his lips into her hair to kiss her head as she weeps. Seeing this tender affection, Robbie swallows hard, trying to conceal his jealousy for not being the one to protect Marcie. His mouth hangs slightly open, wanting to say something but knowing it was better if he didn't. Valentina had just been taken away to face an uncertain fate, and they had all just had guns pointed to their heads. The Russians could have easily killed them right then and there. The fact that they didn't meant they could expect a much worse fate than being shot dead. Robbie presses his head against the cell bars, closing his eyes in defeat. All he could do was feel totally helpless, knowing that Marcie could have been killed just moments ago while he was stuck inside the cell across from her, unable to do anything about it. It was worse to imagine than his own death.

Vasyl moves his lips to Marcie's ear, whispering softly to her. Marcie snivels, looking up at him. He moves one of his hands from hers to wipe a stream of wetness flowing down her cheek, his gaze locked on hers. The corner of his mouth rises into a small comforting smile as he leans in to rest his forehead against hers, just barely brushing his lips across her lips. Marcie hesitates, sensing Robbie's eyes on them, but in her moment of weakness with a strong yearning to be consoled, she lets Vasyl kiss her.

Unable to watch their seemingly private moment, Robbie turns away to sit against the cell wall, swallowing the growing lump in his throat again. Madisyn, sitting across from him, bites the inside of her lip, her eyes soft with sympathy for possibly the first time. He might even assume she felt a little bit guilty now for the dark secret they were harboring. Distraught, Robbie looks away from Madisyn, too embarrassed to let her see how bad he was truly hurting.

Called out of class early, Luka enters the headmaster's office. He approaches the man with hesitance, kneeling respectfully first. "You summoned for me, Headmaster?" he asks, his mind searching for plausible explanations for Grisha's earlier animosity.

The old man clears his throat. "Given your newly appointed position, it is time for us to test your loyalty, Luka. To both myself and to your brothers and sisters." He moves to pick up a long sword sitting on the tall fireplace, vivid blue flames glowing inside of it. He holds the weapon out with both hands to Luka, who takes it, staring brightly at its shine.

"I serve you, Headmaster, and my loyalty is unwavering," Luka assures him methodically. The reply was already engrained in his mind, retrieved from a short list of responses he had been taught were appropriate when engaged in conversation with the headmaster. Disagreement was never an option.

Luka knew what it meant to be gifted a weapon like this—such swords were only used in executions. He lifts the sword, feeling both its weight and the weight of the situation itself. He had noticed over the years that prisoners of the school—and there had only been a few—did not remain long in the prison before they were executed. Luka looks up at the old man's face, meeting his unwavering gaze. Luka only hoped the headmaster could not sense his uncertainty. He clears his throat, pushing his doubts to the corners of his mind. Luka kisses the man's ring and turns to leave.

Luka rushes down the stairs and into the main walkway. His heart pounds so hard in his chest that all he can hear is its beating, even over the blare of the intercom summoning the entire student body to the Great Hall. As students flood from their classrooms out into the busy hallway, Luka begins to pant. Some of them move from his way, seeing the sword in his hand and the dazed look in his eyes, but others linger to get a better look. Luka shoves past them, his impatient canter turning into a full-out sprint. Curious students watch him go by, glancing at the sword in his hand with wild eyes, gasping and pointing.

Luka makes it to the *Vipera* lounge, bursting through the double doors as students in his division come running down the steps from their bedchambers, all hearing the order on the intercom. Luka flies up the stairs two at a time through the sea of students headed for the Great Hall and turns down the male wing.

Pushing through the door to his room, he drops the sword and looks around frantically for the dose of *Uspet'* he had hidden for a rainy day. Luka had been going through the drug rather quickly, and Grisha had ordered his privileges were to be stripped until he learned not to abuse it. Grisha himself had never needed drugs as a coping mechanism—as he was already quite ravenous naturally—and he insisted his appointed leadership take charge with as clear minds as possible. Even while Luka wished he could be this way to further impress the headmaster and his peers, inflicting pain on others was not a task he was mentally prepared to undertake without a crutch.

Scrambling to find the needle, he rips open the drawers to his desk, accidentally pulling one completely off its hinges. Luka lets the broken drawer fall from his grip to the floor with a loud *thunk* as the wood cracks. He moves to the bed and tears it apart, pillows flying across the room before flipping his mattress, but to his disappointment, he can't find it anywhere. Panic overwhelming him; Luka falls to his knees, crying and gasping for air as if his lungs were failing him. He steadies himself on the floor, using the inside palm of his hand to ram himself over and over in the forehead, hoping to force himself to get his act together. He wanted so badly to be the type of person everyone expected him to be, capable of fulfilling the headmaster's orders with ease, but his mind tormented him, telling him that what he was doing was wrong. He knew somewhere deep down in his heart that the headmaster was wicked and had torn his family—his *real* family—apart. He was trapped and should have escaped eleven years ago when he had the chance. If only it hadn't taken him so long to realize the weight of the predicament, he was actually in.

Just as Luka is beginning to feel at his weakest, Ivanna bursts into his room. "Luka, I heard the news! He actually wants you to—" She stops as she sees Luka's fragile state, immediately falling to her knees beside him. Luka shoves her away and tries to stand but ends up stumbling as he gets to his feet. He wipes his face with his arm.

"Not now, Ivanna!" he says, his voice cracking. "You need to leave." To avoid looking her directly in the eye, Luka continues searching his room for the *Uspet'*, but Ivanna runs over and pulls his arm, forcing him to face her.

She throws her arms around him, hugging him tightly. Luka lets her, nuzzling his chin into her neck. The actual killing part didn't scare him. *Everything* did. He had been starting to doubt the lessons he was taught in his classes, and while there were brief periods over the last few years where he forgot about his past, it seemed all that was on his mind recently was his sister. Nightmare after nightmare had kept him from getting sleep at night. He was addicted to *Uspet'* despite the fact that it continuously made him sick. This quiet moment had been the first time ever he could actually take it all in and realize the seriousness of his downward spiral, and it all seemed to circle back to his sister.

Luka never found out if Valentina had ever actually made it out alive. Everyone had told him she was dead, eaten by the forest's predators. For years after her escape, students had gone out to search the forest for any remains of her body, making bets to see who would be the first to find her and which body parts they would bring back—a head being worth the most. It was a game to them, and Luka often felt like his entire existence was a mockery. He held no hope of ever finding a purpose for his life or true happiness, and he could only hope his sister had… wherever she was. The happiest he would ever feel was right then, embracing Ivanna for the first time, letting someone else in to see him in his most vulnerable state.

"I know you're scared…" Ivanna whispers, "… to kill someone for the first time." Her inability to understand his real demons pulls Luka back to his somber reality: he truly had no one.

Luka breaks away from her. "I'm *not* scared." Ivanna only smiles at him, touching his face. He moves his head away. "You have to go," he says, unable to look at her. He longed to be understood, to not feel so alone, but at the moment, he had a job to do, and it would be his head on a platter if he didn't get it done. "Get to the Great Hall. *Go!*" Ivanna nods, seeming to at least understand the heaviness of his appointed task, and leaves without another word.

Feeling pressed for time again, Luka searches through his dresser, ripping clothes from it until he finally finds the needle of *Uspet'*, only a quarter of the normal dose he would usually pump himself with. Wasting no time, he injects himself, sliding down the wall to the floor as his breathing slows. At least he had this small crutch to get him through. He squeezes his eyes shut, exhausted from overthinking, and lets the drug's power take control of his mind. He only hoped it would last long enough to get him through the next full hour.

In the Great Hall, a group of students dragged Valentina through the doors as the rest of the student body start to cram inside, excited to see the execution of a prisoner who had invaded their home. Valentina is forced on her knees in the middle of the room, her arms tied with rope. She looks around at all the eyes on her.

Rurik and Yakov stand among the crowd as Ivanna makes her way over to them. "Where've you been?" Rurik demands. He was running out of time to convince her to run away with them. If he came on too strong, though, he could risk blowing the plan for everyone involved.

"Nowhere," she snaps. "Now, let me through." Ivanna peeks through the crowd, trying to get a look at the prisoner. She gasps when she sees Valentina. "Is that who I think it is?"

Yakov squints. "What do you mean? How would any of us know her?"

"That's her... that's Luka's sister," she breathes, panicking. "I've seen pictures of her! Luka used to look at them all the time after she first left. I could never forget her face. Oh, my God... They're going to make him kill her." She shakes her head. "I have to warn Luka."

She backs up to go, but Rurik quickly snatches her by the wrist, yanking her close and lowering his voice, wanting to settle this once and for all. "Something *bigger* than this is about to go down tonight, Ivanna. And you need to be here so you can decide which side you're on." Ivanna squints at him and looks to Yakov for an explanation, who only nods once in agreement.

At the front of the room, the headmaster stands from his throne, looking around impatiently. Grisha, standing closest on his left, leaves the line of head students to approach the old man. "Headmaster—" he begins. The man holds up his hand to silence Grisha, who huffs in defeat, sucking on his teeth.

After a few moments, Luka enters the Great Hall, sword in hand and eyes glazed over. He moves through the students, who quickly part as he approaches the headmaster. From the center, Valentina's eyes widen as she sees him. Her balled fists shake as if she wants to scream out to him, but she refrains. The headmaster nods to Luka, who spins on his heels to face the woman. He walks toward her, not appearing to recognize his sister, and stops a few feet away.

"Sons and daughters," the headmaster begins. "We are gathered today to destroy an enemy, another traitor to our family. And to do the honors… your brother Luka, who has proven himself worthy of his new position, shall prove himself worthy of greatness."

The room erupts with an earsplitting roar from about half the students, the half most devout to The Trinity and its cause. They remain completely oblivious to the disagreement displayed in silence from the group of rebels among them. This silent group covertly looks to one another to acknowledge their unity in the unfolding plan to destroy the school, and with it, the headmaster and his loyal slaves.

The headmaster holds up a hand to silence the cheering. Valentina stares at Luka with wet eyes, but he only looks through her, clenching and unclenching his jaw. He approaches the woman with his sword, putting one foot in front of the other. He could feel the effect of the *Uspet'* wearing off already, having taken only a quarter of the dose he was used to injecting twice a day. For the first time ever, and at what seemed to be like the worst possible moment, Luka started to realize how his tolerance to the drug had exponentially grown since he had first started using it. His palms sweat around the grip of his weapon. Reality's brutal grasp seemed to ring him by the neck, but he could not crack in front of this many people—not in front of the headmaster himself.

"Luka, *please*," Valentina begs in a low whisper, choking back tears. "It's *me*, Luka. Your sister, Valentina. Please."

Luka comes to stand right in front of her. Blood rushes through his head, ringing in his eardrums as his heart pounds beneath his chest. His mind fills with chaos as vexing thoughts penetrate the weak effect of the drugs.

Don't listen to her! A voice screams inside his head. *She's lying. Kill her already! Don't fuck this up, Luka. Don't you want to be great? Do it!*

He raises the sword slowly in front of his body, hovering it close to her neck.

Valentina lowers her head, tears flooding from her as she begins to sing quietly so that only Luka can hear the words of the lullaby she sang to him as a boy.

Soon night will come, qui-et-ing the sun,

Si-lent the sound of the night com-ing through.

Valentina raises her head to look her brother in the eyes.

Hear the wind whis-per-ring, whisp'ring to you…

Luka cocks his head, taken aback. He gasps, his glossy eyes widening and blinking a few times as if they could be deceiving him. "What is this?" he says under his breath to Valentina. Surely it couldn't be true? He swallows hard.

Sleep, sleep, sleep, good night my sweet one,

Good night my dear one, good night my swe-et one

To you good night.

While staring at her, Luka's vision becomes distorted with a fuzzy memory, seeing his aunt's murder all those years ago in the very place he now stood. He sees himself as a child crying helplessly, Valentina holding him and singing him to sleep at night. The rushing of blood in his ears grows louder again until it is all he can hear... *thump... thump... thump.*

A piercing ringing in his mind, resembling sirens—as if his internal alarms were trying to warn him that his life was in danger—increased in volume. The hazy sound of the headmaster yelling with rage over and over pulls Luka back to reality, now staring at his wholly recognized sister and hearing the headmaster screaming behind him.

"*Kill her already! Unichtozh' yeye!*" the old man croaks.

Luka lowers the sword from his sister's neck, still staring at her with disbelief. His beautiful sister—the one person who had loved him and been there for him all along; the one person who wasn't afraid to risk everything—had come back for him.

"It's her life or yours, Luka!" the headmaster reminds him. "*Davay!*" Grisha fumes next to the old man, itching to act. The students in the crowd remain glued to the pair in the center.

In the back of the room, Rurik sneaks a sly glance over to another student only feet away, who nods once to him before giving the signal to others around the hall. This was the moment that would change everything for them—the moment they would take back their freedom for good.

CHAPTER 18

In another wing of the school, inside the headmaster's office, Aleks stands in front of the glowing fireplace, looking over his shoulder once before extending a long torch into the blue flames. He proceeds to set the drapes on fire and runs from the room as the raging fire spreads quickly beyond it, setting off the alarms throughout the entire school.

At the deafening sound, the guards in the security room scramble from their seats, shouting and trying to figure out what happened as the red lights of the alarms whirl around them. Some of them dash from the room, weapons at the ready, determined to search out the cause for such a disturbance.

Back inside the Great Hall, the alarms blare, suddenly breaking the attention from the center of the floor. Undistracted by this and depleted of patience, Grisha yells with fury, breaking the boiling tension. He grabs a sword from the sheath in the headmaster's throne and bolts toward Luka and Valentina.

Luka turns and raises his sword to fight Grisha. Some of the head students lined up by the headmaster—including Leo, Matvei, and Gavriil—rush at Valentina with their own weapons. Thrusting up from her knees, she quickly gets to her feet just as Matvei gets to her first. With her hands still tied in front of her, Valentina leaps into the air, and round-house kicks Matvei in the face, snatching the sharp end of the dagger from his hand as he stumbles backward. Flipping the dagger in her now bleeding palms, Valentina uses it to block Gavriil's strikes, who slashes the air with his knife over and over like a madman. Valentina leaps up and kicks his wrist at a perfect angle, sending his weapon flying across the room before skillfully slashing him across the face with the dagger.

"*Kill them!*" the old man orders.

Before his loyal students can join the battle, they find themselves in their own brawls as the rebels amongst them turn to fight. Rurik and Yakov throw punches at students next to them. Ivanna looks around in horror, seeing her fellow classmates tearing one another apart.

Viktor, having already taken down some of the head students near the headmaster's throne, jumps in to help Valentina as she fights both Leo and Matvei. With a knife in hand, Viktor grabs Leo from behind by his hair, turning him around to stab him in the stomach. He looks Leo in the eyes for a moment as he bleeds. Leo's face is torn with pain and disbelief as he falls to the floor. Her hands still knotted, Valentina jumps to kick Matvei again, but this time he grabs her by the leg. Yelling to muster all her strength, she twists and flips her other leg in the air and kicks him in the head, a few of Matvei's teeth flying out from the impact. Recovering quickly and livid now, Matvei yells, his bloodied mouth making him look like a beast in the forest. He blocks Valentina's jab and overpowers her, twisting her around to bear-hug her from behind and wrapping his large hands around her wrists to keep her in place. Valentina thrusts backward, head-butting him in the nose and causing him to let go. She tumbles forward away from him and lands at Viktor's feet just as Viktor hurls his knife, striking Matvei right in the forehead.

Viktor bends down and uses Valentina's dagger to help cut the knotted rope around her wrists. With his back turned, a student sneaks up behind Viktor, raising a sword into the air and yelling at the top of his lungs. Viktor twists around quickly, just as Galyna grabs the student by the wrist and stabs him in the side with the other hand. Galyna snatches her knife out and throws the boy to the ground. She turns her stern face on Viktor and nods once, as if to acknowledge that they were on the same side, before moving away to find her sister.

The doors to the Great Hall burst open, and a guard comes through yelling at the top of his lungs. "Fire! The school is on fire!"

Without hesitance, the guard runs from the hall to save himself. Some of the students scream and follow, trampling one another and creating a small stampede, Galyna and Zenya among them. The headmaster, still frozen in place at the head of the room by his throne, twists around, watching many of his once-loyal students abandon him.

"Luka! Behind you!" Ivanna screams amongst the chaos. Luka looks back toward her voice for only a mere second as another student viciously lunges at him from the side and tackles him to the ground.

Foaming at the mouth, Grisha pulls the student off Luka and tosses him aside. "He's *mine!*" Grisha roars, spit flying out of his mouth. He lifts his sword in the air to bring it back down on Luka. Luka rolls out of the way quickly, throwing his own sword back up to block himself as Grisha bounds over to swing at him again. Ivanna starts to run toward them, wanting to help, but Rurik pulls her back.

"Ivanna, come on!" Rurik yells. "We have to go, or we'll be dead too!" Ivanna resists at first but finally lets Rurik pull her from the room. Seeing the oldest Swierczynski brother run from the hall to find his brothers, Yakov breaks out of his own fight to join the dozens of students fleeing the chaos.

Below the burning school in the prison, Pyotr and Viktor run to the last cells, unlocking them and letting the UCOCA prisoners out. "You must save your friends and leave quickly before the school burns down," Pyotr informs them.

"What?" Robbie complains. "Would it have killed you to come sooner?"

They run from the room through the secret passage leading to the kitchen, where Yelena returns their weapons to them. Yelena turns to Marcie, who is closest, and takes her hand into hers, squeezing it as if to communicate their gratitude. "*Spasibo.*" Marcie furrows her brows at the old woman but nods in response. "All of you," Yelena says, turning to face each one of them with a warm smile. "Thank you." The woman releases Marcie's hand.

Vasyl laughs. "We should be the ones thanking *you*, really." The others nod quickly in agreement, and Yelena blushes.

Pyotr gestures for Yelena and the young helper girl. "Head toward the forest. We'll meet you there soon," he tells them, squeezing the woman's hand and kissing her on the forehead. Yelena nods and shuffles the young girl out the back kitchen door that leads around to the barn.

Viktor turns back to the UCOCA team. "Good luck," he says gravely. "You'll need it."

The twins purse their lips at the warning. "Aren't you at least going to help us in there?" Marcie asks.

Pyotr laughs, though his face quickly becomes serious again. "We already have. The rest is on you."

Aleks comes running through the kitchen doors to join his brothers. "Let's get the fuck out of here," he says. Without another word, the three of them leave through the back door.

"Come on, we're wasting time!" Madisyn reminds them, taking off running from the kitchen back into the school. The four of them run down the long winding halls, finally reaching the Great Hall and bounding through the opened doorway.

Robbie, Vasyl, and the twins spot Valentina and Luka fighting for their lives and immediately jump in on what's left of the fight. Madisyn runs straight toward Valentina, who is engaged in a battle against four students. Madisyn rips one of the girls back by the hair and throws her to the floor before moving to the next guy. She kicks him in the back of his knee, causing him to fall to both knees before wrapping her arm around his head and breaking his neck. In a similar fashion across the room, Marcie, Robbie, and Vasyl use their own lethal martial arts fighting skills to overpower their opponents between shots from their firearms.

Busy with his own fight, Luka uses all his strength to take on Grisha, throwing constant jabs and blocks as they move around the room, desperate to kill one another. With a more vicious fighting style, similar to that of a rabid beast, Grisha overpowers Luka with quick slashes and the weight of his sword as he moves Luka backward. Luka stumbles over his heels but quickly moves out of the way from another one of Grisha's mighty strikes. Finding his balance again, Luka brings his sword back up to clash with Grisha's. Luka yells, gaining a short burst of energy to push the commandant backward. He uses his sword to whack Grisha's weapon from his hand.

Grisha skillfully recovers, immediately grabbing an abandoned dagger off the floor and using it to block one of Luka's blows. With both hands on the end of his dagger, the commandant thrusts back, using his strength to knock Luka's sword from his grip and causing Luka to fall backward to the floor. Luka scrambles away quickly, getting back to his feet and dashing toward the center of the room, where he grabs a knife sticking out of a dead body on the floor. He whips back around just as Grisha drops down a massive blow. Luka blocks it with his weapon, but the weight is enough to cause him to stumble to the ground again. Grisha pins him down this time, putting his weight on Luka, who continues to block the commandant's constant and quick jabs, every blow stronger than the last as Luka's strength begins to falter.

Noticing Grisha gaining dominance over Luka while she dodges a blow, Madisyn pulls out her own pistol and shoots Grisha in his side from across the room, continuing her own fight with several other students. She slices two across the chest with her knife and grabs one by the arm to flip him over her shoulder onto the floor, pulling her pistol from its holster to shoot him in the face.

Luka pushes an injured Grisha off him, knocking the dagger from the commandant's hand and finally slitting his throat open after a long unyielding fight, blood spurting as Grisha rolls onto his back, clutching his throat. His rage was taking absolute control of his body. Luka continuously stabs Grisha in the stomach over and over until the commandant's blood covers his face and hands. Luka pants as he examines the damage done to the very person in that very school who had once caused him so much trouble.

Among the havoc, Valentina looks up from just taking out the last nearby student and notices the headmaster still standing at the front of the room, paralyzed and utterly disturbed by his crumbling empire. Grabbing a dagger from a dead girl on the ground, Valentina stands and moves toward the man, her eyes locked on him. The old man sees Valentina coming toward him, and his eyes widen, knowing he is too weak and vulnerable to fight her. He yells angrily at the top of his lungs from his own frustration, as if he knew that this was the end. Getting to him, Valentina effortlessly drives her dagger through his heart, holding it there to watch his eyes grow bigger. She snatches it from his chest, and as he falls over, she slashes the old man across the face in one more lethal blow that leaves his nose hanging off his wrinkled face.

Valentina runs over to her brother and the UCOCA team, who have just finished taking out the rest of the students. She hugs Luka tightly, and he stands there, still in shock and unable to wrap his arms around her just yet. Luka pulls away, trying to catch his breath. "Why did you come back here?" he demands.

Valentina raises her eyebrows, thrown off by his response at first but understanding its origin. She blamed herself for not coming sooner more than he had, but even so, she only hoped they could move past it as if no time had passed. "You're my brother, Luka!" she says, holding his blood-covered face in her hands. "And I love you. I'm glad it wasn't too late." She grabs him again to embrace him.

"Guys!" Marcie shouts, breaking their tender moment. "We should leave right now!" The hall around them begins to fill with smoke from the fire. The five of them run toward the doors, fleeing through the burning school. They run down a flight of stairs and down a long hallway, but turning the corner, the group halt in their tracks as the approaching fire tears through, causing the brick to crumble around them. Spinning quickly on their heels back in the opposite direction, they turn down another hallway only to find it completely filled with black smoke and making it hard to breathe.

"Shit!" Robbie croaks through loud coughs.

"This way!" Luka instructs them. "Hurry!" He leads them down a long, winding hallway and down another set of spiral stairs until they come to an opening in the stairwell that overlooks the school grounds. Without hesitation, Luka leaps onto the ledge. He presses his body against the wall and reaches out for a protruding brick, using it along with similar ones to descend the fifteen-foot castle wall. The others follow suit, all of them getting to the ground with ease. Taking off again in full-out sprints, they head around the grandiose structure—black smoke seeping from its crevices—all the way to the back of the school.

"Look!" Vasyl shouts, pointing ahead as he spots a large opening in the thirty-foot wall. He laughs. "That must be Borysko's doing!" The group heads toward the opening, hopping over the crumbled pieces of brick out toward the forest.

A group of nearby loyal Russians, who had escaped the burning school early on and are now gathered together around the back, spot the team of foreigners getting away. "After them!" one of them calls. They run toward the forest after their escaped prisoners, some of the Russians stopping at a nearby shed first to retrieve *Volk* division's blood-thirsty trained wolves.

Getting to the tree line, Vasyl spots his Ukrainian team ahead—Borysko, Yaryna, Pavlo, and six others. As assumed,

Borysko leans against a tall grenade launcher, which he had used to blast the school's wall to pieces for the UCOCA team's easy escape. "We have to go! Go now! Run!" Vasyl yells toward them, motioning for them to take off. "They're not far behind!"

Robbie, remembering his secret weapon, pulls out the detonator and flips off the protective case to push the button, blowing the school behind them to pieces and instantly killing a few of the Russians nearest the school as well as anyone still inside. The shock wave throws the rest of them to the ground. Lying on his back, Robbie hollers happily at the top of his lungs and tosses the detonator into the air. Marcie groans, holding her head from the ringing in her ears, a few others doing the same.

Struggling to help one another get to their feet, the UCOCA team spots a large number of Russian students safely beyond the wall, who have some trouble themselves getting back up. The team immediately takes off running again, all their strides a little hindered from the explosion. Borysko lingers back a moment with his grenade launcher. He places it on his shoulder and shoots back toward the Russians, striking a significant portion of the group in the front and slowing down the others.

Far into the trees, the rebel Russian students—including the three Swierczynsky brothers, Yakov, Rurik, and Ivanna—take off in a different direction nearby, oblivious to the UCOCA agents running with Luka behind them. In the back of the group, though, Ivanna peers over her shoulder as she starts to trail behind. She spots Luka's blond hair and immediately spins around to run after him. Rurik catches her change of direction from the corner of his eye and breaks away from the group to chase after her.

"Ivanna!" Rurik calls. "Don't be stupid!"

As the Russians and their wolves start to catch up with their escaped prisoners, the Ukrainian UCOCA agents whip out futuristic contraptions manufactured in their own weapons lab back home to look mostly like normal guns but with wide barrels to shoot deadly balls of electricity. They shoot back while running, electrocuting some of the Russians with colorful sparks and instantly killing them. The trained wolves pull ahead of the Russian students with more powerful strides and catch up to the team, one of them leaping in the air toward Yaryna, who turns to shoot it mid-air, the wolf lighting up with fiery blue electricity. Another wolf tackles Pavlo, and Robbie shoots it with his pistol, swiftly helping Pavlo to his feet to keep going. Marcie turns back, noticing Robbie's delay, just as another wolf bounds toward her, snarling with bared teeth. Knowing she doesn't have another choice—shoot or be eaten alive—she stands with both hands on her weapon and unloads ten bullets into the beast's face, blowing its head to pieces. Marcie shrieks at the explosion of wolf guts flying at her, covering her face.

Madisyn runs faster to pass her sister, laughing. "You're such a girl!" she screams.

"Just ahead!" Borysko yells at the group. "Grab the boards!" He points in the direction of their transportation: several metallic flying boards resting against the trees, which had been Pavlo's idea, having been mentally defeated one too many times by his previous long trek through the woods. Alerted by an internal GPS, the boards light up as the team approaches, making them easier to spot in the darkness of the forest.

A few Ukrainian agents speed ahead of the group, grabbing their boards and hopping on while running—the boards sweeping them off the ground and zipping them at lightning speed through the trees. The others behind continue running toward them, with the Russians just on their heels now from being slowed down. Ivanna dodges balls of electricity flying back at her as she catches up to them.

"Luka!" she screams his name. "Luka, wait! *Podozhdi!*" Luka turns his head back while running, Valentina pulling him along by his arm. Rurik, still running behind her, screams after Ivanna to no use—her eyes only ahead on Luka. "Luka, don't leave me! Please!"

Luka stops to turn around. Valentina attempts to pull him near one of the flying boards, but he only stares back at Ivanna, panting and not knowing what to do. He was so confused. He wanted to want her, but he had taught himself for so long that he shouldn't. So why did he feel so conflicted now amidst the danger all around them? Making a decision was crucial for him, and yet, he couldn't. He didn't know what to do.

"For fuck's sake, Luka!" Valentina shrieks at him, pulling him out of his own head. "Don't do this again, *please!*"

"Come on!" Madisyn shouts to them. "Don't slow down!" She whizzes past Valentina and Luka—the twins, Robbie, and Vasyl all grabbing their boards and hopping on them to fly away to safety.

The last of the Ukrainian agents running toward them continue to shoot back when one of their shots hits Ivanna, her body lighting up with green electricity before she falls to the ground. Luka's face twists in horror.

"*Ivanna!*" he shouts. Luka attempts to run to her, but Valentina yanks him by the arm, causing him to fall to the ground. He yells in Ivanna's direction, only now allowing himself to feel the emotions he had wished he could accept just minutes ago before it was too late. His fight weakens, numb to her death, and Valentina—with the help of Borysko and Yaryna—manages to shove him onto a board. The flying board whisks Luka off into the air, and he holds on to the side instinctively, his other arm reaching back toward Ivanna as he cries out her name one last time. Valentina and the last of the UCOCA agents fly out behind him before the Russians can reach them.

"Where'd they go?" one of the Russian students demands. "*Blyat'*!"

Only a few feet back, Rurik reaches Ivanna's body, still sparking with electricity. Her face is frozen in a stunned look with eyes and mouth open, her arm still reaching out toward Luka. Rurik falls to his knees at her side, his teeth clenched and tears spilling from his eyes. Rurik looks out toward the direction he last saw Luka, his nostrils flaring as reality sets in. He had just sealed a terrible fate for himself: he would probably die out there in the middle of the forest with a group of brainwashed students who didn't care about him or even each other, and it wouldn't be anyone else's fault but his own.

Having reached the dirt road on the other side of the forest, the UCOCA agents load into parked vehicles as Luka's board comes zipping out from the trees. The board crashes into the ground, throwing him off, and Luka rolls across the dirt, coughing. Madisyn hops out of her vehicle and runs to help him as Valentina, and the last of the agents come flying in, all landing their boards smoothly and hopping right off. Overwhelmed with emotion, Luka shoves Madisyn away and gets to his feet himself.

"Get off of me!" he yells at her through tears. Madisyn backs away, pursing her lips. Valentina hurries toward them.

"Luka!" she hisses. "She is our friend."

"You shouldn't have come here!" he argues. "I didn't ask for your help!"

Turning his back to them, Luka takes in his surroundings. The empty countryside seems to go on for miles. He bends over, resting his hands on his knees and letting his head fall as uncontrollable sobs flow out of him. Valentina kneels before him, tenderly touching his tear-stained face with her hand.

"I know how long it has been," she says to him, her eyes forming tears herself. "Look at you... I have missed so many years of your life—my sweet, sweet boy. I hardly recognized you. I am so sorry for abandoning you, Luka."

Luka moves her arm away to fully stand up again, Valentina doing the same. He keeps his gaze down as she hugs him tightly, his face contorting as if in pain from holding back more tears. She pulls back, still holding his arms.

"I am so glad I have you again," she whispers, squeezing his arms. "You're safe now, brother. Come, I'll show you." Valentina moves away and heads over to one of the vehicles, hoping for him to follow.

Luka lingers, staring into the dark countryside with torment colored across his cheeks and showing in the furrowed skin between his brows. He didn't know how he was supposed to feel, having his old life ripped away from him and being forced into this new one... one without Ivanna, whom he hadn't even appreciated or possibly deserved in the first place. And now he was being ungrateful for his sister returning to rescue him when he should have been thanking her. Eleven years had passed, though, which was enough time for Luka to harbor a lot of resentment toward his older sister, thinking she had abandoned him once and for all, and thinking she would never return. He hated how much thinking he was doing lately. It had gotten Ivanna killed, and it had almost gotten him killed in front of the entire school.

Luka shakes his head, hoping to wash away the flood of thoughts pouring one after the other into his mind. He squeezes his eyes shut for a moment, hearing one of his rescuers tell the others they had to leave now before it was too late. Luka winces, the feeling taking him back to his first years at The Trinity, surrounded by strangers who insisted they were doing what was best for him. He no longer knew what information to trust, but at that moment, he had no other choice—nowhere else to go. Finally, Luka turns around and heads to the car where his sister is waiting for him and gets inside.

CHAPTER 19

———

Late at night inside the Montevega villa, Mackenzie walks through the dark halls upstairs eating an apple. Moving past the twins' bedroom toward her own, she pauses in the hallway. Her head swivels back, lingering on the doors to the bedroom. She hadn't heard another update on her younger sisters, and the anticipation was eating away at her.

Mackenzie pushes through the double doors to reveal a posh suite much bigger than her own. The twins essentially had their own mini luxury apartment inside the Montevega home. Even though Mackenzie was the eldest, her parents had insisted on giving the more spacious room to the twins since they shared a space and were home more often due to their homeschooling schedule. Mackenzie grimaces as she takes in the grandeur of a room that should have rightfully been hers.

She moves through the dark space lit only by the beams of moonlight pouring in from the balcony doors. Biting into her apple with one hand, she lets the fingertips of her other brush over the soft gray fur draped across a glass banner that separated the rest of the bedroom from the modern lounge area. Moving around it and holding on to its rail, she steps down three stairs—glowing faintly from the light panels underneath—into the sunken living space where a white, leather, three-piece sectional sofa faces an eighty-five-inch flat-screen television sitting inside the wall.

On either side of the television were two rectangular jellyfish tanks. Mackenzie stands in front of one, observing the gentle creatures pulsing up and down inside a glowing tank shifting from green to pink to blue. She moves to the couch and plops down in the middle, accidentally sitting on a remote control wedged between the pillows, which immediately flicks on the television.

Mackenzie leans forward on the sofa's edge, staring at four camera screens showing on the television—two of them inside the room (one staring right at her from the corner of the lounge area) and two in rooms she had never seen before (one which looked more like a lab and the other a room filled with weapons). Her jaw drops. She knew her sisters partook in unconventional self-defense classes but had no idea they owned firearms or that they kept them on hand inside a secret vault! She waves her hand at the camera pointed in her direction, watching herself in the top right corner of the screen.

"Fuck!" she breathes in awe, leaving the television on as she moves back up the stairs to snoop around the rest of the bedroom.

She approaches one of two round, white pillars sitting atop a Corinthian capital, which marked the entrance of the vast, neutral-toned space of Madisyn's boudoir. Above the entrance and printed on the wall in bold black cursive ink lies a famous Vincent van Gogh quote, clearly a motto Mackenzie knew her younger sister lived to the fullest:

I would rather die of passion than of boredom.

Peering behind her, a matching area in pale pink tones marks Marcie's side of the suite. Mackenzie traces her fingers across the intricate gold engravements in the pillar, her finger just stopping short of the switch that would reveal the secret rooms below when the fax machine on the twins' desk whirs to life. Mackenzie locks her gaze on the source of the sound, seeing papers fall from the slim, white machine one after the other into a neat pile. She slinks toward the glass desk, picking up one of the documents as it prints out.

Squinting at the document written exclusively in Russian—she had not learned Slavic languages and opted for French and Italian instead at her boarding school—Mackenzie shakes her head. "Who is Yaroslav Sudnik?" she whispers, reading the name.

Her eyes flutter to the bottom of the page, where she recognizes the Rossi car dealership emblem of two spread wings, but with the word "UCOCA" in the place where "ROSSI" should be. Her forehead wrinkles further, perplexed by the acronym and how it could be connected with her mother's global luxury car dealership. She picks up another page in Russian and sees the same emblem at the bottom, realizing it is printed on every page. Huffing in frustration, she snatches up the first page from the desk and spins around to leave, only breaking her direction toward the double doors to quickly move down into the sunken living space again and flick off the television showing the camera screens.

Moving with purpose through the hallway, Mackenzie reaches her father's upstairs office, a much smaller space with no windows and walls lined with books. She flops down behind the desk and turns on the iMac desktop computer, pulling up an internet browser and searching for the name Yaroslav Sudnik. A Google search pulls up the picture of an older gentleman who looked to be in his late eighties. The caption under it informs her that Sudnik is the headmaster of a boarding school in Russia called The Trinity. Mackenzie scoffs.

"Why on earth would those little brats be involved with a boarding school?" she whispers, squinting at the document again and failing yet again to read its Russian babble. "God, they're such freaks…"

Her gaze drifts for a moment, thinking of how much she despised her younger sisters for always having the best of everything, even if it was learning absurd languages that she had no interest in. She smirks, remembering how little her parents seemed to know of the twins' whereabouts. At least it wasn't personal. They seemed to care about the twins as much as they did for her.

Refocusing, Mackenzie looks at the paper again and the emblem at the bottom. She sets it down, and Google searches "UCOCA," only to find a dead end as the browser pulls up a bunch of links to a musical artist. Mackenzie rests her chin on her hand, knowing there had to be another way to find the information she wanted. She suddenly remembers from early on in her extended "gap year" at home snooping around the mansion; she had been looking around her father's office one day, eager to use his state-of-the-art computer system, and came across a classified government program he apparently had exclusive access to. Uninterested in whatever unsettling reasons were possibly behind her father being given access in the first place, Mackenzie thanked the heavens for her family's high-class standing to be privy to such things.

She pulls up the confidential program, easily entering the saved password, and maneuvers through its intricate setup page to find a search engine. She types in the word again and, this time, finds her search to be more relevant and satisfying, further feeding her flagrant appetite for dirt on her sisters. "UCOCA," she reads. "A possible crime organization responsible for a string of related incidents involving wealthy targets."

After clicking on the group's hyperlink, the program takes her to a list of potential crimes related to UCOCA:

1. *Geneva, Switzerland. Target: Benjamin Cook (Businessman, American asylum seeker), found dead.*
2. *Monte Carlo, the Principality of Monaco. Target: Henri Duchamp (Financial Manager), found dead.*
3. *Vancouver, Canada. Targets: Don Berton (Businessman), body not recovered; Norman Bell (Chemical Engineer), body not recovered.*
4. *Amsterdam, the Netherlands. Targets: Simon Holwarda (Scientist), found alive (sedated); Frederik van Leeuwenhoek (Businessman), found dead.*
5. *Palermo, Italy. Target: Valerio Ramazotti (Software Developer), found dead.*
6. *Mantiqueira Mountains, Brazil. Target: Mattheus Azevedo (Businessman), body not recovered.*
7. *New York City, New York. Targets: Kennedy Hilton (Judge), found alive (sedated); Alfred Peterson Wilkes (Businessman), found dead.*
8. *Los Angeles, California. Targets: Patrick McLean (Senator), found alive (sedated); Jacquard "Jay" Saunders (Senator), found alive (sedated); Giovanni Sacchi (Soccer Coach, Men's National Team), found alive (sedated).*

Mackenzie finds links to all of them, scrolling quickly through each added page of juicy details, except the very last entry in California, which has a small note stating, "Currently under investigation, more to follow." Overwhelmed with information, she sits back in the desk chair, looking from the computer screen to the document on the desk. She couldn't think of a possible explanation to connect her younger sisters with what she was looking at, but somehow, she figured it would do her some good to hang on to all her new findings. The documents had great potential for blackmail if nothing else. The only problem now, as their big sister, was deciding what exactly she wanted in return.

CHAPTER 20

———

Inside his hotel room in Russia, and dressed in a rolled sleeve button-down with jeans, Detective Harding whips out two crystal glasses and a bottle of premium vodka in preparation for his date. He had stayed inside the suite all day, and staring at the map on his laptop had simply driven him out of his mind. He knew that a distraction was just what he needed to pass the time and thus called a highly recommended dating service suggested in an awkward encounter with the man across the hall. He was an overweight Russian businessman wearing a robe much too small for his figure and a mustache that made him look like someone's creepy uncle. The two men had both ordered room service and were given each other's dinners by accident, stepping out into the hallway to run down the hotel dining staff at the same time. Harding was just grateful this encounter would lead to a night with a companion of a more feminine charm than with his overly hairy across-the-hall mate.

He sets the alcohol on the table in front of the television and flips on the stereo. "Brianstorm" by Arctic Monkeys—a band that made him feel like he was twenty again—blasts a cool, jazzy tune from the stereo as he struts to the bathroom mirror to smooth his hair with some gel. He pops open one of the top buttons on his shirt to reveal a little chest hair.

A knock comes from the door, making him whip around. He moves to his laptop on the desk first, ensuring for the last time that the trackers had not moved on the map before partially closing the lid. Another knock sounds and Harding takes a deep breath, moving toward the door. He opens it to reveal his late-night guest: a busty blonde escort leaning seductively against the doorway in a tiny, shimmering dress.

A HALF HOUR LATER
Laughing obnoxiously together on the couch, Harding takes the drunk prostitute's glass away and sets it down on the table. He pulls her in for a long drunken kiss, trying not to think about how long he had gone without human touch.

HOURS LATER
Both Harding and his guest are passed out, half-naked, and sprawled across each other on the couch. Across the room, the laptop *pings*—an alert he had set to indicate sudden movement of the red dots on the map. The blinking red dots travel north of Krasnodar and through Ukrainian borders, settling for less than an hour in Kiev and then continuing west over Poland.

EARLY MORNING
Harding stirs awake mid-snore. In a haze, he looks around the room as if to remember last night's events. His cloudy gaze makes its way over to the sleeping woman next to him, impressed even in his sober state of his absolute catch—even with her heavy coat of makeup smudged, she was stunning…

and quite possibly younger than the detective would typically deem appropriate for a bachelor of his age.

Flipping on the television, he slides out from under the woman, donning his briefs before moving to the kitchen area to fix a pot of coffee. He holds his face in his palms, moaning from his killer vodka-induced hangover as the coffee brews, its soothing rumble into the carafe calming him, and the pungent aroma filling his nostrils. He impatiently grabs the carafe mid-brew and pours the brown liquid into a mug, replacing the glass and causing the machine to hiss and whir as it brews the rest of the ground beans.

With his hot cup of coffee in hand, Harding moves to sit on the couch again. He grabs the remote and flips through the channels, settling on a local news station, the woman next to him stirring from her sleep as the television flashes "Breaking News" banners. A reporter rambles in Russian as Harding follows the English subtitles across the screen:

"The Trinity boarding school, roughly thirty kilometers outside the city of Krasnodar, was found burned to ashes earlier this morning. The smoke could be seen from the city, attracting the attention of nearby construction workers who called in the report. Local law enforcement and firefighters made their way out to the school and to put out fires, which spread quickly through nearby forests. Many seared bodies were found dead inside the school and in the forest, including several students as well as what the police believe to be Headmaster Yaroslav Sudnik..."

Harding chokes on his coffee, spilling it all over himself and the woman, who screams and shoves him away. She scurries to grab her clothes from the floor, but her dress is already stained brown.

Rushing over to his laptop, Harding opens it to see the moving dots on the map, moving at a steady pace over Germany. "*Fuck!*" he yells, slamming his fists on the desk.

Holding her soaked clothes, the woman runs up behind him. "What the hell is your problem?" she says in Russian. The detective does not understand her words but winces at her tone. "You're paying for my clothes, asshole!"

Harding rushes past her to grab his wallet, figuring he should compensate her for the night and her ruined clothes. He grabs a few large bills and shoves the money at her, guiding her to the door.

"You have to go now," he says, opening the door and pushing her through it. "I have a plane to catch." The woman hits him and curses in Russian as he slams the door in her face, leaving her in her underwear in the hallway.

CHAPTER 21

———

Having parted ways with their Ukrainian comrades, the UCOCA team finds themselves inside their private jet with their new guest. Luka stares out the plane's window, every now and then peering over to the twins and Robbie with heightened suspicion. The three teenagers remain focused on their phones and new-age social apps, something Luka simply could not relate to.

"Hmm, that's strange," Madisyn says, tinkering on her mobile device. Marcie looks over at her. "Someone's been snooping inside our room." She shows her sister the phone screen, having accessed the cameras to show Mackenzie moving about.

"Did she get into the armory?" Marcie asks, her eyes wide. "I thought you locked our doors!"

"I thought *you* locked them," Madisyn retorts defensively.

Valentina comes out of the cockpit and walks over to them. She holds out her own mobile to the twins. "Your sister called me eight times," she informs them blankly. "Call her back."

Marcie's jaw drops. "She *never* calls. What should we do?" She looks to her twin for an answer. "She's supposed to think we're studying for A Levels, for Christ's sake!"

Madisyn rolls her eyes and snatches the phone. "Snap it together, Marcelle. She probably just got arrested for doing something stupid with those stuck-up friends of hers, and now she's calling us to bail her out." Valentina purses her lips and moves to sit in a seat across the aisle from the four of them. "Mackenzie is harmless. Don't get your knickers in a twist." Marcie rolls her eyes and stares out the window.

Luka watches the twins, studying them closely and comparing them to the girls he knew at The Trinity. His eyes land on Marcie—who sits across from him next to the window, oblivious to his staring—though Madisyn looks up from both mobiles in her hand. She watches Luka ogling her sister and furrows her brows, slightly offended that he wasn't ogling her instead. Across from Madisyn and next to Luka, Robbie looks up and catches Madisyn's gawking. He looks over to the boy next to him as well but quickly turns back to his phone as Luka's stare shifts over to Madisyn.

The two hold their gazes on each other, neither backing down nor succumbing to the other's intimidation. Luka tilts his head curiously, observing Madisyn and wondering what kind of freak she must have thought he was. A sly smirk sneaks across Madisyn's lips. This was the first time she had really looked at him, and maybe the first time he had really seen her too. Luka was cuter than she had expected him to be with the blood cleaned off his face: he had a chiseled jaw and tousled blond hair, with gray eyes as piercing as a wolf's hungry gaze.

Robbie looks back up at Luka and Madisyn, shifting uncomfortably in his seat. He shouldn't have cared as much, but he still hated seeing Madisyn ogle other guys, though not as much as he hated seeing Marcie ogled by other guys. He clears his throat loudly, causing Marcie to finally turn her gaze from the window and also notice Luka and Madisyn's locked eyes on each other now. Marcie narrows her eyes at her sister's gall. Who did Madisyn think she was? Coming on to Valentina's little brother like that!

Valentina looks over, noticing silent tension in the air-craft's cabin. "Luka…" she calls to her brother. He slowly breaks his gaze with Madisyn, looking over to his sister. She motions for him with her hand. "Come sit by me for a while."

Luka turns back to the three of them as if to get the final glance of their stare down but then gets up to sit by Valentina, the two siblings engaged in a hushed conversation in Russian.

Madisyn huffs and gives her sister and Robbie one last scolding glare before turning her attention back to the second phone in her hand. She dials their older sister's number and waits for her to answer.

Back inside the Montevega villa, Mackenzie eavesdrops behind a doorway, listening to her mother argue with Detective Harding on speakerphone when her own cell phone vibrates. Seeing Valentina's number on her screen, she steps further away from the room to answer it.

"Hello, Mackenzie," Madisyn addresses her in a bored tone.

"You two are in a world of trouble," Mackenzie says, surprised at hearing her sister's voice instead of Valentina's.

"Whatever do you mean," Madisyn says in more of an uninterested tone. This was not a question she was actually interested in knowing the answer to.

Mackenzie puts a hand on her hip, holding her chin up with a satisfied smirk. "I just hope you weren't lying about where you were. You see, Mum and Dad had a detective track you both down, and they don't seem to like the news he's giving them right now."

Madisyn laughs cockily at this. "You're lying," she says firmly. "Why would Mum and Dad even *care* about where we were? And how would some silly detective even begin to 'track us down,' hmm?" The others immediately cease their outside conversations to stare at Madisyn, who only rolls her eyes and waved the comment off. "She's full of shit," she mouths to a worried-looking Marcie.

"You only *wish* I was lying!" Mackenzie says in a strained tone. She looks over her shoulder cautiously to make sure her mother is still occupied. "Our parents put tracking devices in both of your teeth ages ago and had you sedated so you wouldn't even remember. And now this detective is on the phone telling Mum how you guys are involved in some kind of criminal activity in Russia! He says you burned down a school! And then I found these weird documents in your room talking about some headmaster over a boarding school in Russia. Is that just supposed to be a coincidence? And what on earth is UCOCA? And why is it using the same emblem as Rossi? You sure do have a lot of explaining to do!"

While paralyzed in her seat, the phone still pressed to her ear, Madisyn does not speak. Her eyes dart up to meet Robbie's across from her, who is leaning in rather hard, straining to hear their conversation. Madisyn sucks on the inside of her cheek, knowing they were in quite the predicament if people as clueless as her older sister and her mother knew what they were up to, let alone a detective—someone with a more threatening position to take them down. She had always assumed law enforcement were just as ignorant to their actions as their family. They were always careful to be discreet on missions, though she remembered seeing some of the tabloids which aimed to accuse her and her twin of always being in the same location as a high-profile murder. Those damn sleuthy gossip columnists...

"Um, hello?" Mackenzie says into the phone. "Are you still there? Have you gone bloody mute?"

Madisyn swallows hard before speaking, lowering her voice this time while attempting to speak rather calmly. "Are Mum and Dad in the room with you?"

From the hallway of their home, Mackenzie's face distorts. She scoffs at the question. "No. Do you think I'm stupid?" She waits but receives no answer from her younger sister. "Since when did you lose your will to speak, Madisyn? You're usually a very outspoken girl. It's quite annoying, actually but I've become rather used to it, so *spill*." She examines her cuticles, flexing and bending her hand in front of her, quite satisfied with the corner she had surely backed her sisters into.

Madisyn pauses again before speaking, four sets of eyes glued to her. "We never had this conversation," she says calmly to her sister.

"What?" Mackenzie asks, not understanding. "What are you going on about, Madisyn?"

"I said we *never* had this conversation!" she repeats quickly. Madisyn slams her finger on the phone to end the call, everyone in the cabin of the plane looking at her.

On the other end, Mackenzie puffs, not realizing her sister had hung up. "Don't think I don't know what you're up to because—I *know*!" She rips the phone from her ear and stomps down the hallway to brew up her next attack.

Madisyn glances from her twin to Robbie to Valentina and even over to Luka. Robbie leans all the way forward, practically falling off the edge of his seat. "*What the fuck?*" he mouths slowly.

"Madisyn, what's happened?" Marcie translates for him.

She opens her mouth to speak but then closes it, taking a deep breath first. She closes her eyes and swallows. "There are tracking devices on our molars. Mine and Marcelle's," she reveals, opening her eyes finally and watching the rest of theirs grow.

"*What?*" Robbie shouts.

"Wait!" Marcie interjects, thinking quickly. "Maybe it's not an issue. I mean, it's not like anyone was looking for us, right?"

Madisyn swallows hard again before answering. "About that…" Robbie lets his head fall back with a groan. "There's a detective involved," she continues. "Who *may* have been tracking us while we were in Russia."

"Maybe he doesn't know anything," Marcie says, naive hope in her voice. Robbie's face distorts at her utter stupidity.

Valentina shakes her head quickly, everyone looking at her. "We have to get them out."

"*What?*" Marcie shouts. Madisyn only fidgets with her fingers.

"We don't know what this detective knows," Valentina adds. "But if we get the devices out, if this person has evidence connecting your location with the school—which it sounds like they do," she looks to Madisyn, who only refuses to look over at her, confirming the answer she needed. "Then it will no longer be valid because we'll make it so the devices were never on you. If they can't find them in your teeth, all of their evidence becomes invalid."

Robbie breathes loudly. "That sounds wicked insane, V."

"There are no other options," Valentina says firmly. "We'll get them out. Before the plane lands." Marcie sighs and looks at her sister. Madisyn's eyes float up to meet Valentina's.

"How, exactly?" Madisyn asks cautiously, not actually wanting to know the answer. Valentina doesn't respond and instead gets up and moves to the back of the plane, disappearing behind the curtain. The others exchange anxious looks.

After a short moment, the flight attendant, an older Ukrainian woman, comes through the back door of the plane with Valentina. Everyone turns to face them. "I am not a licensed dentist," the woman confesses with a thick Ukrainian accent. "But I have worked with teeth."

Robbie breathes loudly, wheezing with amusement. The twins stare at her, their mouths dropping open in scoffs. "Absolutely *not*!" they protest in unison.

Valentina shakes her head at them, her face stern. "You don't have a choice."

Only moments later, Madisyn finds herself strapped to a chair, leaned all the way back. Luka keeps her mouth pried open with a metal contraption as the flight attendant stands over them, holding a sharp tool. The woman flips on the tool, and it buzzes loudly. Madisyn's eyes widen at the sound, and she squirms in her seat. The others stand around her, watching, Marcie covering her mouth to keep from screaming. Leaning in, the woman gives a toothy grin before getting to work, Madisyn letting out an earsplitting squeal and squeezing her eyes shut.

Recovering from a horrific and painful episode, the twins sit back in their original seats, holding ice packs to their sore cheeks. Valentina comes out of the back of the plane. She extends her hand toward them, revealing two microchips.

"Your tracking devices," she says. The twins moan and roll their eyes, refusing to take them. Robbie laughs, both grateful and amused that no such foreign object was found in his mouth.

"We have to get rid of them," Luka suggests in English. Everyone turns to him, surprised at his sudden will to speak without his native tongue.

"Yes… yes, you're right, Luka," Valentina agrees. She gives him a warm smile. "What do you suggest?"

"Improvised explosive?" Robbie says quickly.

Luka furrows his brows at the suggestion, taking the microchips from his sister. He goes to the back of the plane and rummages through the cabinet. Pulling out a set of brass knuckles from the twins' secret stash of emergency weapons, Luka slides them onto his hand. He pops out a small table from inside the cabin wall and places the microchips on it, immediately bringing his brass-covered fist down and crushing the devices to tiny bits. Scooping the pieces into his palm, Luka moves over to an opening on the floor and slides back the door, the wind blowing up in his face. He opens his fist and lets the crushed devices drop into the English Channel below them. Luka secures the door again and stands up, suddenly halting as he notices the eyes staring at him.

"Well…" Robbie breathes, quite impressed at Luka's rather simplistic but efficient approach. "That certainly works."

Luka moves to sit back down in his original seat next to the window. Marcie removes her ice pack from her cheek, looking at him. "Has my face gone back to normal?" She beams at Luka, who only looks at her rather oddly. He turns to stare out the window instead. Marcie frowns at this, Robbie pursing his lips with raised eyebrows.

"Well then," Robbie concludes. "I'm going for a quick nap." He moves to the back to rest on the couch, mostly to avoid being next to the strange boy. Madisyn gets up to talk with Valentina, leaving her sister alone with Luka. Marcie looks at him again.

"What are you thinking right now?" She asks him in Russian.

Luka turns to her hesitantly at first. He studies her face before responding in his native tongue. "Everything I knew—my entire way of life... it's all gone now. And I don't know how to... I don't know what to think."

Marcie frowns sympathetically. "This can't be easy for you. Honestly, I didn't think you could be turned over to our side in there... none of us did really, except Valentina." Luka winces. Marcie leans in closer. "You understand that there is no headmaster for you to follow anymore, Luka. You're free."

His eyes narrow, and he leans in closer to her. "You don't understand what it's like to have everything you've ever known stripped away from you. All in less than a day. And to just be expected to go along with some new life and 'freedom' a couple of strangers think they can give you." He shakes his head.

"Are you saying your sister is a stranger?" Marcie questions. "Because a stranger couldn't have gotten you to turn against those people that you thought were your family for your entire life—"

"You don't know anything," Luka snaps.

Marcie sits back in her seat. Luka sits back, too, keeping his eyes on her. He couldn't help feeling envious of the girl—of all of them actually. They seemed to live a life so utterly filled with choices, so much that they had made the decision to come to rescue him. But that was just it—Luka hated being the one to be rescued. He should have been able to take care of himself.

"You only have us now, Luka," Marcie says. "You have to trust us. Or else it's you, against the entire world."

Luka shakes his head again, his mind muddled by the entire situation. They couldn't have been normal teenagers for them to carry out an act like this. They were gutsy, sort of like spies in a way, but they were also nothing like the people he once knew his whole life. "What are you guys anyway?" he asks.

Marcie smiles at him. "We're your friends now."

Less than an hour later, the jet slows on the runway as Robbie stirs from his nap and peeks out the window. "Shit!" he exclaims, fully awake again. "What are *they* doing here?"

The twins and Valentina move to the other side of the plane to look out the windows, spotting Reese, Bill, and Mackenzie standing outside in front of two black town cars.

"No one ever meets us at the airport!" Marcie says.

"They can't know about Luka," Valentina adds. She turns to her brother, speaking in Russian. "Wait in the back of the plane. I'll devise a plan to get you soon." He nods and hops up, disappearing behind the back curtain.

The others start to gather their bags. "Leave the money," Madisyn advises. "And the weapons. We'll come back to get them later." Robbie grabs the duffel bags from their trip to L.A. and stashes them in the back with Luka.

The four of them exit the plane and head over to the parked cars. "What's going on? Is something wrong?" Madisyn calls out in her most polite voice. Robbie and Marcie stare at her, surprised to hear such a girly, high-pitched tone coming from Madisyn. She shoots them a dirty look in return to act normal.

Reese embraces her daughters as they come up to her. "No, we're just here to take you home," she informs them. "Some awful man used very personal information to try and frame you all for some horrible crime."

The twins feign shock, gasping loudly. "What*ever* do you mean?" a wide-eyed Marcie says. Robbie rolls his eyes but offers Reese a concerned look himself.

"It doesn't matter anymore," their father adds. "Your mother almost had him fired when he came to us with the preposterous story! But we settled for a *very* long unpaid probation, didn't we, sweetheart?" Bill coos at his headstrong wife.

"Only after he agreed to drop those lousy accusations," Reese clarifies. "I would have had that man's life *destroyed* if it wasn't for your father."

"Oh Reese, imagine what the poor man makes in a year..." Bill says, clicking his tongue.

Robbie stifles a laugh. "I'm curious. How many millions did you drop on our behalf to clear such charges, Mrs. M?" The twins' and Valentina's heads swivel around to glare at him. "*What?*" he says, shrugging. "I'm just curious."

"That's not important, Robbie," Reese says with a smile. "The fact is you *all* come from substantial wealth, and no lowlife detective's word will *ever* be taken seriously against families like ours. Oh, and Robbie, we've mentioned none of this to your parents. No need to go getting them all worried over nothing." She raises a threatening eyebrow and turns to get inside the first car.

Robbie laughs, his gaze following Reese. "God," he breathes. "Your mum is so cool." Marcie scoffs, though Madisyn smirks in agreement.

Bill purses his lips and sighs. "Your mother was actually very worried, despite her hardened exterior. That psycho was saying you guys burned down a boarding school in Russia!"

Madisyn gushes, feeding off her father's energy, almost making fun of his complete ignorance. "Well, thank *God* you guys handled it! That's terrifying. However, could we get into Oxford with a crime like that on our records?" The twins and their father laugh while Robbie and Valentina exchange amused glances. Bill gets into the first car with his wife, and the twins follow.

Mackenzie rolls her eyes and scoffs, her gaze following the twins with suspicion. She turns back to Robbie and Valentina with crossed arms, looking them up and down. Without saying a word, Mackenzie spins on her heels and gets into the second car.

"Come, Robbie," Valentina says. The driver packs their bags inside the trunk. Valentina starts to get inside the second vehicle as well, but Robbie hesitates.

"I—I think I forgot something back in the plane," he stammers.

Valentina clears her throat, looking back slightly to see Mackenzie busy on her phone inside the car. "Why don't you go grab whatever it is, then, hmm? Quickly," she says. Robbie nods and runs back to the plane. Valentina slides into the backseat next to Mackenzie, who looks up distrustfully at her.

"So…" Mackenzie starts. "Where exactly *were* you guys?"

"Ukraine," Valentina answers firmly. "I have family there."

Mackenzie squints her eyes, sucking her cheeks in. "But Valentina, if you're Russian, how come your family lives in

Ukraine?" She asks, a little too sweetly. "Aren't there political issues between the two countries? Ukrainians *hate* Russians."

Valentina twists the corner of her mouth into an annoying smile. "My family moved there for a better life. Do you really believe those lies that detective spread?" she asks. "Maybe you should learn to start trusting your family."

"Why on earth would he *lie*?" Mackenzie retorts.

"Foolish Mackenzie…" Valentina sighs, shaking her head. "There are a lot of people out there who dislike your parents just because they're an extremely wealthy and powerful inter-racial couple. Don't think that people *wouldn't* try to use silly rumors to bring your family down."

Mackenzie sinks in her seat, unable to look at her. "Don't try to guilt me into believing you…I'll be keeping my eyes open," she warns weakly. She turns her attention back to dawdling on her phone.

Robbie comes running back out from the plane to join them in the car, leaving the door open behind him. He clears his throat, fidgeting with his hands. Mackenzie looks over at him after a few passing moments.

"Well…" she begins. "What did you forget?"

Robbie's mouth opens to speak, but he closes it. He digs into his pocket for a prop he can use, and to his dismay, he snatches out a pen—perhaps the plainest pen in the world if there ever was one so plain. He holds it up, chuckling at his own stupidity but going along with it. "My *lucky* pen," he states firmly, grinning at Mackenzie to keep from laughing.

Valentina squeezes her eyes shut, utterly irritated by his hopelessness, and Mackenzie narrows her eyes at him, tilting her head. She looks away from them both. "You're all completely full of shit," she retorts, rolling her eyes. Sighing, Robbie tucks his pen away, her gaze lingering on him. "What are you waiting for, then?" Mackenzie demands. "Close that door! Chop-chop! Mum and Dad's car already left!"

Valentina sucks on her teeth to keep from saying anything to either of them and reaches out to grab the door, pulling it shut. She throws Robbie a confused look, but he just gives her a small nod and pokes his lips out with absolute certainty.

The car begins to pull away when the pilot suddenly comes running from the plane with Luka trailing behind him, wearing a gray beanie to hide his distinctly blonde hair along with a pair of Robbie's black designer shades. The car comes to an abrupt halt, and Valentina's eyes grow at the sight of her brother. Smiling from ear to ear, Robbie rolls the window down.

"I am so sorry to bother you all," the pilot begins, as instructed. "But I was just wondering…" He grabs Luka by the shoulders and pulls him to the window. "I have an emergency and have to meet someone in a half hour. I was hoping maybe you could take my *nephew* home with you. I'll be back to pick him up as soon as I can. He shouldn't be any trouble."

Mackenzie looks at them all in disgust. Valentina instinctively forces a smile. "Of course!" she says to the pilot, trying to go along with Robbie's plan, even with how risky it was exposing Luka to an already suspicious Mackenzie. "He can stay in the guest house with me so as not to disturb the Montevegas." Luka gets inside the car, sitting across from Valentina and next to Robbie.

"Thank you so much!" the pilot exclaims dramatically. He smiles at Robbie, having done his part perfectly, and then turns to Luka once more. "I'll come to get you as soon as my meeting is over, all right then?" Luka nods, staying quiet. The man smiles at him and turns to the others. "He's quite shy. He probably won't speak much at all. Practically mute, this boy! And here is his luggage. I'll just load it into the trunk then, and you can be on your way." The pilot puts the duffle bags of money and weapons in the trunk of the vehicle and taps the back of the car, indicating they're good to go.

Inside the vehicle, Mackenzie stares at Luka, who avoids her by looking out the window, keeping his sunglasses on. Robbie leans forward to whisper to her. "Stop staring at him, Mackenzie," he scolds. "He's shy, remember?" Mackenzie scoffs at him, turning to stare out the window as well.

CHAPTER 22

Inside Valentina's home—across the glass bridge from the Montevega villa—Luka sits up in bed as his sister hooks his arm up to an IV, hoping to relieve him of his withdrawal symptoms from the *Uspet'*. "This should help stabilize your system," she speaks to him in Russian. "But you'll need treatment. I can pick something up in the morning to help for a while until we can find you a center."

Luka watches his sister's face, ignoring her comments about his health. "So, you trust them?" he asks.

She looks up at him and nods. "They're good people, Luka. I've been with them since I left. I raised the girls and Robbie. Their family is now my family. And with time, they'll be yours too."

His face scrunches in pain at this wild assumption. "The Trinity..." he says, "is all I know."

"You have to want to change, Luka," Valentina says. "Mentally, you have to want it. I was in that school as well. It will be hard at first, but I will help you to adjust. You just have to let me."

Luka's face falls away from hers. "It's just that..." He sighs heavily. "Ivanna..."

Valentina leans in close to him. "She was your friend?" Luka winces at the word. Valentina reaches out and squeezes his hand in hers.

"I don't know anything about love," Luka says. "But I cared for her." His eyes fill, but he clenches his jaw to hold back his tears. "Or at least I used to," he says, a tear escaping down his cheek. "I just—I don't know."

Valentina sighs. "I'm so sorry, Luka," she says softly. "And maybe it is selfish of me to say, but I'm glad you are here with me instead. You're my baby brother—and I should have never left without you."

She stands, leaning in to kiss his forehead before leaving.

In one of the reading rooms of the Montevega home, Mackenzie pretends to read a tabloid on the couch. She couldn't really fall asleep with everything on her mind. In fact, she could hardly read the pages she was staring at. All she could think about were the secrets her sisters were hiding, and how they might be more dangerous than she had thought them capable of. She begins to wonder when the right moment might arise for her to approach them about this UCOCA mystery just as the twins enter the room—almost as if they had read her mind. Mackenzie peers over her magazine as Madisyn and Marcelle come to stand right in front of her.

"I was waiting for you two," she informs them. "It's a miracle you aren't in prison by now, isn't it?"

Madisyn narrows her eyes at her older sister, ignoring her comment. "Mackenzie, we need your word on something."

Their older sister shuts the magazine and sits up, a sneer taking over her face. "Every secret has its price," she teases.

"We need you to *never* bring up that conversation about those tracking devices to anyone outside this family," Marcie says. "As far as you're concerned, you never even told us." Mackenzie narrows her eyes, looking from one twin to the other.

"And also, whatever documents you think you saw in our room," Madisyn adds. "Drop it. No one will believe you anyway."

Mackenzie glares at the two of them. "I don't know what horrible thing you two and Robbie and Valentina *actually* did, but I'll have you know—"

"If you tell anyone," Madisyn says, raising her voice, "then your little summer 'escapade' in Kavos last year might just slip out of our mouths to Mum and Dad. Or perhaps, the press? That would probably hurt you the most, wouldn't it?" Mackenzie jumps from her seat with balled fists, fuming.

"And we have the tape to prove it too," Marcie adds. "Naughty, *naughty* girl." She shakes her head, smirking.

"How do you even know about that?" she hisses.

Madisyn takes a step closer to her older sister, lowering her voice. "We're very skilled in finding useful information. So, if you know what's good for you, dear sister, you'll stay out of this," she warns.

Mackenzie shrieks. "*Ahh!* You two are *monsters!*" She grabs her magazine from the couch and storms past them, leaving the room.

The twins watch her go, a dark smile on Madisyn's face. Marcie frowns, though, turning back to her sister. "You don't think they'll be able to trace everything back to us, right?"

Madisyn snorts and laughs. "You have to stop worrying so much. Let's just be thankful our sister made a sex tape, and it just so happened to land right in our hands." They both laugh, though Marcie remains a little uneasy. Madisyn turns to go, but Marcie hesitates again.

"Don't you ever get scared?" she asks. "I mean, what would they do to us… if they *did* find out? We'd go to prison or something? Doesn't it worry you that a detective is on to us?" She lowers her voice. "What if they find out about V's brother?"

Madisyn grabs her twin by the shoulders. "No one is smart enough to beat us," she reminds her, narrowing her eyes. "We're indestructible. UCOCA, our legacy, is *gold.* We're in charge now." She drops her hands to squeeze Marcie's. "It's like I always told you, Marcie. If we want something, we take it. *We* rule the world. And the people around us are all too daft to do anything about it." She winks at her sister and turns to leave.

Marcie watches her go, anxiously fiddling with her hands. She didn't know how her twin could be so sure all the time. Mackenzie would be easy to keep quiet, but somehow, Marcie couldn't help thinking that their encounter with this detective would not be the last, and that if they weren't careful enough, it might just ruin them.

Lurking behind a corner and watching Madisyn go, Robbie steps inside the room. Marcie smiles warmly at him, grateful to have someone who could take her mind off everything. He comes up to her, his hands in his pocket. She had never seen him so shy before.

"What is it?" Marcie asks him with a laugh. "I thought for sure you had gone home," she lies, her gaze falling to her fidgeting hands. Robbie watches her carefully, his mouth open as though he wanted to say something but didn't know the exact right words. He steps closer to her, removing his hands from his pocket, and comes to stand right in front of her. Her gaze flickers up to his, his face mere inches from hers. She swallows hard.

Reaching out to touch her face tenderly, Robbie leans in and kisses her. Marcie feels her body sink into his in a way she hadn't felt before. Marcie raises a hand to touch his face as well, the two of them intertwined. Robbie gently pulls away, keeping his forehead pressed to hers. He takes a deep breath to calm his rapid heartbeat, letting his hands drop as Marcie takes them into her own and gives them a squeeze.

"Can we just... put everything that's happened before behind us?" she asks, embarrassed and ashamed of her behavior over the last couple of weeks—from rudely kissing Vasyl in front of him when Robbie was already in such a vulnerable state, to what Heidi had said to her at the football game about being too innocent and holding back. He had to be getting impatient with her by now after all that.

Robbie sighs, a laugh slipping out with it that causes Marcie to blush. He nods, his eyes flickering down for a moment and then back up to land on her. He should have wanted to tell her the truth—that she wasn't the one who had something to be sorry for—but at that moment, all he could do was be grateful to let the past be the past. "I'd like that."

Outside, in front of the Montevega villa in the circle driveway, Madisyn hops inside a sleek, yellow luxury sports car, brand new off the lot from the Rossi London dealership—just a little something she had treated herself to after completing two more successful missions. She pushes in the engine start button and listens as it roars to life, a smooth rumble that sends a rush of tingles down her spine. The Bluetooth from her mobile connecting with the vehicle, she turns up the volume as her professed anthem "Fade Away" by Logic comes on, the suave jingle in the background paired with seamlessly spoken lyrics that resonated with her goal of eternal fame and power pulling a smile across her lips.

Pressing smoothly on the gas—and with nowhere in particular in mind, as she had the whole world at her fingertips—Madisyn speeds down the long, winding driveway and off into the night.

ACKNOWLEDGMENTS

———

At the start of my publishing journey, I never knew how many people would be involved in the process of getting my novel on the shelf. As a writer, most of the time, you're alone through the process of getting your thoughts all out onto paper, but with more experience—and as you dive further into becoming a published author—you start to realize just how critical it is to have a strong support system.

First and foremost, thank you to my amazing family for being behind me no matter what. My parents have always supported my love of writing and my overall dreams of becoming a published author, and without them being there to back me up, I would not be where I am today. Thank you to my nana—a diehard lover of mysteries—for also encouraging me from the beginning to follow my heart. I will never forget that pink framed poster she had made for me as a child that affirmed my passion for writing stories and the importance of always keeping pen and paper on hand.

To my big sister Alexandria—the bookworm—thank you for exposing me to great books as a kid (even though I couldn't stand reading back then!), including some of my favorites that have inspired my writing: *The Luxe* series by

Anna Godbersen and *Artemis Fowl* by Eoin Colfer, to name a few. And Alex, thank you for being my most dedicated editor and beta reader—aside from my actual editor. Your opinion of my writing has meant so much to me. To see you pick up this manuscript and dive so far into this story, and actually care about it almost as much as I do, has allowed me to produce a work even greater than I had originally imagined. I appreciate you, sis!

Thank you to my amazing editor Kristin Gustafson for believing in my book since first reading chapter one! Having your praise was the first time I had actually heard someone's thoughts on this story, and it meant a lot to hear someone's unbiased opinion for once (I love my family but hearing someone other than my mom tell me how great my book is really struck an emotional chord).

To my best friend Yulia Bychkovska, gosh... where do I even begin? Thank you for not only your friendship and believing in my writing (before actually ever reading any of my writing!), but for being the person to lead me to my current publisher, New Degree Press. You know how much it meant for me to get my books published, and just when I had hit a wall and wanted to give up on submitting my work, you came through with this amazing reference to the Book Creators (Fall 2020) course led by Georgetown professor Eric Koester. Just from meeting with Eric and asking if I could submit my manuscript to NDP, who worked directly with the best writers from his book course, my book was greenlit for publishing! I would not be publishing this soon if it weren't for you, Yulia, and for that, I am forever grateful. Secondly, thank you for helping me with the Russian translations of this book. Google translate has nothing on you and Ester—I love you guys! To show my appreciation for the positive impact you've had on my life and book publishing journey, I last-minute created a character in your honor (if you can't guess, it's Yaryna Borisova from UCOCA-Ukraine, *obviously*) that I hope you love.

To my English professors at Columbia College—specifically Professor Christina Ingoglia and Dr. Pete Monacell—thank you all for believing in my talent! Even as a Communication major, my Creative Writing classes were my absolute favorite because they allowed me to explore my love for making up stories. I remember in our Creative Writing Fiction class, I actually worked on one of the scenes from this book (the one where the character of Luka Dementiev is first introduced in the Russian boarding school) and had so much fun letting the class workshop it, even while they didn't know it was part of a bigger novel! Professor I. and Dr. Monacell have played such a crucial role in honing both my writing (in the classroom) as well as my editing skills through my time as an editor for the Columbia College Literary Review. And like my own parents, while sometimes I may not have always seen eye-to-eye on their feedback, I know now just how important it was for them to be brutally honest with me. I would not have made it all the way to editor-in-chief of CCLR without their mentorship, and I would not be a published author either if it weren't for them helping me to find and develop my writing style.

To my Communication professor at CC, Dr. Amy Darnell, thank you for both the time as my teacher in the classroom and often my therapist (I mean, "college advisor"). Thank you for putting up with me as a Comm major who just couldn't contain her love for the English department! As a teacher, you were one of the first to help me realize how there is so much more to college and learning than just getting A's—while this was a hard lesson to learn GPA-wise, I really learned to appreciate this so much. Thank you for being there with me while I went through finding my love for filmmaking, directing, and screenwriting, even while I turned back around and came to realize my passion was more in writing books instead! Being able to go through all those film classes and my Senior Seminar project allowed me to have a newfound appreciation for the art of filmmaking and to realize I should leave it to the professionals—ha! I will never forget your undying love for *Thelma & Louise* and all the other action movies we never saw eye-to-eye on, though I hope one day when this book and the rest of the series are made into movies, it'll be one great film we can agree on.

Thank you to my bosses, both past and current. To Sarah Naji from Columbia College Student Affairs, thank you for taking me under your wing and allowing me to explore my passion for film at the time. Even while I may not go on to make movies, the time I spent as a leader in Student Affairs and making videos for our college has allowed me to develop my appreciation and love of this creative skill, which in turn has helped my writing tremendously. To Cydney Campbell Webster, Melissa Clements, John Webber, Sarah Baltzell, and the rest of the GLP Attorneys family, thank you for supporting me as an author even without me ever asking! As my first full-time job and being in a new city, I never knew a work culture could be so inclusive and supportive of one another outside of work, and I am forever grateful to work with such a powerful team.

Thank you to Anna David, *New York Times* bestselling author of eight books and my mentor! I discovered Anna's podcast Build Your Business with a Book (which was then called Launch Pad, after her publishing company) right after being picked up by New Degree Press. She is the first author I have seen to spill *so* many great secrets of what getting published is actually like, especially when it comes to traditional publishing, as so many new authors strive to do. As a first-time author, her marketing advice for my book was so incredibly insightful that I reached out to her through her publishing company's website and was able to meet her via Zoom! Since then, I have followed her podcast, read her books, and used her Book Launch documents religiously to help build my audience and market my book. Without her, I would be completely lost, and for that, I am so grateful she has come into my life and has supported my journey of publishing.

Thank you to my publisher New Degree Press, who is truly unlike any other publisher. They have taken the time to walk their publishing authors through the process by holding weekly courses and making author coaches constantly available for our every need—on top of our editors! NDP really has an amazing thing going with how they approach publishing, and I highly encourage anyone who wants to get their book published to check out their website and consider applying to Eric Koester's Book Creators class. While I didn't personally go through the class itself and jumped right into publishing my finished manuscript, I can vouch that Eric is a phenomenal teacher with the way he has organized his sessions and sets up new authors for success.

To my loving and sweet partner-in-crime, Aidan Pazan, thank you for jumping into this crazy journey of publishing and being so supportive throughout the entire process—even in the moments where you saw me struggling and overwhelmed. I wouldn't have been able to do this without you.

Lastly, I want to thank each and every person who supported my book through the presale campaign. I would not be publishing today if it weren't for all of these amazing people below, who believed in my book and myself as an author before everyone else:

Abby Bailey

Abby Cape

Adriana Nieman

Aidan Pazan

Alexandria Kirsten Macaluso

Alexis Balausky

Allison Krieg

Allison Mallory

Amelia Williams

Amy Darnell

Andrew Shinsako

Angelina McLaughlin-Heil

Anna David

Ben Brea

Benjamin Gabel

Benjamin Hurt

Brenda J. Hearn

Brenden Holmes

Brenetta Ward

Brittany Quansah

Brooke Mallory

Caleb Rieger

Cameron Hinkley

Carlie Cunningham

Catherine Oldt

Cerise Akins

Chase Stephenson

Christina M. Ingoglia

Christopher Cooper

Cindy Ostrander

Cydney Webster

Darin B. Windsor

David McReynolds

David White

Deborah Macey

Denis Julio

Don Foster

Donny Garrett

Drakke Hearn

Dustin Springer

Easton Banik

Elizabeth A. Brooks

Elizabeth Hill

Ellie Senft

Emily Campbell

Emily E. Holt

Emily Ngo

Ethan Cowell

Evelyn Hillman

Faye Burchard

Gary Kerr

Genoveva Gomez-Lince

Gillian Grimsrud
GLP Attorneys
Greg Allen Woods
Haley Bryant
Helen Day
Jade John
Jake Peak
Janetta Woods
Jeanne Naeger
Jennifer Winfrey
Jessica Bernhardt
Jessica Marron
Jessica Rains
Joey Gorombey
John Webber
Jonny Weischedel
Jordan Cole
Jordan Copeland
Juanita M. Simpson
Judy Saurwein
Kayla Motl
Kirk Matthew Daffon
Kobe Smith
Kristen Dowell
Laura Weiss
Lauren Alexander
Lauren Goldberg
Lindsey Pfluger
Lolita Woods
Luke Wernette
Lynette Gallon-Harrell
Madison Best

Magen Mintchev
Maisy Borden
Malwina Najbar
Mandy Eckerle
Marcus Rader
Marinda Allen
Marissa Ritter
Mary Bristow
Matthew Peniston
Melissa Clements
Melissa Hearn
Michele Mizia
Minnie Moore
Mirrande Morgan
Mitchell Willyard
Morgan Caban
Naomi Payne
Nicole Futch
Phakisha Horne
Phyllis Ramsey-Monroe
Prince Chingarande
Quewon Smith
Ralph G. Kenner
Robert Dettmer
Rory Cunningham
Rotshak Dakup
Ryan Shank
Sarah Baltzell
Sarah Naji
Sarah Risinger (Richardson)
Sharon, Melvin & Shawna
Ward

Shelley Bonczek

Sitney E. Day

Steven Lilley

Sydnie English

Tiara Williams

Tony Bonnagio

Tonya Malone

Tyler Hightower

Varon Martinez

Wendy Flanagan

Wendy Severiche

William Idleman

Yulia Bychkovska

Zach Beyar

Zachary Wesselmann

Zinda Foster

CPSIA information can be obtained
at www.ICGtesting.com
Printed in the USA
FSHW020623160521